Praise for the works of Cade Haddock Strong

Mailboat

The author is a skillful writer who knows how to bring readers into her story and hold them enthralled from the first page to the last. Strong has created two characters, one a successful author and the other a mailboat captain, who will capture the hearts of readers and have them rooting for the two characters to make the relationship work even though readers know the book will have a happy-ever-after ending. Both characters are strong, intelligent, and looking for a relationship that will complete their lives. Strong's descriptions of life on the river are vividly drawn and will have readers Googling possible vacation destinations in the Thousand Island area.

If you like your romances between two well-drawn strong and intelligent characters without constant angst, this book is for you, and should be put at the top of your to-be-read list.

-Abbott F., *NetGalley*

Jackpot

This is my first time reading a Cade Haddock Strong book, and I must say if they are all as good as this then I shall be looking for more. What I really loved about this book is that it starts at the beginning for both Ty and Karla, it's not a story of they meet and flash back. It starts at the beginning and you get to read their story as they move along. There are many layers to this sweet story which is well written and kept me keen.

-Cathy W., *NetGalley*

Fare Game

The author nails intrigue/thriller and romance in this book…The whistle-blowing storyline is plausible, logical, tense and interesting, the romance believable and sweet, the ending satisfying. With all other elements done well, this one makes a second good book by Haddock Strong. I liked it, and will definitely check out her next offering.

-Pin's Reviews, *goodreads*

This author is new to me but I'll be looking for more of her work because I really liked this story. It's a romantic thriller with two likeable leads, some well-done minor characters and very interesting plot that kept me interested from start to finish.

-Emma A., *NetGalley*

My belief is that when readers pick up this book, they will be enamored by a carefully and skillfully plotted story line that's also well written and doesn't sacrifice moral complexity to the demands of a fast-moving narrative. Ms. Haddock Strong does such a great job…

-Diane W., *NetGalley*

The plot has many layers—lust, a whirlwind relationship, intrigue (where is the money going?)—and desperate characters on both sides of the law.

-Ginger O., *NetGalley*

I loved how Haddock Strong gets her readers into the story. Her writing is clear and persuasive, and she manages to explain airline financial irregularities, price-fixing, and whistleblowing without ruffling a single one of my feathers. She introduces them slowly as part of the story, mostly in dialogue, and they become one of the many layers of the story. Likewise, the relationship between Kay and Riley is also layered, their professional and personal lives, their exploration of each other and their difficulties. It is beautifully done. This book is a must for readers like me that need a bit of something on the side of their romance. It gives a good read, good romance as well as some very hot sexy moments. An excellent combination.

-The Lesbian Review

The Schuyler House

...is a story about learning valuable life lessons from painful circumstances, opening one's heart to love and making positive changes in one's life. This story captivated me on so many levels because I was taken on a wild journey with Mattie! The numerous twists and turns in the plot kept me wondering about what was going to happen next. I also entertained insane thoughts of just forgoing sleep so I could continue to read on to satisfy my curiosity. If you enjoy a storyline with unique twists and angst filled situations coupled with a dash of slow burning romance, then this is certainly the story for you!

-The Lesbian Review

THE
ADVICE
COLUMNIST

CADE HADDOCK STRONG

Other Bella Books by Cade Haddock Strong

The Schuyler House
Fare Game
Jackpot
On the Fence
Mailboat

About the Author

Cade spent many years working in the airline industry, and she and her wife have traveled all over the world. When not writing, she loves to be outside, especially skiing, hiking, biking, and playing golf.

While her roots trace back to Upstate New York, Cade has lived all over the US and abroad. From the beautiful mountains of Vermont and Colorado to the bustling cities of DC, Chicago, Boston, and Amsterdam. She now calls Charlottesville, VA home.

Cade has authored six sapphic fiction novels, spanning the realms of suspense, romance, and mystery. But her passion for sapphic fiction doesn't stop at the page. As a founding member of the Sapphic Lit Pop-Up Bookstore, Cade is on a mission to shine a spotlight on the genre she loves.

Website: cadehaddockstrong.com

THE
ADVICE
COLUMNIST

CADE HADDOCK STRONG

BELLA
BOOKS

2024

First Edition - 2024

Editor: Ann Roberts
Cover Designer: Kayla Mancuso

ISBN: 978-1-64247-533-3

Acknowledgements

The Advice Columnist marks my first foray into the realm of true mystery writing. It's been an exhilarating journey, and I owe an immense debt of gratitude to my stellar cast of beta readers. I'm looking at you, Louise McBain, Nan Campbell, Rita Potter, and my remarkable wife, Lisa. Their keen insights and invaluable feedback served as the secret ingredient in weaving together all the twists and turns in this story.

Writing mysteries is a tricky business. Dreaming up all the puzzle pieces, and then trying to juggle them. Strategically planting red herrings to keep readers on their toes. Crafting unpredictable characters. But, gosh, writing this book was so much fun. I got to play with anagrams and cook up riddles.

Writing a mystery requires a special kind of finesse. Keeping the reader hooked without leaving them tangled in a web of confusion. Luckily, I had the mystery guru Ann Roberts as my editor. Thank you, Ann, for helping me shape this story into something more gripping. And, as always, thanks for weeding through all my grammar snafus. No doubt you wore a hole in your garden gloves!

My heartfelt appreciation extends to Linda, Jessica, and the rest of the Bella crew for their support and guidance. It's hard to wrap my head around the fact that this is my sixth book. Thanks for making the journey so incredible.

The idea for this story came to me over two years ago while I hiked along the Potomac with author Louise McBain. After scribbling down a rough outline, it gathered dust on my shelf for months. I didn't write at all during that time. It was like my creative juices took a vacation without me.

Then, one day I dusted off the outline, and bam! Inspiration struck. I started typing like a woman possessed. Before I knew it, I was back in the writing groove. This book was like my lifeline, dragging me out of my writing funk and back into the game.

P.S. To my wife, Lisa. Every day I am grateful to have you by my side. Without you, I wouldn't have written one book, let alone six.

CHAPTER ONE

As Lydia waited her turn in the meandering line, she gazed around the café's eclectic surroundings, pausing on a haphazard stack of newspapers piled near the worn counter. *The Washington Post*'s front-page headline was tragically all too familiar: "The Red Scarf Murderer Strikes Again, Claims High School Chemistry Teacher in Silver Spring." The details were grim. The victim had been slain in his own home as he and his wife slept. She'd woken to the gruesome discovery of her husband's lifeless body, his throat slit, and a red scarf tied around his neck.

Lydia's spine tingled at the thought of waking up beside a corpse. She snatched the paper from the rack and thrust it toward her friend Jen who stood beside her.

"I hope they catch that guy soon," Jen said. "This makes four murders, and no one has a clue how the victims are connected. It creeps the shit out of me, you know? A killer roaming around DC like he owns the place." Her eyes darted around the bustling café. "He could be here right now."

Lydia tucked the newspaper under her arm, casting a glance at the people around them. The guy standing behind them exuded an eerie vibe. He totally had a serial killer look about him. When he flashed a tight-lipped smile in her direction, the hairs on her arms stood on end. She quickly averted her gaze, exchanging a glance with Jen.

"According to what I read online," Jen said, "the police can't establish any link between the victims. That's what makes it even more unnerving. Maybe this guy is picking targets at random." She blew out a breath. "I might seriously consider getting a dog."

"At least you don't live alone," Lydia said, brushing a strand of unruly hair from her face.

Jen placed a hand on Lydia's shoulder. "Maybe it's high time you and Carrie moved in together. You've been dating what? A year and a half now?"

Lydia buried both hands in the pockets of her jeans. "I've brought it up a few times. Carrie doesn't think her apartment is big enough for two and she doesn't want to move again until she's ready to buy a house."

Jen raised an eyebrow. "A house, huh?"

Lydia sighed. "Yeah, Carrie's fixated on the idea that we're almost thirty, and it's time to *adult*. But truthfully, as much as the idea of a house sounds appealing, my bank account is nowhere near ready for that."

Jen looked poised to ask another question, but it was their turn to order.

Lydia smiled at the barista and ordered a double espresso.

When the barista stepped away to prepare her beverage, Jen nudged Lydia's arm. "Since when do you drink espresso?"

Lydia shrugged. "Carrie not-so-subtly implied that grown women don't drink hot chocolate, not if they want to be taken seriously."

Jen rolled her eyes. "Whatever."

They found a table toward the front of the café. Lydia hesitated before she sat down. "Oh, gosh," she exclaimed, reaching for the copy of *The Washington Post* tucked under her arm. "I didn't mean to take this. I've got to go pay for it. Be right back."

On her way back to the counter, she narrowly avoided a collision with a man wielding a cup of coffee in both hands. "Watch it, honey," he growled.

Rather than point out that it was in fact he who needed to watch where he was going, Lydia bit her tongue. No need wasting her breath on a rude stranger.

She returned to her table and delicately sipped her espresso before setting it back on the hockey puck-sized saucer.

"You know," Jen said, "you grimace every time you lift that little cup to your lips."

"I do not."

"Uh-huh, you so do." Jen leaned forward and whispered, "Why don't you go up and get yourself a cup of hot chocolate. I promise I won't tell Carrie."

Lydia sneered at her and forced down a few more tiny sips of espresso.

Jen gave her a questioning look. "By the way, how are things with you and Carrie? You haven't talked about her much lately."

"Everything's great, why wouldn't it be?"

Jen placed her hand over Lydia's. "I mean it, Lyd, are you happy?"

Lydia gave her a dismissive wave. But the truth was, things with Carrie hadn't been that great lately. "Well, sometimes…"

"Sometimes what?"

"Sometimes, I wonder if maybe I'm more in love with the *idea* of Carrie than I am with her." Lydia sucked in a breath. She couldn't believe she'd admitted that. Sure, Jen had been her best friend since third grade, but still, she hadn't intended to vocalize her concerns.

Jen's bright blue eyes widened. "What do you mean?"

"I don't know. Carrie checks all the boxes, and I generally enjoy spending time with her." Lydia dabbed her lips with a paper napkin. "I shouldn't have said anything. It's just me being silly. The last thing I want is to be single again. Can we forget I even mentioned it?"

"There's nothing wrong with being single."

Lydia laughed. "Yeah, right. Easy for you to say. You and Eric have been together since college."

"I don't want you to settle, that's all."

"I'm not settling," Lydia assured her. "Carrie's good for me. We do lots of cultural stuff, she motivates me to go to the gym, and she introduced me to this keto diet she's been on—"

"Wait." Jen held up her hand like a traffic cop and made a show of looking Lydia up and down. "You're on a diet? I'd kill to have your body."

"Spare me." Lydia pinched her stomach. "I could definitely stand to lose a few pounds."

Jen leaned forward. "Um, I hate to point out the obvious, but aren't you sort of the pot calling the kettle black?"

"What do you mean?" Lydia feigned innocence, although she was keenly aware of the point Jen was making. As the advice columnist for *Forté*, a women's magazine, Lydia often emphasized the importance of positive body image when responding to the letters and emails she received.

Jen rapped her finger on the table. "You know damn well what I mean. You should listen to your own advice."

Lydia leaned back in her chair. "Fine, point taken."

"Speaking of advice, have you heard anything more from Maudie Zeller at the *Post*?"

Lydia nodded. "Yep, I'm having lunch with her later this week."

"Have you decided what you'll do if she asks you to become the next Dear Birdie?" Jen asked, referring to the coveted advice column in the *Post*.

"No, not yet. You know, becoming the advice columnist for *The Washington Post* is like a dream job for me. Problem is, I'm not sure I'm ready. It would be a big step up, a much bigger audience, a fatter paycheck, but I've only got five years of experience under my belt."

"What does Carrie think about the opportunity?"

"She's all for it. Honestly, I think she mostly likes the idea of telling people I work for the *Post*. She considers *Forté* to be a second-rate publication."

Jen gave her another eye roll. "Well, it's no secret how I feel about it. If the woman who currently holds the job wants you to replace her when she retires and is trying to convince you it's a good fit, then it's probably a good fit."

"I guess."

"Come on, Lyd. You told me Maudie has been impressed with your work at *Forté*."

Lydia blushed. It was true. Maudie had in fact said that, although Lydia still had a hard time believing it. She cracked her fingers and let out a long sigh. "I know I'll regret it if I turn the position down. I may never get an opportunity like this again, but what if people hate me? And what if moving to *The Washington Post* is too big a leap?"

"I totally get that you're anxious about it," Jen said. "But it would kill me to see you pass up the opportunity."

Lydia finished the last of her espresso. By now it was cold, and she winced as she swallowed the bitter black liquid. She laughed. "Okay, I'll admit it. Espresso tastes like tree bark."

Jen cackled. "It sure as shit does."

"Maybe next time I'll get a mochaccino or whatever it's called. You know, half coffee, half hot chocolate."

"That seems like a happy medium to me. And mochaccino sounds sophisticated, so I'm sure Carrie will approve." Jen stood and pulled her jean jacket off the back of her chair. "I need to run, but let me know what you decide about the *Post* thing, okay?"

"Sure," Lydia said, checking her watch. "Actually, I'll walk out with you. If I don't hurry, I'll be late to the English Center."

Jen patted her on the back. "It's fantastic that you're still volunteering there."

"I wouldn't give it up for anything. I absolutely adore teaching there. Tonight's the first night back after summer break and I can't wait to see everyone—all my favorite students and the other teachers."

Once they stepped outside, Jen gave her a hug goodbye and whispered, "You're a good egg, Lydia."

Lydia stepped back and huffed out a laugh. "I'm a scrambled egg, that's what I am." Waving goodbye to her friend, she started up the hill toward the church that housed the Washington English Center.

Lydia tugged open the heavy wooden door to the church. Her sneakers squeaked on the gleaming linoleum floors as she wound her way to the section of the massive old building that housed the Washington English Center, the WEC. Because tonight marked the beginning of a new semester, a welcome reception was being held in the auditorium before everyone dispersed to their respective classrooms.

Lydia greeted a cluster of fellow volunteer teachers with warm hugs. A tap on her shoulder drew her attention to Miray, one of her returning students.

Miray gave Lydia a broad smile. "Hi, Teacher!"

"Well, hello, Miray," Lydia said. "It's nice to see you back this semester."

"Please," Miray said.

Lydia smiled. Although they'd gone over it many times, Miray still managed to mix up please and thank you.

WEC's executive director, Gabrielle Alvarez, beckoned from inside the auditorium. "Welcome, everyone, please take your seats."

Once everyone was assembled, and the idle chatter settled down, Gabrielle delivered a few opening remarks before introducing the evening's keynote speaker to the stage. A petite woman with beautiful wide brown eyes bounded up the steps and slipped behind the podium.

A mixture of pride, admiration, and yearning gushed through Lydia. Although she'd had minimal interaction with the woman, a latent crush had taken root during their brief encounters in the halls of the school or in the WEC's computer lab. Lydia pegged her to be somewhere in her late twenties or early thirties and had heard through the grapevine that she'd come to the US from Venezuela.

The woman tucked her long brown hair behind her ears, tapping the microphone as she scanned the crowd. "My name is Sofia and I've been a student here at the Washington English

Center for three years." Her infectious smile filled the room. "This semester I'm taking on a new role at the school. Instead of being a student, I will be a teacher."

The room erupted in sustained applause with many rising to their feet.

Lydia couldn't help but be in awe. Sofia's incredible journey from a non-English speaker to teacher in a short span was miraculous. In prior semesters, Sofia had been a constant presence in the school's small library, scribbling on a notepad or burying her nose in a book.

Sofia continued, sharing her personal transformation and the initial trepidation that almost derailed her journey. "Three years ago, I was so scared to walk in the front doors of this building. In fact, one day, I took the bus here but only got as far as the front walk before I left and went home. The second time I came, I made it as far as the front stoop and nearly bolted again. I probably would have if it hadn't begun to rain cats and dogs." She laughed and pointed to one of the teachers in the audience. "That's an idiom he taught me."

After a beat, Sofia said, "Part of the reason I was so terrified to come here is because no one thought I could do it. No one thought I could learn English, and I almost believed it myself." She paused for a long moment. "If you are to succeed as a student, you have to be here for yourself, nobody else. And don't listen to anyone who says you can't do it. You can."

Microphone in hand, Sofia walked to the far edge of the stage and peered out at the crowd. "Now that I can speak English, people see me for who I am—a smart, educated woman—not who they thought I was—illiterate and stupid." She waved her hand toward the section where a large group of students sat. "You've taken the hardest step. You're here today. I won't lie. English is one of the toughest languages to master. Learning it will take time and can be frustrating." The muscles in her arm tensed as she pumped a hand into the air. "But don't worry, we're all here to help you on this journey."

Lydia pulled a tissue out of her bag and dabbed her eyes.

The teacher sitting beside her nudged Lydia's arm. "Geez, I didn't expect this assembly to be such a tearjerker."

Lydia smiled, glancing at the amazing woman on the stage. "It's stories like hers that make teaching here so rewarding."

CHAPTER TWO

Lydia descended the steps into the intimate, softly lit cocktail bar. It was a "reservations only" type place and the maître d' dutifully checked for her name on his iPad before letting her pass into the inner sanctum. Lydia couldn't fathom how Carrie had secured a reservation. Based on what Lydia had seen on social media, the place was booked solid for the next nine months.

A smile graced Lydia's face when she spotted Carrie, perched in a tall, plush purple chair at the far end of the bar. In this sea of beautiful people, Carrie stood out. She was the most attractive woman in the room. Tall and thin, but not too thin, with perfectly tousled short blond hair.

Lydia still marveled at the fact that a stunning, successful woman like Carrie had chosen her. Although Carrie claimed to love her, the thought of losing her haunted Lydia. Her stomach churned at the possibility. She absolutely could not let that happen. She and Carrie were perfect together. They shared the same dreams—a house in Upper Northwest DC, kids, a dog, and a Tesla SUV parked in the driveway. Of course, these dreams were still years away from being realized, especially given Lydia's meager salary at *Forté*. Still, she was determined to attain them.

As she navigated the room toward Carrie, glances followed her, prompting a bout of self-doubt. Was something wrong with her dress? Had her curls gone into frizz mode? She patted her hair. It felt okay. She straightened her posture and held her chin high as she passed through the impeccably dressed crowd. "I'm as good as they are," she silently reassured herself, though her conviction wavered.

She greeted Carrie with a kiss on the cheek. "Hey, babe." She ran a hand down the arm of Carrie's perfectly tailored black suit. "You look like a million bucks. Is that outfit new?" Although Carrie had spent the previous night at Lydia's apartment, she'd gone home in the morning to get ready for work, as she always did.

Carrie waved her hand dismissively. "Gosh, no. It's at least two seasons old."

After she slid in beside Carrie, Lydia ordered a cosmo and scooped some cashews from the small bowl in front of them. "Oh, wow, these nuts are warm."

Carrie smiled. "Like in first class on an airplane."

"Yeah," Lydia said, although she had no clue. She'd never flown first class in her life.

After Lydia's cocktail arrived, Carrie shifted in her seat. "You know how I have that big firm party next week…"

"Of course," Lydia said. "It's been on my calendar for months." Carrie's law firm planned to throw a big shindig in celebration of their one-hundredth anniversary.

Carrie winked. "Will you wear that hot red cocktail dress?"

"Um, sure, I guess, if you think it's appropriate."

"It's borderline inappropriate, but that's kind of the point. I want to watch the men at my firm drool when I walk through the door with you."

Oh, so I get to be a piece of meat? Lydia immediately chastised herself for having this thought. She'd had a similar thought when she'd entered the bar. *There you go again, calling the kettle black.* Yet doing what Carrie was asking was a small price to pay. Carrie's biggest goal in life was to make partner at the firm and Lydia would do whatever she could to help her get there. "Do you have a vision for which shoes I should wear?"

Carrie stroked Lydia's leg. "Well, I'd love it if you wore my four-inch Louboutins, unless you think that would be over the top?"

"Probably," Lydia said. "Assuming we're going for sexy, not streetwalker. Plus, your shoes would be a size too big for me."

"Yeah, good point," Carrie said. "Let's save the shoe question for the weekend. I'll inventory your closet, but it's possible we'll need to hit the stores."

"Yay." Lydia clapped. "Shopping."

Carrie pouted. "Come on, be a sport. You know this firm party is a massive deal to me."

Lydia picked up Carrie's hand and kissed it. "I know. Anything for you, babe."

Carrie beamed. "That's the spirit." She paused before adding, "While we're on the topic of calendars"—she dug into her large orange Goyard bag for her phone—"the opening for the Berenice Abbott exhibit is coming up. Do you have it on your calendar?"

Lydia pulled out her phone too. "Where and when is the opening? I don't recall you mentioning it."

Carrie rolled her eyes. "I've mentioned it a few times. It's at the Phillips Collection, silly. It's sponsored by the Contemporaries Committee, you know, the group I recently joined?"

Lydia didn't fully comprehend what the contemporaries group was, but Carrie had been very excited when she'd been asked to be part of it. It was probably very prestigious. "When did you say the opening was?"

"Tuesday, October seventeenth."

"Tuesday?" Lydia shook her head. "You'll have to count me out. I teach at the English Center on Tuesday nights, you know that."

Carrie tossed her phone back in her bag and crossed her arms. "Come on, Lyd. This is important. I'm sure your students can survive one week without you."

"I'm sure they can, but I made a commitment to them and to my co-teacher. I'm not abandoning them unless it's a life-or-death type of situation."

"Spare me the drama. You won't be abandoning them."

Lydia clasped her hands in her lap and looked Carrie straight in the eye. "I'd love to join you for an opening at the Phillips, just not when it falls on a Tuesday night."

"I just don't get it," Carrie whined. "You spend so much time at that ridiculous school, not to mention all the hours you put into lesson planning. And for what? They don't even pay you."

"The school is *not* ridiculous," Lydia said as evenly as she could. "And yes, I'm a volunteer, but I get far more from the students than they get from me. In fact, I'd pay to teach there if I had to."

Carrie threw back the last of her martini and mumbled something about Lydia being idealistic.

Lydia didn't take the bait. They'd had this conversation before. Carrie would never get how amazing it was to work with the students at WEC. Many had come to the US to escape horrible situations in their home country. Lydia considered it an honor to be able to teach them. To steer the conversation away from WEC, she forced a smile and said, "So, are we still going to Annapolis this weekend to see your friends? What are their names, Bethany and Rita?"

Carrie nodded and her demeanor brightened immediately. "Oh, yes. The weather is expected to be exquisite, and they've offered to take us sailing. I mentioned that you had experience with boats."

"I do," Lydia said, "but certainly not with one as big as theirs…Still, I should be able to hold my own when it comes to sailing." She laughed. "After all, I grew up on a lake."

Carrie winked again. "It'll be so sexy to see you at the helm."

"I'll do my best to make you proud in front of your friends."

Carrie nudged Lydia's leg with her own. "Oh, I'm sure you will."

"I'm really looking forward to the weekend. It'll be really nice to get out of the city for a change."

"What time can you leave on Friday? I want to be in Annapolis by dinnertime. We need to hit the road early before traffic gets horrendous."

Lydia took a moment to consider her schedule on Friday. "Probably two-ish. I've got lunch with Maudie Zeller, the woman from *The Washington Post*. I can leave right after that."

"Right, the lunch interview."

"I'm kind of anxious about it and I don't want to be looking at my watch."

"Of course," Carrie said. "Just make sure it doesn't run past two."

Is she even listening to me? Lydia bit her lip and looked down at the floor. "I'll do my best."

Carrie patted her leg. "I hope that gig at the *Post* pans out."

"Um, yeah, me too," Lydia replied with a hint of uncertainty.

"I mean, if you insist on being an advice columnist, you might as well work somewhere prestigious like the *Post*."

Carrie's casual reference to the *Post* job as a mere "gig" pissed Lydia off. When Lydia had initially mentioned the position to Carrie, she'd expressed concerns about stepping into Maudie Zeller's substantial shoes. Carrie had dismissed her reservations, suggesting that, in her opinion, the bar for an advice columnist— whether at the *Post* or elsewhere—was relatively low.

Despite Carrie's dismissive attitude toward her profession, Lydia had always taken immense pride in her work, investing considerable effort into helping *Forté*'s readers. Many of those who wrote to the advice columnist at *Forté* genuinely needed help, whether it was overcoming past trauma or navigating challenging situations in their lives. Lydia harbored the hope that, with time, Carrie would come to appreciate the significance of her role.

The success of her relationship with Carrie held profound importance for Lydia. Together they would build that idyllic life Lydia had envisioned since childhood.

CHAPTER THREE

The maître d' greeted Lydia when she stepped inside the stylish confines of Le Diplomat, a French restaurant nestled in Logan Circle. She fiddled with the edge of her napkin, stealing glances around the bistro as she waited for Maudie to arrive. At the stroke of noon, she spotted her lunch companion at the door. Her vibrant scarf fluttered behind her as she made her way through the crowded tables. With graceful elegance, Maudie approached Lydia's table, a warm smile lighting up her face.

"Lydia, darling, it's so lovely to see you." Maudie's voice carried a crisp yet warm tone, reminiscent of a seasoned newscaster. "Thank you for joining me."

Lydia rose from her seat, her heart fluttering as she extended her hand. "Thank you for inviting me, Maudie. I'm truly honored."

After they placed their orders, Maudie leaned forward, her sharp eyes assessing Lydia. The clinking of cutlery and soft hum of conversation surrounded them. Lydia tried not to fidget, with Maudie's eyes lingering on her. She absentmindedly stirred her iced tea and sat up straighter, anxiously waiting to hear what the seasoned journalist had to say.

"I've followed your work at *Forté*, Lydia," Maudie said finally. "You have a knack for unraveling life's complexities with grace and perceptiveness."

A flush of pride warmed Lydia's cheeks. "Thank you, Maudie. Your own work has always been an inspiration to me. Your ability to tackle tough subjects with compassion and insight is beyond admirable."

Maudie's eyes softened. "A healthy dose of intelligence, empathy, and integrity—those are the hallmarks of a good advice columnist." Without missing a beat, she said, "Now, tell me more about your role at *Forté*."

Lydia leaned back, clutching the napkin in her lap as she recounted her time at the magazine. "Um, let's see…When I first came to *Forté* five years ago, my role was strictly as their advice columnist. I had limited prior experience, but they took a chance on me. For that, I am eternally grateful. Anyway, before long, I developed a large and loyal following, and the executive editor began to seek my input around other magazine content."

"Other magazine content…Can you elucidate?"

"Well, just last week, she asked me to come up with a new idea for a regular feature. I came up with what I've dubbed 'Sisterhood Stories.' It will spotlight women who have forged lasting friendships in unconventional circumstances or through unique experiences. For example, women who met through unusual hobbies or life-changing challenges. Basically, highlighting the power of female friendship and how it allows women to overcome obstacles and achieve their goals."

Maudie tapped the table with her hand. "I adore it. What a wonderful idea."

Once their meals arrived, they exchanged anecdotes about the dynamics of being an advice columnist. Lydia found herself captivated by Maudie's words of wisdom and stories of navigating the world of journalism with poise and tenacity.

"Not everyone understands it, but what we do is very important, Lydia. Never doubt the power of your words to touch the lives of those who seek solace in them."

"Oh, I don't," Lydia said. "I take my job very seriously. And, well, on that note, I wanted to ask you about one of my responses to a letter last week…It was about a woman grappling with loss and uncertainty, and I couldn't help but wonder—"

Before Lydia could finish her sentence, Maudie reached across the table, her hand resting gently on Lydia's arm. "I read your response to that letter. It was heartfelt and poignant, Lydia, like so many of your replies." She pulled the white cloth napkin from her lap and dabbed a dollop of salad dressing from her chin. "Which is why I invited you to lunch."

Lydia stiffened and held her breath, awaiting Maudie's next words.

"As you're aware, I plan to retire soon. I'd like for you to be the next Dear Birdie."

Lydia nodded appreciatively. "I feel ready for the challenge, Maudie." It wasn't entirely accurate, but Lydia didn't want to reveal the anxiety that had loomed over her since Maudie first reached out.

Maudie clasped her hands. "Excellent, excellent." She pulled a white index card from her purse. "This is the salary range the *Post* is prepared to offer you."

"Excellent, excellent," Lydia replied as she glanced at the figures on the card. *You idiot, why are you parroting her?* "Um, would you mind if I took the weekend to think it over?"

Maudie seemed mildly taken aback, but she nodded her head and said, "Of course." After a beat, she added, "Are there any other questions I can answer for you about the position?"

Lydia cleared her throat. "Could you tell me a little bit about your team?"

"Absolutely. There are three people who work directly for me. An intern and two full-time staff, all of whom have indicated they plan to stay on after I retire. Sally, the intern, and Noah are both relatively new, but I've found them both to be exceptional. Whip-smart and earnest. Then there's Tisha. She's been with me almost since the day I started at the *Post*. A real firecracker. I honestly don't know what I would have done without her all these years." Maudie chuckled. "But you better stay on her good side."

"Oh, gosh, okay."

Maudie patted Lydia's hand. "Don't worry, you'll be fine. She'll adore you."

"A team of three, that sure will be nice. I'm a team of one at *Forté*."

"Well, until recently, we were a team of four," Maudie said. "I recently had to let someone go, it was an unfortunate but unavoidable situation."

"I see." Lydia was curious about the circumstances surrounding this person's termination, but she hesitated to ask, unsure if it would be appropriate.

The waiter dropped the check on the table. Maudie reviewed it, pulled some cash from her wallet, and rose from her seat. "I'm sorry, I need to run. Please call me on Monday to let me know your decision about the position."

Before Lydia could reply, Maudie was already on her way to the door, her scarf trailing behind her.

Lydia used the ladies' room and emerged from Le Diplomat a tad past two p.m. Shielding her eyes from the afternoon sun, she strolled to the corner, scanning the vicinity for Carrie's hunter-green BMW. There was no trace of her. It wasn't unusual for Carrie to be late but departing for Annapolis at two p.m. had been non-negotiable. Leaving later than that would ensnare them in the gridlock that was DC traffic.

That morning, Carrie had even gone so far as to suggest Lydia reschedule her lunch with Maudie to ensure their timely departure. Although Lydia resisted, Carrie only dropped the idea after bemoaning the traffic nightmare they'd face.

And now it was 2:07 p.m. and there was still no sign of Carrie. Maybe she'd texted to say she was running late? Lydia fumbled in her bag for her phone. Nope, nothing from Carrie. There was, however, a message from Jen asking about the meeting with Maudie. Rather than reply, Lydia called her.

Jen's ecstatic voice filled the line after the first ring. "How'd it go?"

"The job is mine if I want it," Lydia replied, the words still sinking in.

Jen squealed into the phone. "Oh, my, God. That's fucking amazing. I'm sooooo proud of you."

"I told Maudie I needed the weekend to think about it."

"What's there to think about? Becoming the *Dear Birdie* advice columnist at *The Washington Post*. Dude, you said it yourself, it's a dream come true."

"I know. I didn't want to come off as too eager, and this is a monumental step up for me. What if I'm not ready?"

"Oh, you're ready, Lydia. Like I told you the other day, fucking Maudie Zeller reached out to you about replacing her, not the other way around. You've always revered her, so there's absolutely zero reason to doubt her judgment. If she believes in you, you need to believe in you."

"I guess." Lydia shuffled her feet on the sidewalk. "Oh, and the salary she quoted, it's more than double what I'm making now. I'm inclined to accept the job for that reason alone. A fatter paycheck would make everything better."

"More money is certainly icing on the cake, or whatever that phrase is," Jen chuckled.

"One thing struck me as a little odd, though."

"Oh yeah, what was that?"

"Well, I asked Maudie about her team. It sounds like she recently had to terminate someone. She hinted that it got a little messy but didn't elaborate. It was probably no big deal, but—"

The blare of a car horn interrupted Lydia's thoughts. "Oh, gosh, Carrie just got here. I gotta go. I'll call you when we get back from Annapolis."

"Wait, hold on one more sec," Jen said.

"What is it?"

"Did you hear about the most recent murder?"

Lydia's hand went to her heart. "You mean there's been another one since the chemistry teacher in Silver Spring?"

"Yeah, they found the body this morning. It's all over the news."

Lydia's anxiety spiked. "I had my phone off during lunch. I'm almost afraid to ask. Who is the victim this time?"

"Some guy in Vienna, Virginia. Hotshot real estate agent and apparently the king of youth soccer around the DMV," Jen replied, using the acronym for DC and its surrounding Maryland and Virginia suburbs.

Lydia pinched her eyes shut. "That's horrible."

"I know, right?"

Carrie laid on the horn again.

"Listen, Jen. I really need to go."

"You tell that woman to buy a big ol' bottle of Champagne to celebrate your new job."

Lydia hurried toward the curb. "Celebrating before it's official might jinx things. Bye, Jen. Have a good weekend."

"Who the hell were you talking to?" Carrie asked as soon as Lydia opened the car door.

Well hello to you too. Lydia slid into the passenger seat and tugged the door closed. "I was talking to Jen. She wanted to know how my interview went."

"Well that's just great. Now we're ten minutes behind schedule," Carrie muttered, peeling away from the curb before Lydia had even buckled her seat belt.

Lydia opted not to point out that they were behind schedule because Carrie was late. No need to start the weekend off with a fight.

CHAPTER FOUR

Lydia strode across the pristine, cavernous marble lobby, joining her colleagues as they awaited the elevator. Colleagues, *Washington Post* colleagues, she thought to herself. It had been almost two weeks since she'd started the new job, and she still hadn't grasped that it was all real. That she really was the new Dear Birdie.

The elevator crept upward, stopping at every floor along the way. I really need to find the stairs, Lydia decided when she stepped off on seven. Her office was small, but it had floor-to-ceiling windows and got great morning sun. Honestly, though, she was just stoked to have an office of her own. At *Forté*, everyone had been crammed into one room, and although she'd made some good friends there, she wouldn't miss the obsessive knuckle-cracker whose cubicle was behind hers or the "I must eat loud crunchy things that smell weird" colleague.

She dropped her bag on the spare chair tucked in the corner of her office, hung her coat on the back of the door, and eased into the fancy office chair behind her desk. It had a bajillion knobs and levers, and what they all did was still a mystery, but Lydia didn't have time to fiddle with them now. Her email inbox beckoned, the number of unread messages seeming to multiply by the minute. If she wanted to weed through it before she met with her team at ten, she'd better get busy.

The team she'd inherited from Maudie Zeller was proving to be a stroke of luck. They'd made Lydia's transition into the new job smooth and consistently provided invaluable input, particularly in handling the deluge of letters Dear Birdie received. Lydia valued their collective judgment when selecting letters for the column and appreciated their counsel on crafting responses to the letters they featured.

Ultimately, of course, the final decisions rested with Lydia, but she had immense respect for her team's opinions, especially Tisha's. With nearly two decades under Maudie's wing, Tisha demonstrated a unique talent for pinpointing the most captivating letters Dear Birdie received. She also had a knack for selecting letters that touched on topics that resonated deeply with their readers. Why Tisha hadn't been tapped to replace Maudie was a mystery to Lydia. It was something she planned to discuss with Tisha. Lydia had always been one for full transparency in the work environment. Best to ensure Tisha didn't hold any lingering resentment.

At 9:57 a.m. Lydia went to the small office kitchen to top off her coffee before making her way to the conference room for the morning meeting with her team. They'd spend two hours going through letters, choosing the ones to feature, and strategizing about how to answer whatever questions the letter writer posed.

Following the meeting, Lydia would use her notes to craft the responses slated for publication. However, before any content saw the light of day, it would be scrutinized by editors and potentially undergo legal and medical review. Lydia had a bachelors in English and a master's in psychology, but there were still plenty of subject areas where she appreciated a review by experts, and then of course, there was the fact that the *Post* required it. The last thing they needed was a lawsuit.

When she reached the conference room, Lydia found Tisha firing up her laptop. The screen at the front of the room lit up when Tisha projected a reader's letter. Once the rest of the team had assembled, Lydia signaled to Tisha that they could begin.

Tisha cleared her throat. "This letter is from a woman whose boyfriend struggles to hold a job. It's noteworthy because we receive a striking number of letters concerning deadbeat spouses, boyfriends, girlfriends. It's definitely a topic our readers care about and one that elicits passionate comments."

With that, Lydia and the rest of her team directed their focus to the screen, each reading the letter to themselves.

Dear Birdie,

My boyfriend and I have been together for two years. Everything is great except that, in the time we've been together, he's mostly been unemployed. I have a small business that does pretty well and we're able to live off what I bring in, but "Joe" spends most of his days playing video games. I've even caught him watching porn a few times.

He's an able-bodied twenty-seven-year-old and I'd like him to work, but whenever I ask about his job search, it turns into an argument. He was fired from his last job after only two weeks. I'm sure that was a major blow to his ego.

My friends think he's a deadbeat and have urged me to move on, but I love him, and honestly, I'm not thrilled at the prospect of being single again. That, and running my business is very stressful and requires me to work long hours. The last thing I have time for is dating. I feel like I'm cheating on Joe by even writing this letter.

The other problem is, if I break up with Joe, I'm not sure where he'll go. He lives with me and doesn't have much in the way of savings, at least that I'm aware of.

Maybe I should also mention that Joe's a very talented artist. Even though he hasn't painted much lately, I've seen some of his work and it's incredible. He's promised to reach out to some galleries about showing some of his pieces, but so far, he hasn't done so.

Joe has some great attributes, but I wish he was more driven. Is that enough reason to tell him to take a hike?

Sincerely,

Gainfully Employed Girlfriend

After Lydia and her team had a moment to digest the letter, she glanced around the room. "Thoughts?"

"Total deadbeat," the intern, Sally, said.

Tisha nodded in agreement. "There's a lot to unpack here. It's possible Joe"—she used her fingers to indicate quotation marks when she spoke his name—"has some emotional issues. It appears he lacks confidence, but, and I'm only speculating here, he doesn't appear willing to help himself."

Lydia took a few sips of coffee as she mulled over how they should respond to the letter. Although there was generally no right answer to the questions readers sent in, it was important to thoughtfully consider every reply. Only a fraction of the emails and letters that they received were selected for *Dear Birdie*. Typically, though, the theme in a published letter would be applicable to situations faced by hundreds, if not thousands, of other readers.

Lydia offered, "The girlfriend doesn't mention anything about Joe physically or emotionally abusing her, but my intuition tells me that may be the case. Her comment about feeling like she's cheating by writing the letter and hinting that Joe may have money tucked away that she's not aware of…"

"I'm with you," Tisha said. "We need to help this woman extricate herself from this relationship, ASAP, although I sense we need to tread carefully."

Everyone else on Lydia's team agreed. Joe needed to go. Collectively, they came up with the steps they thought the letter writer could take to make that happen. Lydia would incorporate these steps into the response she drafted later that afternoon. She nodded to Tisha. "Okay, what else do you have for us today?"

"This next letter will strike a chord with all of us," Tisha said as she brought it up on the screen.

Dear Birdie,

I'm caught in a never-ending cycle of fear and anxiety due to the constant media coverage of the Red Scarf Murderer. It feels like every time I open my computer or turn on the TV, there's news of another murder. I'm living in a perpetual state of dread, 24/7.

These feelings have taken over my life. I've become a recluse in my own apartment. The idea of stepping outside, even to grab groceries, paralyzes me with fear. What if I'm destined to be the next victim?

I desperately need advice on how to alleviate these feelings. They have pretty much taken over my life and they're eating me up inside. It's taking a toll on my mental and emotional well-being. I can't sleep at night. My mind races.

The whole situation has left me feeling despondent. What drives a person to commit such heinous acts??? How can such evil exist in our society, right in our own backyard?

Sincerely,

Anxious, Anxious, Anxious

When Lydia finished reading the letter, she looked around at her team. "I imagine all of us are experiencing some of the same reactions as this letter writer?" Her question was greeted with a series of nods.

"No surprise, we've gotten a lot of letters like this lately," Tisha said. "I chose this one because it touches not only the person's emotions, but also on the evil that is the murderer."

"My girlfriend could have written this letter," replied Noah. "She's pretty much afraid to leave our apartment. Fortunately, she's able to work from home."

Sally raised her hand. "Unlike many of the other letters we get, this one will resonate with practically every single *Washington Post* reader."

Lydia gave her a reassuring smile. "That's a good point, Sally. Our response to this letter should speak to our entire readership." She waved her hand around the room. "Thoughts on how to reply?"

"Well," Tisha said, "first we should assure Anxious, Anxious, Anxious that it's completely natural to feel…anxious. There's a freakin' psycho roaming around the DC region."

"I agree," Lydia said, "I think it's essential that we address the gravity of the situation—emphasize to our readers that having a serial killer in our midst is terrifying, potentially one of the scariest things we may experience in our lives. The Red Scarf Murderer is, without a doubt, a truly deranged and evil person. In our response, let's not mince words about that. The person responsible for these actions has demonstrated a level of cruelty that's difficult to fathom."

Tisha rested a hand over her heart. "To help bring some peace of mind, we might also want to mention that the Red Scarf Murderer will eventually be caught and justice will prevail."

"Let's hope so," Sally mumbled under her breath.

For the remainder of their morning session, the team talked through their reply to Anxious, Anxious, Anxious. It wasn't every day that the sentiments expressed in a letter to Dear Birdie touched everyone on Lydia's team. Before they adjourned, she reminded them that the *Post*'s employee mental health hotline was always there as a resource if they felt overwhelmed with anxiety.

As the sun dipped below the horizon, casting a warm glow across the *Washington Post* building, Lydia made her way through the lobby and pushed through the revolving door. There had been a recent spell of unseasonably warm weather, and when she stepped out of the air-conditioned building and onto the sidewalk, it was as if she'd opened an oven. Her curly hair immediately shifted into frizz mode. Using the elastic around her wrist, she promptly pulled it off her neck.

She slipped off her cotton blazer, tucking it around the strap of her new leather shoulder bag. While a few other workaholics trickled out of neighboring office buildings and a city bus chugged by, K Street was relatively quiet. The immediate area boasted several very good and very expensive steakhouses—no doubt full of lobbyists and expense account executives—but otherwise, the business district typically emptied out when the clock struck five.

Ever since she'd started her new job, Lydia had made it a habit to walk home from work each night. Tonight, however, the one-and-a-half mile, predominantly uphill trek felt particularly daunting, especially with the oppressive humidity. Her apartment sat almost equidistant from two Metro stations, making the bus the most sensible option if she wanted to avoid the walk. Lydia stepped inside the partially enclosed glass bus shelter on the corner and settled on the metal bench to wait.

After five minutes, she stood and scanned the street. No bus was in sight. Given the hour, the route had probably shifted to its off-peak schedule. Yanking her leather bag up on to her shoulder, she mumbled, "Might as well at least begin the walk home." As she trudged up Connecticut Avenue, her phone vibrated in her back pocket. She tugged it out and stared at the screen. It was a text from Carrie. Lydia read and reread the message, blinked a few times, and read it again.

Lyd, I think we should break things off and stop seeing each other. You're a great person - I just don't see us together long term. No hard feelings, but it's time we both move on.

The city noises around her vanished, and all she could hear was her heart pounding in her chest like a relentless drum. A lump formed in her throat, making it hard to breathe and her emotions swung from hurt to anger and back again. Although she was numb, she didn't cry.

Suddenly not trusting her legs to hold her up, she inched under the awning of an office building and leaned against the cool brick wall. After she sucked in a few deep breaths to steady herself, anger bubbled to the surface, overpowering the pain she felt.

She clutched her phone and stabbed the icon next to Carrie's name. "God damn it," Lydia said when the call went to voice mail. She stabbed the phone again to end the call without leaving a message, stomping her feet like a three-year-old having a tantrum. This garnered a few looks from people passing by, but right now, Lydia didn't give a hoot. She jammed her phone into her pocket but immediately tugged it back out again. She needed to talk to Jen, pronto.

"You are *not* going to believe this," Lydia said as soon as Jen picked up. "Carrie, my marvelous girlfriend, just broke up with me, by text! What the hell. Who does that? I mean, Jesus, we've been together for a year and a half. When I tried to call her, it went to goddamn voice mail. She doesn't even have the guts to talk to me. Can you—"

"Whoa, calm down," Jen said.

"How the hell am I supposed to calm down? My girlfriend dumped me. Apparently, she doesn't see a future for us."

"Where are you?"

"A few blocks from my office. Thank God I didn't get Carrie's message while I was at work…"

"Have you had dinner?"

"No, and I think I forgot to eat lunch."

"Meet me at Al Tiramisu in fifteen minutes," Jen said, referring to their favorite Italian restaurant. "I'll call them now and tell them to save us a booth."

Lydia didn't argue. With her shoulders slumped, she slowly put one loafer-clad foot in front of the other and began to make her way toward the restaurant. The sidewalk got busier as she approached Dupont Circle and turned onto P Street. There were women with yoga mats slung over their shoulders, bar patrons gathered on outdoor patios, and couples—freakin' happy couples—out walking their dogs or lugging bags home from the grocery store.

The tears finally came. Lydia stopped beside a lamppost and pulled a tissue from her bag. *Why doesn't anyone want to be with me?* She'd tried so hard to give Carrie everything she wanted. Her lip quivered and tears rolled down her cheeks. Pedestrians cast concerned glances in her direction. *Pull it together, Lydia.* She blew her nose and dabbed her eyes.

A text came in from Jen. *Where are you?*

Lydia stuffed the tissue in the pocket of her pants and stomped the last block to the restaurant.

Jen stood outside Al Tiramisu and wrapped Lydia in a big bear hug. After a good cry on the sidewalk, Lydia pulled out a fresh handful of tissues and tried to clean up her face. "Do I look like a complete mess?"

Jen gave her a lopsided smile. "Luckily, the restaurant is dimly lit."

"Bitch," Lydia muttered as she followed Jen inside.

After they'd ordered dinner and each had a glass of wine in front of them, Jen said, "Okay, tell me what happened with Carrie."

Lydia threw her hands in the air. "What's there to tell? She sent me a text saying we were over, that it was time to move on." Tears welled up in her eyes again. "I thought things were good between us. She was happy as could be when I landed the job at the *Post*. At last, I had a real job that paid a decent salary."

"Your job at *Forté* was a real job too."

Lydia shrugged. "I guess, but you know Carrie never thought so." She went to stuff her fistful of tissues into her leather shoulder bag and let out a muffled chuckle. She patted the side of the bag. "I bought this hideous thing for Carrie. She didn't think my old messenger bag was appropriate for a columnist at the *Post*. I'm such an idiot."

"You're not an idiot," Jen said.

"Yes, I am. At the *Post*, I feel like a total imposter. I'm positive that even Sally, the intern I inherited, thinks I'm in way over my head."

"May I remind you that you were the most popular columnist at *Forté* and you have a huge social media following. You've got a gift, Lydia. You give it to people straight without hurting their feelings or pissing them off. That's not easy. You're empathetic and pragmatic."

"I appreciate your kind words, I really do, but I'm no Maudie Zeller," Lydia said with a pout.

"Here we go, ladies," their waiter said as he placed a steaming plate of Laganelle with mushroom ragu in front of each of them.

When he was out of earshot Jen whispered, "Do you think he finds it odd that we always order the same thing?"

"Right now, I honestly don't give a crap what he or anyone else thinks."

Without even being asked, the waiter returned a moment later with two more glasses of wine.

Lydia pushed her pasta around on her plate with her fork and took a small nibble here and there.

"Penny for your thoughts," Jen said.

"I'm just wondering if I'll ever find that special someone. I tried so hard with Carrie, but no matter what I did—landing a reputable job, learning to like martinis, giving up hot chocolate, buying more girly clothes—it was never enough. I was never enough."

"Maybe you tried too hard."

Lydia was about to tell Jen to take a long walk off a short pier, but although it hurt to hear, there was probably some truth in Jen's words. "It's possible," she admitted and took a gulp from her wineglass.

"Are you going to try and call Carrie again?"

"I don't know. Probably not. It would make me look desperate."

"Fair enough," Jen said.

"And may I remind you, she broke things off with me via text, that's how little she thinks of me."

"I think it's more of a reflection on her, on what a chickenshit bitch she is."

"You want to know what's pathetic?" Lydia asked.

"What?"

"I've been combing the real estate listings in Cleveland Park, hoping to find the perfect house for us. All the while, Carrie was probably killing time by swiping right, waiting for the opportune moment to dump me. You know, now that I think about it, she was kinda off when we visited her friends in Annapolis a few weeks ago. I should've clued in."

"Don't be so hard on yourself, Lyd."

Lydia threw her hands in the air. "I can't help it." After downing the rest of her wine, she said, "Anyway, thanks for giving me a shoulder to cry on."

Jen reached across the table and squeezed her hand. "Anytime. You've been there plenty of times for me."

CHAPTER FIVE

The next morning, Lydia stared out her kitchen window, aimlessly shoveling Honey Nut Cheerios into her mouth. Before she'd gone to bed the night before, she'd removed all traces of Carrie from her phone, deleted her as a contact, and unfollowed her on social media. Maybe not the most mature thing in the world, but so what? Lydia was embarrassed and hurt and sad.

And one thing was for certain, she wasn't going to let Carrie drag her down. *No sireee.* Tonight, when she got home from work, she planned to create a profile on Sapphire, a lesbian dating app, something she swore she'd never ever do, but desperate times called for desperate measures.

She'd wait a few weeks before she went out on an actual date, allow herself a little time to wallow, but then she'd put herself out there. In the meantime, it couldn't hurt to at least explore the women on Sapphire. It would allow her to acclimate to the whole dating app scene.

Lifting her cereal bowl to her lips, she slurped up the last of the milk and set the bowl down with a thud. Carrie would have grimaced if Lydia had done that in her presence. So childish, not to mention terrible table manners. "Go to Hell, Carrie," Lydia bellowed into her empty apartment before letting out an audible belch. Damn, that felt good.

After she showered and dressed, she rushed off to work. Although she'd barely started her new job at the *Post* and continued to battle persistent imposter syndrome, she did love what she did. For that, she was immensely grateful. Right now, work was the perfect distraction, and it was encouraging that not every aspect of her life was a complete shit show. Sure, her personal life was in utter shambles, but at least she had a good job. No, not a good job, a *great* job.

During their morning meeting, Lydia and her team reviewed the first three letters Tisha had selected for them, followed by their usual discussion. When it came time to consider the fourth letter, Tisha paused and placed a hand over her heart. "I saved this next one for last. Once you read it, I think you'll understand why." Tisha picked a piece of paper off the table and waved it in the air. "This final letter for today came to us in the old-fashioned way—snail mail." She laughed. "We don't get many that way anymore."

Although Tisha had scanned the letter and displayed the electronic version up on the screen, Lydia was drawn to the actual handwritten letter. She lifted it off the table and leaned back in her chair to read it. It was written in pencil and nearly a full page long.

Dear Birdie,

My name is Ana and I hope you can help me. Five years ago, my husband, Bobby, and I came to the US from Venezuela. Life here was very good for us, much better than in Venezuela. Bobby got a job doing construction and we had a beautiful baby girl. Her name was Beatrice.

This past year some very bad things happened. First, our daughter died. A car hit us while we were crossing the street. The driver didn't even stop.

Then, a few months later, there was an accident at Bobby's work. They took him to the hospital, but he didn't survive.

Bobby and Beatrice were everything to me. I've tried to remain strong but sometimes it is difficult.

Not only did I love Bobby very much, but I also relied on him for everything. I know this was not smart. Now that he is gone, I am in a bad position. I don't speak English (my neighbor helped me translate this letter for you) and Bobby and I didn't have much money.

I must now provide for myself. I work hard at my job, but it doesn't pay much money. People will not hire me for better jobs because I don't know English, only Spanish.

The apartment where I live is not fancy, but it is clean and safe, and I have many friends in the building. They have helped me through this terrible year, but if I don't find a better job soon, I will have to move out and I don't know where I will go.

My friend's daughter said I should write to you. You might have some ideas about what I can do given my situation. I am reliable, and I will do any job that will allow me to cover the rent.

Sincerely,

Ana

When Lydia finished reading the letter, she set it aside and wiped a tear from her cheek with the back of her hand. "Wow," was all she could say. Of all the letters she'd received in her years as an advice columnist, this one took the cake—the poor woman had been through so much. Everyone in the room reached for the box of tissues on the table and dabbed their eyes. Lydia did the same and blew her nose before asking, "Thoughts on how to respond to Ana?"

"The dear soul," Tisha said. She balled up the tissue in her hand and stuffed it into her sleeve. "I guess a good place to start would be for her to learn English."

Lydia nodded. "I had a similar thought, Tisha, and I happen to know the perfect place for her, the Washington English Center."

"I'm not familiar with it," Sally said.

"It's on the edge of Kalorama, just north of Dupont Circle," Lydia replied. "I'm a volunteer teacher there. It's an incredible place. Full of strong people like Ana who are trying to make a better life for themselves. Tuition is very low, and it's often waived for students who can't afford the fees."

Tisha raised a finger. "It appears Ana has an excellent support network—she says she has a lot of friends in her building—but she must be suffering from unfathomable grief." She gestured toward Noah. "Can you research some low or no-cost counseling options. I believe the DC government recently launched a new program."

"I'm on it," Noah said.

They brainstormed other ideas about how to help Ana, including some job resources she could explore.

When Lydia returned to her office after the meeting, the first thing she did was draft a response to Ana's letter. Rule number one for advice columnists: don't become emotionally invested in the stories people write in about. While always empathetic, Lydia had generally been able to compartmentalize the letters she received. In the case of Ana's letter, though, it was virtually impossible not to be deeply impacted by her tragic story. Lydia drafted and redrafted her response, taking extra care to hit what she thought was the right tone.

That evening, when Lydia eventually stood from her desk to go home, she was bone tired. By the time she hit the sidewalk, the dusky hues of twilight filled the sky. Grateful for the refreshing coolness after a stint of warm weather, Lydia opted for the scenic route home. Her walk brought her past a towering red-brick church that, according to the sign outside, dated back to the 1890s. Three sets of ornate metal doors marked its entrance, one of which was ajar, as if beckoning her inside.

Drawn by curiosity, she paused and stared up at the dome perched above the church. The crisp and clear night sky and the moon's silhouette peeked through the darkness. A flicker of light from inside the church caught her attention, bringing her focus back to the open door.

She ascended the steps, crossing the threshold into the hallowed interior. Lights shone over the colorful sanctuary, but otherwise the church was dark and there didn't appear to be anyone else around. Guided by an inexplicable urge, she followed the red carpet down the aisle and sat in one of the empty wooden pews. She bowed her head in a silent prayer for Ana. When she was done, she stood but before she exited the pew, she heard a door click shut. Turning, she noticed the door she'd come through was now closed. Was she trapped inside?

She spun around. A shadow crept along the wall near the altar. "Hello, is someone there?" No answer came. She raced out of the church, exhaling in relief when she pushed through one of the rear doors and it swung open.

When Lydia stumbled through the door of her apartment, her brain felt like a bowl of overcooked oatmeal. All she wanted to do was sink into her couch and binge-watch something on Netflix. First though, she had to address the growl in her stomach. There was some leftover spaghetti and meatballs stashed in the fridge and she tossed it into the microwave. As the food warmed, she opened her laptop to skim the latest news headlines. That's when she saw an unwelcome reminder—the sticky note she'd left herself that morning: *Create profile on Sapphire* ☺ She groaned. What had possessed her to add the peppy little smiley face? When the microwave beeped, Lydia surprised herself. Instead of succumbing to the couch, she scooped up her laptop and ventured toward her desk with her steaming plate of food.

Immediately, she plunged into creating her Sapphire profile, hunched over her computer as she crafted her online alter ego. By ten o'clock that evening, Lydia had not only fashioned an online persona but had also compiled a list of ten self-improvement goals, most of which she thought she could accomplish in short order. Improvements she hoped would transform her into a better person and primo girlfriend material.

The list kicked off with *improve muscle tone*. This goal would likely take the longest, but Lydia had a lead on a good personal trainer who, she hoped, would kick her into shape lickety-split.

Excited to share her accomplishment with Jen, Lydia fired off a text. *You have a minute to chat?*

Her phone rang a few minutes later. "What's up?" Jen asked.

"I created a profile on Sapphire and I need your opinion."

"Sapphire, the lesbian dating app?"

"Yes." To preempt any concerns, Lydia added, "I know it's only been a hot minute since Carrie and I split. I don't plan to dive in right away. I'll give myself a little time. Having the profile in my back pocket will be handy. I'll just pull the trigger when I'm ready."

"Ready for what?"

"Ready to dip my toes back into the dating pool. Let's FaceTime so I can share my screen with you," Lydia suggested, maneuvering her phone to showcase her Sapphire profile.

Upon glimpsing Lydia's profile picture, Jen said, "Oh, my, God...That picture of you, where on Earth was it taken? Wait, don't tell me, a Halloween party in college."

"Ha, ha, very funny. It's from Carrie's sister's wedding last spring. Everyone got their makeup done and I didn't want to be the odd one out."

"Okay. Still, that doesn't explain why you chose this photo for your Sapphire profile."

"Ignore the photo for now. Let me walk you through the rest of it."

Lydia proceeded through each section of the profile—hobbies, likes, dislikes, and her aspirations for a partner.

When she was done, Jen asked, "What exactly are you going for here?"

"I'm trying to portray the person I aspire to be."

"Why not aspire to be yourself?"

Lydia glared into her phone. "What are you implying, Jen?"

Jen sighed audibly. "Listen, Lyd, all I'm trying to say is that you should create a profile that reflects who you are, not who you think you should be or what you think someone else wants. You've been my best friend since we were seven. You are kind, smart, and incredibly giving. I wish more people could see that side of you."

"What do you mean?"

"When it's just the two of us, you're authentic, funny, a bit dorky. Generally, all around awesome."

"Thanks, I guess."

"But you act differently when other people are around."

Lydia shook her head. "No, I don't."

"Let me give you an example. A few weeks ago, when you and I were at the arboretum, we were having a blast, running around, taking goofy pictures..."

"That was fun."

"It was, until we ran into those two women who knew Carrie and they hiked part of the trail with us. Instantly, you transformed, got all serious. Even your voice changed. It was like this mask had come down over your face."

"You're so full of it."

"I'm not, but if you don't want to listen to me, let's take a hard look at this dating profile you've assembled. Under hobbies you list writing poetry, attending the symphony, hiking, and cooking."

Lydia shrugged. "Yeah, so?"

"When we went to the symphony last fall, you fell asleep."

"I did not."

"Um, yeah, you did, drool and all. You even let out a few muffled snores."

Lydia threw her hands in the air. "I'd probably had a long week."

"I'll give you a pass on the writing poetry part. I know you were an English major and I remember when you went through that bizarre phase where you kept quoting Emily Dickinson. But do me a favor, open your fridge. Tell me what's in there."

"You know darn well what's in there. Frozen pizza and beer."

"So instead of listing cooking as a hobby, perhaps you should say, 'enjoy warming up pizza.'"

Lydia flipped her the bird playfully. "Just because I don't have the makings for a gourmet meal in my fridge, doesn't mean I don't like to cook and don't aspire to do it more. Carrie liked going out to dinner. Anytime I bought fresh stuff at the farmers' market, it spoiled."

Jen rolled her eyes. "Whatever. Moving on…Hiking is probably your only honest answer. I know you love to be outdoors. But what about sailing, biking, and softball? Why aren't they on your list?"

"I don't know."

"Weren't you the star pitcher of the *Forté* softball team?"

"Yeah, I guess."

"I don't want to be harsh, Lyd, but maybe take another crack at your profile, including the profile picture. Although, honestly,

I don't know what the big rush is. You and Carrie broke up what, like twenty-four hours ago? Take time to settle into your new job, reflect on what you really want in life and in a partner. Heck, maybe you can even learn to cook. If you need a guinea pig to test out some of your gourmet creations, I'm your girl."

"All right, all right, I'll make some edits to my profile, but no promises on hitting the pause button to reflect or whatever. Although, if I do try out some new recipes, you'll be the first to know. No promises they'll be edible."

After they ended the call, Lydia flopped on the couch and stared at the ceiling. Was Jen onto something? Did Lydia act differently around other people? Was she too focused on being what she thought others expected? Lydia yawned. These were deep questions, ones that she probably needed to ponder, but not now. She was too tired.

CHAPTER SIX

On Tuesday evening, Lydia left work a little earlier than usual. Before she went to the Washington English Center to teach, she had to make a quick pit stop at Target to grab some additional school supplies. Although WEC provided its teachers with more than ample resources, Lydia and her co-teacher, Arleen, had a few special things they liked to have on hand in their classroom.

She reached the elevator at the same time as Tisha. When it arrived at their floor, Tisha stepped in first and hit the button for the underground parking garage. She glanced over at Lydia. "Lobby?"

"Nope, not tonight," Lydia said. "Parking garage for me too. I borrowed my neighbor Callie's car. Gotta make a quick run to Target."

Tisha and Lydia walked through the musty, dimly lit garage together and bid each other a nice evening when Lydia reached Callie's red Volvo.

Lydia tore through Target like a tornado, weaving through aisles with practiced finesse. Mission accomplished, she hurriedly parked the car back in Callie's designated spot and began her ascent up the hill toward the school. When she got to her classroom, she set her backpack down and enveloped Arleen with a hug. "Ready for class?" she asked.

Arleen hesitated before answering. "Yes, although…" She retrieved her phone from a nearby desk and held it up for Lydia to see. "I just got a notification. There's been another murder."

Lydia slumped into a chair, a heavy sigh escaping her. "Oh, no, not again."

Taking a seat beside her, Arleen delved into the grim details. "They haven't released too much yet, but it sounds like some high school kids found the body in a park out in Maryland."

"Geez, that's awful."

"I know. Apparently, the kids had just finished playing soccer and were waiting in the parking lot to be picked up by their parents."

Lydia blew out a breath.

"When a reporter interviewed one of the kids, he said they'd seen the victim talking with some guy near the edge of the park about an hour earlier. They thought maybe he'd been trying to buy drugs—I'm not sure why—but anyway, when they discovered the body, it had the telltale red scarf…" Arleen shuddered, pinching her eyes shut as if trying to erase the haunting images from her mind.

The door to their classroom clicked open and a few of their students trickled in. Arleen and Lydia scrambled to their feet. They'd have to finish their discussion about the latest murder later.

While Lydia outlined the lesson plan on the whiteboard at the front of the classroom, Arleen pulled out her copy of the textbook and flipped it open to the first chapter.

Lydia wrote out the final activity they'd planned for tonight and faced her students. By now, seven of the ten seats were occupied. She and Arleen always made sure to have a few extra chairs at the beginning of each semester. It wasn't unusual for new students to be added to their roster even after classes had officially begun. People's lives didn't always coincide with the WEC school calendar.

They'd organized the desks in a horseshoe shape, and starting with the first student on the left, Lydia and Arleen personally welcomed each student to the class. When they finished, Lydia checked her watch. She'd give it a few more minutes in case anyone else filtered in, but then they needed to get started. They had a lot to cover in a short period of time.

Using magnets, Lydia attached a few images to the whiteboard and Arleen circled the room again to make sure everyone had their books open to the correct page. Lydia checked her watch again. It was time to begin. She wrote her name on the board and then pointed to herself. Arleen began to do the same but paused when the door to the classroom clicked opened.

In stepped a slender woman with straight black hair that fell to her shoulders. Her large brown eyes darted around the room before settling on Lydia. Lydia smiled and went over to greet her. "Hello and welcome. My name is Lydia."

Digging into the cloth bag slung over her shoulder, the woman withdrew an index card.

Lydia accepted it and read the neat print. "Ana Delgado. Class 1B, Tuesday 6 p.m."

The woman nodded.

Could this be the Ana, the poor soul who had penned the letter to Dear Birdie? *Had she lost her husband and child?* The Washington English Center offered classes of all levels, on weekdays, weeknights, and weekends. Was it too much of a coincidence for the letter writer—assuming she'd even enrolled in the English classes as Dear Birdie had suggested—to end up in Lydia's Tuesday evening class? Lydia dismissed the idea and motioned toward one of the vacant chairs. "Please, Ana, have a seat."

Based on the class list Lydia and Arleen had been given, all their students had either completed the Basic and the 1A intro classes that WEC offered or they had tested out of them and into 1B. It was, therefore, safe to assume they were all familiar with the English alphabet—the native language for many students at WEC was either Chinese or Arabic—and they knew at least a handful of English words and phrases.

Once the class had gone through the first section of the lesson, the students practiced dialogue in small groups before working individually on a worksheet. Lydia and Arleen moved around the room reviewing their work and offering hints to help the students fill in the blanks.

Lydia stopped at Ana's desk and peered down at her worksheet. In neat handwriting, she had completed all the questions. After Lydia scanned her answers she said, "Great work. Everything is correct."

Ana beamed up at her. "Thank you. I like class. I come back next week."

The magnificent smile on Ana's face warmed Lydia's heart. Although they'd spent only a short time together, Lydia could tell she was intelligent and good-hearted.

The premonition returned and Lydia wondered, was this Ana, the woman sitting in front of her, the same Ana who had written in to the *Post*? If Lydia was a betting woman, she'd say that she was, and although she was dying to know for sure, she would never come right out and ask her. There were all sorts of privacy rules regarding the letters that Dear Birdie received. Plus, although Dear Birdie's identity wasn't a secret, it was generally best not to blatantly broadcast it.

What mattered most was that, if Ana was *the* Ana, she'd been brave enough to enroll in English classes at WEC and actually show up. Countless people took the first step—they signed up— but then failed to appear on the first day of class. Regardless of who Ana was or wasn't, Lydia would do all she could to help her learn English, as she did with all her students.

Once class was over, Lydia and Arleen rearranged the chairs back into a horseshoe, wiped the whiteboard clean, and collected their belongings. The lively hum of conversation echoed through the hallway as students spilled from their classrooms.

Lydia had a book to return to one of the teachers on the upper floor. Like a salmon swimming upstream, she battled her way up the wide staircase to the second floor where most of WEC's advanced classes were held. Halfway up, her bag slipped off her shoulder, and without pausing, she turned to yank it back into place. Bad idea. Her foot missed a step and sent her teetering. Two hands swooped in and caught her.

Lydia glanced up, ready to express her gratitude, only to find herself locked in a gaze with two captivating brown eyes. Her breath caught in her throat. It was Sofia, the student turned teacher who had spoken at the welcome reception a few weeks before.

"Are you okay?" Sofia asked, concern etched on her face.

Lydia's cheeks flushed with warmth. "Yeah. I wasn't paying attention to where I was going." She gave Sofia a sheepish grin. "Total klutz."

Sofia's eyebrows arched up her forehead. "Klutz?"

Despite Sofia's near-perfect English, it wasn't surprising that the term "klutz" wasn't in her vocabulary. "Um, yeah, sorry. It means clumsy or awkward."

"Klutz," Sofia repeated as if she was filing the word away in her mind. A broad smile crossed her face, causing the corners of her eyes to crinkle. "I was actually on my way to find you."

Lydia's stomach stirred. *God she's beautiful.* "You were?"

"Yes." Sofia gestured to a small bench in the upstairs hallway. "Do you have a minute to talk?"

Lydia nodded. "Yes, of course."

As they settled onto the bench, Sofia said, "I heard from one of my students that you take each of your classes on a field trip."

"Yes, every semester. I take them shopping as a way to practice their English in the real world. We go to the grocery store, the farmers' market, maybe a boutique, stuff like that."

Sofia rested a hand on Lydia's arm. "It's a great idea."

The casual touch sent a small shock through Lydia. There was a subtle quality to Sofia that drew her in. Sofia was undeniably attractive, but it was more than that. The way Sofia carried herself—an air of confidence, yet an underlying vulnerability that tugged at Lydia's curiosity. Or perhaps it was the genuine warmth in her smile or the kindness in her eyes. Lydia cleared her throat. "Um, thanks. The students really seem to enjoy it."

"Would you mind if I tagged along on your next field trip?"

"No, of course not."

"I'd like to do something similar with my class and I think it would be helpful to observe what you do with your students before I try it on my own."

That made complete sense to Lydia. "I plan to take my class a week from Saturday. We usually meet here at the church and then venture out on foot. I can text you the details once we firm up a time."

"Great, thank you."

After exchanging phone numbers, they both stood, and Sofia treated Lydia to one more of her brilliant smiles before turning and heading down the hallway.

Lydia watched until she disappeared into a classroom. Their brief encounter left her yearning for more, a desire to know Sofia, to discover the stories behind those brown eyes. The field trip could not come soon enough.

CHAPTER SEVEN

Lydia whistled as she walked home from the English Center that evening. Teaching class always left her on a bit of a high, but tonight she was especially blissful. Was it because of her encounter with Sofia?

Before she had time to give it further thought, her cell phone vibrated in her back pocket. She groaned when she peered at the screen. It was a text from Carrie. Although Lydia had deleted her as a contact, she'd forever recognize her phone number.

WTF does she want? It had been radio silence from Carrie since she'd ceremoniously dumped Lydia the previous Monday at 6:33 p.m. *Not that the time is seared in my brain or anything. Of course, it is. How can it not be?*

With a dramatic swipe, she deleted the text, but before she had time to return her phone to her pocket, it rang. It was Carrie. "What in God's name?" she said out loud. "Answer it or let it go to voice mail? Oh, what the hell." She stabbed her phone to accept the call and barked, "Hello."

"Hey, babe," Carrie replied.

Lydia almost responded in kind, but fortunately, she caught herself before the endearment slipped out. Just hearing Carrie's voice stirred so many emotions. Sadness. Yearning. Anger. She tried to keep her voice even when she responded. "Why are you calling me?"

"I miss you."

Lydia pinched her eyes shut and sucked in a breath. A sliver of her heart wanted to tell Carrie she missed her too. But did she really? And even if she did, how could she even consider forgiving the woman who'd tossed her aside?

Lydia must have gone too long without responding because Carrie asked, "Did you hear me, Lydia? I said, I miss you."

"I heard you."

"I made a mistake," Carrie said. "I'm sorry I broke things off with you."

"By text," Lydia reminded her.

"Like I said, it was a mistake. Can you forgive me?" Without waiting for Lydia to respond, she said, "I've got a big work function Thursday night. Will you be my date? You know I hate going to those things alone."

"So, you're calling me because you're desperate for a plus-one."

"Don't be like that, Lyd. I said I missed you. Please, come with me."

For a second, Lydia almost said yes. Although she hadn't yet posted her profile on Sapphire, the mere thought of doing the online dating thing made her nauseous. She took another deep breath and gathered every ounce of willpower she could muster. "No, I will not go with you." The words came out easier than she expected, and it felt good to say them. It felt good to say no to Carrie.

"Don't make me beg, Lydia."

"I said no, Carrie, and I meant it. No amount of begging will change my mind." Lydia paused for a moment before adding, "Although, I must admit, I'm surprised you don't have a new girlfriend yet." It was a snarky thing to say, but Lydia wasn't feeling especially charitable at the moment.

"It didn't work out."

"What didn't work out?"

"This other woman that I was, um, interested in."

Lydia nearly tripped over the uneven sidewalk and bile rose in her throat. When Carrie had dumped her, it hadn't even crossed her mind that it was because there was someone else. *You idiot, of course there was someone else.* She was such a naive nitwit. She clutched her phone so tightly that it was a miracle the screen didn't shatter in her hand. "Answer me this, Carrie... Were you seeing this other woman when you and I were still together?"

There was a long pause before Carrie spoke. "No, I mean yes, but it's not—"

"Forget it, Carrie. I don't want to know," Lydia said with more conviction than she felt.

"Please, let me explain."

"Go fuck yourself."

"Lydia," Carrie pleaded.

"Have a nice life," Lydia said and ended the call. She stuffed her phone back in her pocket and marched up the front steps to her building.

When she got upstairs to her apartment, she dropped her bags on the floor in the small foyer and hung her coat on the hook near the door. She wandered into her bedroom, suddenly desperate to rip off her work clothes and slip into something infinitely more comfortable.

Normally one to take care of her belongings, she opened the door to her closet and flung off her right shoe, sending it sailing into the full-length mirror on the back wall. She did the same with her left, except this time the sole hit the mirror with a "thwack," sending a long splinter from the base of the mirror all the way to the top. Lydia slapped her forehead. "Oh, crap!" That was all she needed, seven years of bad luck. She stepped forward, examined the mirror, determining she was off the hook. It was cracked, not broken. The superstition clearly stated a *broken* mirror brought seven years of bad luck.

Stepping back from the mirror, she stabbed a finger toward her reflection. "You go, girl. Ain't nobody's the boss of you. You deserve better than that cheating wench Carrie."

She spun away from the mirror on the ball of her socked foot, yanked her sweater over her head, stepped out of her skirt, and ceremoniously tossed both garments on the floor. "I'm such a badass," she bellowed and pumped her hand in the air.

After adding her bra to the heap on the floor, she pulled on a T-shirt and sweats and closed the closet door, only to reopen it a second later. She laughed as she gathered her clothes from the floor and hung them up. *I'm a neat badass, nothing wrong with that.* For good measure, she scooped her shoes off the floor and placed them carefully inside their box.

She wrangled her curls into a ponytail and made a beeline for the kitchen to pour herself a large vat of wine. It was nearly nine o'clock and she hadn't eaten anything since lunch. Still, the thought of food repulsed her. For all her professed badassedness, learning that Carrie had most probably cheated on her, or at least considered it, stung, a lot. No, it stung astronomically. Without question, it further emphasized what a royal piece of shit Carrie was, although that did nothing to ease the knot in Lydia's stomach. It made her even angrier at Carrie, and it also made her even angrier at herself. *How could I have been so blind?*

She stomped her foot. Falling into a funk was not the answer. Doing so would only end up hurting herself in the long run. A moment like this required strength—and music. She reached for her phone, fired up Spotify, and scrolled through her playlists. A dose of Taylor Swift was just what the doctor ordered. Lydia cupped her hands around her mouth and bellowed, "The next chapter of my life starts right now!"

With the infectious beats of Taylor's tunes filling her apartment, Lydia danced around as she finished off her glass of wine. Eventually, she turned down the volume and poured herself a tall glass of water. Settling at her desk, she opened her laptop and logged into the Sapphire site. As she scrolled through her profile, she pondered whether she was truly ready to hit that publish button.

Jen's words echoed in her mind...*Aspire to be yourself. Reflect on what you really want in life.* Humming into her empty apartment, Lydia reluctantly made edits to her profile. Out went the glam profile photo, replaced by one of her steering a sailboat. Opting not to remove any of the hobbies she had listed—writing poetry, attending the symphony, hiking, and cooking—she did add sailing and softball. After a few more tweaks, she hovered her mouse over the submit button, closed her eyes, and counted to three. On three, doubt crept in, causing Lydia to yank her hand away from the mouse as if it had heated up like a curling iron. *Should I heed Jen's advice? Should I embrace singlehood and take time to reflect and find my inner self?* Her brain knew the answer to these questions was an unequivocal yes. It was her damn heart that always mucked things up.

She held her breath, scrolled to the top of her profile and hit the delete button. Poof, her Sapphire profile vanished. She marched back into her bedroom, opened the closet door, flipped on the light, and stared at herself in the splintered mirror. "Who am I? What makes me happy?" Her dark-brown eyes stared back at her as she leaned in closer.

She asked the questions again, this time louder. "Who am I and what makes me happy?" The truth was, she didn't have the slightest clue. "This must be rectified," she declared to her reflection before stepping back and slamming the closet door shut.

For the next two hours, she immersed herself in research—self-help books, seminars, and retreats. After that, she dug through the old columns she'd written for *Forté*, hoping the advice she'd doled out to others could guide her now.

Around midnight, she closed her laptop, having ordered five self-help books, registered for a daylong seminar on finding your inner self, and committed to a three-day retreat in Arizona over the upcoming weekend. Sure, it was a splurge on her budget, especially with a last-minute Columbus Day weekend airline ticket. But so what? It would be well worth it if the retreat helped her figure out exactly who Lydia Swann was.

She couldn't wait to tell Jen in the morning. Not only had Lydia decided against posting her profile to Sapphire, at least for the time being, she'd also embarked on a journey of self-reflection. Hopefully, Jen would be proud of her.

CHAPTER EIGHT

Lydia strutted to work with her head held high, fueled by a pep talk she'd gotten from an enlightening podcast that morning. The podcast was titled *The New You*, and over breakfast she'd listened to an episode about confidence. The podcaster, Cherie, claimed that simply exuding confidence not only convinces others you've got it together, but it also persuades you into being more confident. It's like a confidence placebo effect. According to Cherie, confidence was the secret sauce on the journey to becoming a new and improved version of yourself. Seemed pretty straightforward.

Lydia soaked up Cherie's every word, eager for more. She thought about queuing up the next podcast episode for her walk to work but decided against it. First, she had to put Cherie's confidence-boosting theory to the test. No distractions allowed, not even music. She had to stride into the day like she owned it.

A few minutes after she sat down behind her computer, Tisha knocked on her open door. "Got a minute?"

Lydia waved toward the two chairs opposite her desk. "Of course, please, come in."

Tisha stepped in her office, closed the door, and took a seat. From the look on her face, one might guess that she'd eaten a batch of three-day-old sushi for breakfast.

"Is everything okay?" Lydia asked.

Tisha shook her head. "No, not really. There's something you need to see."

Lydia hesitated. "Um, okay. What is it?"

"A *Dear Birdie* letter came in late yesterday. I just forwarded it to you."

Dear Birdie received hundreds, if not thousands, of letters every day, and given how long Tisha had worked at the *Post*, Lydia had to assume she'd seen just about everything. That made the expression on Tisha's face even more unnerving.

Lydia turned toward her computer and scrolled to the top of her email inbox. Tisha stood and came around behind her and together they read the letter in question.

Dear Birdie,

I'm "Joe." My girlfriend of two years recently wrote to an advice columnist—can you guess who—about our relationship. The dumb bitch columnist convinced my girlfriend that I was a deadbeat and encouraged her to dump my ass. Guess what? She did.

Not only that, but she kicked me out of her fucking house. The breakup came out of the blue. No warning signs, not even a hint. So, there's only one explanation—the fucking advice columnist put crazy ideas in my girlfriend's head.

You know what I think? I think the advice columnist should keep her goddamn mouth shut and mind her own fucking business, that's what!

Thanks to the advice columnist, I'm now stuck sleeping on my friend's couch, AND I've got no girlfriend. It sucks royally!

So, smart-ass, you got any advice for me? Like any bright ideas about how to get my fucking girlfriend back?

Sincerely,

Now Single "Joe"

Lydia leaned back in her chair and crossed her arms over her chest. "Wow, swell guy."

"Yeah, a real charmer," Tisha agreed. "Let's hope he's all bluster. As you may know, the *Post* has a psychiatrist on retainer,

Dr. Fern. To be safe, you might want to run the letter by her. Presumably, she'll advise us to ignore it and not reply to him, but we'll see."

"Okay, thanks. Definitely a good idea to run the letter by Dr. Fern." Lydia twirled her hair. "Although, I'm sure it's nothing to worry about."

Tisha headed toward the door. "I'll let you get back to what you were doing." Before she stepped into the hallway, she paused and turned back to face Lydia. "By the way, your hair looks really nice like that."

Lydia's hand instinctively went to touch her straightened locks. "Thanks. This morning I decided to go that extra mile when it came to my hair and makeup."

"What's the occasion?"

Lydia cocked her head and gave her a confused look.

"I thought maybe you did your hair because of a special occasion," Tisha explained.

"Oh," Lydia said. "Nope, not unless you call being newly single a special occasion, which I certainly do not."

Tisha placed a hand over her mouth. "I apologize, I didn't mean to pry."

Lydia had been at the *Post* for less than a month, and she hadn't divulged much about her personal life to her coworkers. Everyone on her team was aware she was gay—it had come up when they'd answered a letter from a closeted queer woman during her first week on the job—but that was about it. "It's okay. You're not prying. My girlfriend, Carrie..." Lydia was about to say "dumped me" but then she remembered her new motto: be confident, no more pity parties. "Um, my girlfriend, Carrie, and I broke up a little over a week ago."

Tisha pressed her palm to her chest. "Oh gosh, I'm sorry."

Lydia waved her hand through the air. "Ah, it's okay. It was for the best." She touched her hair again. "Anyway, now that I'm single, I thought I should make a little more effort. I'm not getting any younger, you know? Gotta find that special someone."

Tisha raised her eyebrow but didn't say anything.

Lydia had noticed the simple gold band Tisha wore on her ring finger. "What about you? How long have you been married?"

Tisha's face lit up. "My Harold and I have been together for twenty-seven years."

"Wow," Lydia said. "That's wonderful. I envy you. When you said his name, you got a little twinkle in your eye."

Tisha gave her a broad smile and nodded. "As for you, Lydia. Be patient. That special someone will come along."

"I hope you're right. Being single is the pits." Lydia reminded herself again of her new motto and her pledge to discover her inner self. "Uh, what I mean is, being single can be a drag, but I'm going to make the most of it. Use this time for some self-care and reflection."

"Good for you," Tisha said. "That's the spirit." She turned to leave. "See you in the meeting at ten."

Lydia gave her a wave goodbye and began to sort through her emails. Before she knew it, the team meeting reminder popped up on her screen. After refreshing her coffee, she went to the conference room. Once everyone on her team was present, Tisha brought up the first letter of the day for them to review.

Dear Birdie,

A few years ago, my husband and I experimented with an open marriage. We both enjoyed it, and although we eventually decided to stop doing it, we remain friends with some of the people we met during that time. We've become very close to one guy, Blake.

Blake is single and a really great person. Funny, smart, kind. My husband and I had a lot of fun with him in the bedroom and although the three of us are no longer intimate, we all hang out together pretty regularly and there's never been an issue.

A few weeks ago, we hosted a few friends for dinner, Blake among them, and one of our single female friends expressed interest in Blake. We adore both her and Blake, so I encouraged her to ask him out. They recently had their first date, and it appears to have gone very well.

So, my question is, should I tell my female friend how my husband and I know Blake? She knows he's a dear friend of ours but does our history with him matter?

Sincerely,
One Time Swinger

After she read the letter, Lydia leaned back in her chair and addressed her team. "In my experience as an advice columnist, I've seen my fair share of letters that touched on the theme of open relationships or a desire to try a threesome or foursome. Typically, a man, or occasionally a woman, writes to say they want to inquire whether their spouse/partner is open to trying "something new" in the bedroom. Usually, they aren't sure how to bring up the topic."

"I'm with you," Tisha said. "If I had a dime for every letter we got on this topic…" She tapped her finger on her chin. "Although, I've got to say, this letter offers a unique twist, one I don't recall encountering before."

Lydia nodded in agreement and addressed the whole team. "Ideas on how we should respond?"

Sally raised her hand. "Um, yeah." Her cheeks turned bright red. "If I was the friend, I'd want to know the truth. In my opinion, One Time Swinger should have been up front about her past with Blake right from the beginning, right when the friend first expressed an interest in him. I mean if the friend and Blake get serious, or get married or something, the truth will eventually come out."

"I think you're right," Tisha said. "The friend definitely needs to be told. She may not like that aspect of Blake's history, or maybe she will, but either way, it's information she should have as she assesses her relationship with this guy."

Noah sat up straighter in his chair and cleared his throat. "No doubt about it, the friend needs to hear the truth ASAP. However, I think that before One Time Swinger goes telling her friend, she should offer Blake the chance to inform her first."

Lydia smiled at Noah. "You're exactly right." She scanned the room. "Thank you all for your input. Let's move on to the next letter."

Everyone returned their attention to the front of the room. The next letter Tisha had for them came from a woman who had a strong urge to become Amish although she had no connection to the Christian religion. Lydia and her team surmised that what the woman desperately needed was to unplug from social media, especially videos on TikTok, even if it was only for a few weeks.

The final letter they reviewed was from a man named "Bob" whose coworker, "Sue," had a prosthetic leg and walked with a cane. Bob didn't know Sue well and had never socialized with her outside of work, but by coincidence, they both ended up at the same hotel while vacationing with their families at Disney World. Although Sue had not seen him, Bob spotted her strutting across the hotel lobby in shorts, no prosthetic leg or cane in sight. In his letter to Dear Birdie he asked, "Should I confront Sue and let her know I'm on to her prosthetic limb charade?"

"Wow," Noah said. "The stuff people write in about is insane. You couldn't make this stuff up if you tried."

Lydia stifled a laugh. It was important that she remain serious. She didn't want to encourage anyone on her team to make fun of the people who wrote in to Dear Birdie.

"I think Bob should continue to play along," Tisha said. "The whole thing is too bizarre. He should keep his nose out of it."

"I agree," Sally said.

Lydia nodded. "I tend to agree as well but let me mull this one over a bit more. There are so many people out there who really do have artificial limbs, and for this woman to pretend she has one…It doesn't sit right with me. All I can think is that she's doing it for attention and needs to be called out." Lydia jotted down a few final notes and adjourned the meeting.

On her way back to her office, she grabbed her lunch from the fridge in the staff kitchen. Usually, she'd sit with her coworkers and chat while she ate, but not today. Instead, she hunkered down at her desk to get some work done. Soon, she would jet off to Arizona for her retreat and she had a long to-do list to conquer first.

While chomping down on her kale salad—part of her newfound effort to embrace a healthier diet—she sketched out ideas on how to respond to the slew of letters they'd reviewed that morning. If nothing else, it was a distraction from the dull, tasteless abyss that was her meal.

With the last leaf of kale conquered, she dove into her emails. And then, bam! She got to the unsettling letter from Now Single Joe. A pit formed in her stomach as she read it through again. Heartbeat racing, she whispered, "It's nothing to worry about."

After work, Lydia met Jen outside Off the Record, a bar below the iconic Hay Adams hotel across Lafayette Park from the White House. The bar was primo for people-watching. You never knew which bold-faced names might be lurking in the corner. Jen's fixation with the place was their cardboard coasters. Each one was adorned with an original political cartoon. Whenever Jen got wind that a new coaster had been released, she and Lydia ventured to the bar with a sole mission: snag a coaster to add to Jen's ever-expanding collection. And that's why they were there tonight.

"Score," Jen said when they crossed the threshold of the bar. "We've got real estate." In Jen-speak, this meant there were still a few open seats at the horseshoe bar.

They claimed two of the plush stools and ordered their drinks. After the bartender poured them each a martini, Jen gently hoisted her full-to-the-rim glass. "Happy almost three-day weekend."

"I'll drink to that," Lydia said before taking a sip.

Jen delicately set her drink back down on the bar. "So, how's your week been?"

Lydia shrugged. "Busy, but good. You?"

Jen swung her head from left to right, cracking her neck before she replied, "A total shit show. One of our interns fat-fingered some numbers. It almost cost our firm a mega-big client."

"But, let me guess, you saved the day?"

Jen grinned. "I did, but it was a little hairy there for a bit." She pouted. "The poor intern. It was an honest mistake, and his supervisor totally threw him under the bus, the jackass."

"What a prick."

"Yeah, I can't stand the guy. Thankfully, I don't have to work with him much." Jen took the olives out of her drink, slid them off the toothpick one by one, and popped them into her mouth. "Oh, my God. You have your retreat this weekend, right?"

Lydia twisted back and forth on her barstool. "Yep. I fly out of National at ten a.m. on Friday."

"It's an introspection retreat, right?" Jen asked.

"Uh-huh."

"And what is that exactly?"

Lydia shrugged. "Beats me. According to their website, the retreat will help me identify my true nature and discover who I am deep down. During my time there, we'll reflect on our strengths and weaknesses and improve the worst parts of ourselves, face our inner demons, deal with insecurities…stuff like that."

"Gotcha," Jen said with a smirk. "That's a lot for one weekend."

To further her point, Lydia added, "This woman named Cherie will run the retreat. I've listened to all her podcasts and she's so inspirational. She promises we'll walk away with the tools to enable us to become the best version of ourselves. Once we're secure in who we are, we'll be more confident, and it'll boost our self-esteem."

Jen looked at her with raised eyebrows. "It all sounds very… ambitious."

"I agree," Lydia said. "I really hope it's not a bunch of mumbo jumbo because it ain't cheap. Plus, I'm eager to figure out the puzzle that is me."

Jen gave her a reassuring pat on the thigh. "I'm sure it will be amazing."

Lydia played with the stack of coasters the generous bartender had given Jen. "I haven't the faintest idea what to pack."

Jen pulled the coasters out of Lydia's reach. "What sort of activities are on the agenda?"

"Yoga, meditation, workshops, meals, of course, nature hikes, sound bathing—whatever that is—and chanting. I think that pretty much covers it."

Jen took another sip of her martini. "Okay, so I'm guessing the dress code will be pretty casual?"

"Beats me," Lydia shrugged. "But I really need to think about what image I hope to convey."

Jen rolled her eyes.

"I'm serious, Jen. I must consider whether I want people to think I'm smart and nerdy, funny and colorful, a born leader, or something else?"

"I'm not even going to dignify that with a response. You're going there to find yourself, not to don persona costumes. Just be you."

"We've had this conversation," Lydia said. "And it still doesn't help me figure out what to pack."

Jen faced her. "I'm sorry I harp sometimes. I only do it because I love you, Lyd."

"I know."

"And to quote Alex Morgan, 'You must stop looking out. You can only get where you want to go by looking in.'"

"She said that?" Lydia asked.

"Yeah, in some ad for the World Cup."

"Huh, I don't remember it, but I like the quote."

"Me too," Jen said. "Now, about packing. If I were you, I'd pack some yoga clothes, hiking boots, jeans and T-shirts, a sweater—it can get cold in the desert at night—and maybe a nicer outfit in case there's a more formal dinner or reception one night." Jen snapped her fingers. "And don't forget a toothbrush, oh, and underwear."

Lydia poked Jen in the arm. "You are so not helpful."

"But I so am," Jen said with a laugh. "How about this? How about after we finish our drinks, we go back to your place and have a little packing party."

"That would be awesome. I can try on a few outfits for you. Even if I don't attempt to convey an image, I at least want to make sure I look good. Who knows? Maybe I'll meet the woman of my dreams while I'm there?"

Jen rested her hand on Lydia's arm. "Please tell me that's not the real reason you're going to Arizona, because you hope to meet someone?"

"No, of course not. Don't be ridiculous."

CHAPTER NINE

Lydia closed her eyes as the American Airlines flight to Phoenix barreled down the runway and lifted into the air. Once they reached cruising altitude, she pulled her backpack out from under the seat in front of her. During the more than five-hour flight, she reviewed the documents she'd received from the Saguaro Sanctuary, the resort that would host her mindfulness retreat.

The packet Cherie had emailed to the attendees included details about what to expect from the retreat, tips on how to get the most out of it, and a handful of suggested preretreat exercises. There was also a very long list of general house rules.

It was a lot of information to digest and given that Lydia had booked the retreat on a whim only a few days earlier, she hadn't yet had time to complete any of the recommended exercises. The first item on the list was to practice journaling. Lydia pulled a pen from her bag, but her search for something to write on came up empty. An American Airlines cocktail napkin would have to do.

Journaling had never been her thing, but she did her best to focus while simultaneously fighting off multiple attempts by her neighbor to start a conversation. Lydia didn't mean to be rude, but when she got to the retreat, she didn't want to waste a single second. Given how much money she'd shelled out, she had to hit the ground running.

Upon arriving in Phoenix, she took the Sky Train to the rental car center and was handed the keys to a Subaru Outback. After circling the vehicle to check for any damages, she climbed in to make the two-hour drive to Saguaro Sanctuary on the outskirts of Sedona.

The heavy metal gates of the resort swung open when Lydia rang the bell. She followed a long dirt road up to the main building. A valet greeted her and pulled her suitcase from the back of her car. Before she followed him inside, she took in her surroundings. Giant cacti dotted the landscape, and the final rays of the sun cast red and orange bands across the sand. Although her decision to attend the retreat had been a bit impulsive, she was now grateful she'd taken the plunge. Life was short and she needed to get on with hers, ASAP.

The temperature had already begun to drop. Lydia shivered as she mounted the wide stone steps to the reception area. The lobby was cavernous but welcoming. Textiles adorned the walls and rustic furniture was arranged in small seating areas, most of which were full of people.

Once she'd checked in, she hurried to her room to freshen up and unpack. According to the agenda in her welcome packet, the opening reception began in thirty minutes. She changed into her favorite jeans, a long-sleeve, cotton T-shirt, and Converse high-tops before making her way back to the main lobby.

A sign pointed her to an airy room where the reception was well underway. She migrated to a spot on the far wall and snagged a glass of white wine off the tray of a passing waiter. There were people of all different shapes and sizes, more women than men, and although a good portion of them were white, a fair number also appeared to be Black or Brown.

Lydia hadn't given much thought to who else might be at the retreat. Did that mean she was self-centered or self-absorbed?

She'd never considered herself to be either of those things, but what if she was? She sighed and took solace in the fact that, although she'd only just arrived at the retreat, the introspective questions were already flowing. *Maybe there are contemplation-inducing juices in the wine?*

Most of the people in attendance were talking in small groups. Not having the gumption to interject in one of their conversations, Lydia stayed on the fringe and continued to assess the crowd. Her eyes kept returning to a woman who stood in the center of the room. Aside from the color of her hair, her resemblance to Carrie was uncanny—athletic build and tall, towering over the smattering of people gathered around her. Although the woman appeared to be deep in conversation with the man beside her, she kept catching Lydia's eye...*And, holy crap, she's heading in my direction.*

Lydia's first instinct was to bolt from the room. A gulp of her wine served up the courage she needed to stay firmly planted on the hideous brown carpet.

"Hey, there," the woman said, reaching out her hand. "I'm Vanessa Redding." Her voice had this gravelly edge to it, and there was an air about her, one that made her very intimidating.

Lydia shook her hand and squeaked out, "Lydia Swann."

Vanessa tightened her grip. "It's a pleasure to meet you, Lydia."

When Vanessa let her hand go, Lydia unconsciously stuffed it in her front pocket, perhaps in fear that Vanessa might try to recapture it.

Vanessa asked Lydia where she was from and what she did for a living, and Lydia, in turn, asked Vanessa the same questions.

"I live in Northern California," Vanessa replied. "For a brief time after college, I was a member of the US Olympic Swimming and Diving Team. Now, though, I'm a professional cliff diver."

Lydia nearly dropped her glass of wine. "You're a what?"

"A professional cliff diver," Vanessa said, as if she'd instead conveyed that she was an accountant for an insurance firm.

"Wow, I had no idea that was a thing."

"Oh, yes. It's a very big thing," Vanessa assured her. "There are competitions all over the world. In fact, I recently returned from one in Polignano, Italy. It was sponsored by Red Bull."

"Red Bull, that's cool." Lydia considered herself somewhat worldly and had a decent handle on geography, but she'd never heard of the place where the competition had been held. "Where is Polignano exactly?"

"It's a small town on the heel of Italy's boot."

Before Lydia had the chance to ask Vanessa another question about her unusual occupation, a woman at the front of the room called everyone to attention. For the next thirty minutes, a string of speakers approached the podium to welcome them and officially kick off the retreat.

Lydia was left to wonder why a woman who appeared as confident as Vanessa was attending this retreat. Perhaps she'd been stricken by a case of acrophobia. In her line of work, that would certainly be concerning.

* * *

The first two days of the retreat flew by. Lydia tried her best to absorb everything, but ever since the opening reception on the first night, she and Vanessa had become practically attached at the hip. Often Lydia spent more time thinking about Vanessa than she did about the content being presented at the retreat. She replayed their conversations and interactions repeatedly in her mind when, instead, she ought to have been listening to the long line of speakers.

But really, who could blame her? If one were to look up the word charisma in the dictionary, Vanessa's picture would surely be there. And although they hadn't yet shared a kiss, the electricity between them was off the charts, at least in Lydia's mind. At night, as she lay alone in her room, she imagined how their first kiss might come about.

When she wasn't dreaming about kissing Vanessa, Lydia was busy Googling topics Vanessa had mentioned over the course of the day. She should have been practicing the lessons from the retreat workshops, but instead she spent hours digging deep into the Cuban Missile Crisis, Vermeer's preoccupation with light, and the dot-com bubble. If Vanessa happened to raise these topics again, Lydia wanted to be ready to discuss them intelligently. She wanted to be certain that, in Vanessa's eyes, she appeared smart and knowledgeable about the world.

Naturally, her foolish brain had to chime in. Was she falling into the same hole, trying to be someone she thought others wanted her to be? No, she was simply going the extra mile to prove her intelligence, that's all. Nothing wrong with that.

During one of their breaks during the day, Lydia subtly slid a mention of Vermeer's use of light into the conversation and she earned an approving glance from Vanessa. At least all Lydia's Googling had paid off.

At dinner on the second night, Vanessa jockeyed to grab the seat beside Lydia, casually scooting her chair a few inches closer so their thighs touched. But then, after dinner when people gathered for drinks in the bar, Vanessa pulled a one-eighty, acting as if Lydia didn't even exist. She brushed off her attempts to join the conversation and ultimately turned her back on Lydia completely.

Lydia did her best to brush it off and not be offended. It made sense that Vanessa wanted to chat with other people. No big deal. Lydia smoothly shifted gears, striking up a conversation with a couple from Albuquerque like it was no sweat off her back.

At the tail end of the evening, Vanessa magically appeared at Lydia's side. "Shall we call it a night?"

"Oh, yes." Lydia winked at the couple from Albuquerque. "If you'll excuse me. I need to get my beauty sleep."

As they strolled back across the elaborately manicured grounds to their rooms, Vanessa slipped a hand around Lydia's waist. This kicked Lydia's libido into high gear. *Maybe tonight we'll share a first kiss...and more.*

"Would you like to come in?" Lydia asked when they reached her cabin door.

Vanessa laughed. "We need to get our beauty sleep, remember?" With that, Vanessa abruptly bade her a chaste farewell and disappeared into the dark night.

Lydia spent hours tossing and turning in bed. Why was she so fixated on Vanessa? She'd paid a small fortune to attend this retreat but had hardly done any self-reflection at all. Instead, she'd directed all her mental energy on Vanessa.

A growing apprehension had also sprouted legs in the back of her mind. Was she drawn to Vanessa because of her resemblance to Carrie? There were so many similarities between the two women, not only in their appearance but also their personality—electrifying, charismatic, confident...self-absorbed.

Lydia punched her pillow. She'd worked so hard to move past Carrie and here she was, once again, being tugged back into the realm of unhealthy relationships.

She flipped over onto her stomach and screamed into her pillow. For once in her life, she was trying to focus on herself, pursuing personal growth. But what had she done? Fallen into the same old trap. Lydia had shoved aside her own goals, focusing instead on trying to be the person she thought someone else wanted her to be. What was wrong with her?

"Tomorrow I will do better!" Lydia announced into the dark hotel room. "I will distance myself from Vanessa and give the retreat my utmost attention."

While she got ready the next morning, Lydia peered at herself in the mirror and gave herself a pep talk. "You got this, girl. Today is about you, and only you. Don't let thoughts of Vanessa clutter your mind."

To boost her confidence and resolve, she stood as tall as she could as she strode into the dining room for breakfast. She scanned the room for an empty table. Invariably her eyes landed on Vanessa. In a single instant every ounce of her willpower evaporated into the dry desert air. It was as if her legs had a mind of their own, carrying her directly toward Vanessa's table.

"Hello." Vanessa gave her a not so obvious up and down. "You look beautiful this morning. That top suits you."

Lydia blushed. "Um, thanks."

Vanessa waved toward the long buffet at the back of the room. "Shall we get ourselves some healthy nourishment to propel us through another incredible day in the desert?"

Lydia nodded and dutifully trailed behind her. They walked wide of all the good stuff—chafing dishes full of bacon and waffles—and went straight to the section loaded with the fresh fruits, veggies, and a mound of tofu.

Even though her resolve had crumbled during breakfast, Lydia did manage to pay closer attention during the morning sessions. For at least a few hours, she was able to suppress thoughts of Vanessa, focus on the speakers, and take copious notes. If nothing else, she'd at least have good documentation of the various behaviors the retreat leaders encouraged them to follow. Once she was back in DC and no longer in constant proximity to Vanessa, Lydia vowed to practice them religiously.

Unfortunately, things went downhill in the afternoon. Lydia's mind utterly betrayed her. During a meditation session, her brain did the exact opposite of what it was supposed to do and went into overdrive. Would she and Vanessa remain in contact after the retreat? When would they see each other again? Would they ever share a kiss? Did Lydia really hope for something more between them?

At Vanessa's urging, Lydia enrolled in an afternoon yoga class. She'd never done yoga in her life, and although she spent half the class three steps behind or doing an upward dog instead of a downward dog, she liked it more than she thought she would.

Later that night, all the retreat attendees converged outside around a massive two-story-high bonfire. Away from the flames, the darkness of the desert surrounded them. Vanessa was perched on a stump to Lydia's left and the flickering light from the fire danced over her face. She, and everyone else, seemed mesmerized by the fire, and initially, few people spoke.

Eventually, Vanessa struck up a conversation with the man on her other side. Much to Lydia's dismay, their conversation shifted to the Cuban Missile Crisis. She supposed the topic held relevance given the war in Ukraine, but didn't these people ever talk about anything normal, like the *Barbie* movie or *Ted Lasso*?

Lydia made a comment about JFK in an effort to join the conversation.

Vanessa glared at her. "Please don't interrupt."

The shock on Lydia's face must have been evident because Vanessa rested a hand on her knee. "I'm sorry. Why don't you go mingle. Maybe you can find someone else to talk to."

Lydia didn't need to be asked twice. She stood, wandered over to the other side of the bonfire, and joined a group of women sitting in a circle of Adirondack chairs. The woman next to her gave her a warm smile and they fell into easy conversation.

About an hour later, Vanessa strolled over and leaned down to squeeze Lydia's shoulder. "Should we call it a night?"

Lydia stood and looked Vanessa directly in the eye. "No, I think I'll stay a little longer." As she watched Vanessa disappear around the building, she whispered to herself, "I deserve to be treated better."

CHAPTER TEN

On the flight home from Phoenix, Lydia pulled her legs to her chest and curled up against the wall of the aircraft. Out the plane's small oval window, billowy clouds stretched into the horizon. Her mind drifted back to the days she'd spent at the retreat. She couldn't help but question whether it had truly been the transformative experience she had anticipated.

If she were brutally honest with herself, it hadn't lived up to her expectations, but much of that had been her own doing. She'd allowed thoughts of Vanessa to occupy her mind for far too much of the time. Still, it wasn't that she hadn't gained anything from the experience, right? Sure, most of what she'd taken away mirrored the advice Jen doled out in her pep talks. So, if nothing else, the retreat had driven home one point: Lydia needed to pay more attention to her best friend. Listening to Jen was definitely cheaper than flying across the country to hang out in the desert and listen to podcasts celebs with large social media followings.

She pinched her eyes closed, but immediately blinked them open. *Oh, my, gosh.* Had she used Vanessa as an out? Had she latched onto Vanessa because she was a welcome distraction, allowing Lydia to dodge deep introspection? Lydia cringed. It was a strong possibility.

What am I so afraid of? Out of nowhere, or maybe from some dark corner of Lydia's subconscious, a mental snapshot of her stepmother, Melody, barged into her thoughts. Melody had died four years earlier, and Lydia rarely thought of her. Actually, she went out of her way to keep Melody out of her thoughts. But suddenly, she couldn't erase the image of Melody's face from her mind.

Lydia hunched over, unzipped her carry-on bag, and yanked out the latest issue of *Vanity Fair* from her bag. Even the glossy images splashed on its pages couldn't rid her brain of the Melody invasion. She closed the magazine and set it in her lap. *Why am I thinking about Melody now?* Lydia closed her eyes again and let her mind run.

Her parents had divorced when she was two and her father quickly remarried. From that point on, Lydia only saw her birth mother occasionally—Christmas, Mother's Day, and if Lydia was lucky, on her birthday. Her father was a kind man, but he literally worked himself to death.

This left her father's new wife, Melody, to basically raise Lydia as she pleased. This was not a good thing, at least as far as Lydia was concerned. It was best not to speak ill of the dead, but her stepmother had been a raging bitch, and that was being generous.

In her youth, Melody had donned the dual crowns of a beauty queen and spelling bee contender. She never missed an opportunity to remind Lydia of her impressive feats, runner-up in the Little Miss America pageant—twice—and securing a fifth-place finish in the hypercompetitive Scripps National Spelling Bee.

These early triumphs became the driving force behind Melody's life mission: to sculpt Lydia into a simultaneous champion of beauty pageants and spelling bees. Beginning at a very young age, Melody imposed an intense regimen on Lydia, forcing her to memorize words for hours after school. On the weekends, she zealously escorted her to every beauty pageant under the sun.

All Lydia yearned to do was play soccer and baseball outside with her friends. But Melody didn't care. It was as if Lydia had unwittingly become Melody's real-life embodiment of a nerdy American Girl Doll.

Lydia fared okay in the spelling bees, once advancing to the third round of the Scripps Bee. However, no matter how many pageants she entered, Lydia never came close to winning. This drove Melody insane. On the car rides home from each failed pageant she would berate Lydia. In Melody's mind, Lydia was, by far, prettier than all the other girls. She didn't win because she carried herself like a linebacker while all the other girls floated like ballerinas. Melody also never hid her disdain for Lydia's unruly curly hair. "Your hair doesn't do you any favors," she'd mutter.

"Would you like something to drink?"

Lydia opened her eyes. A tall, thin flight attendant stared down at her.

"Um, yes, please," Lydia said. "Do you have sparkling water?" The dry heat in Arizona had left her lips cracked and she licked them in anticipation of a cool beverage. The flight attendant was kind enough to give her a full can. Lydia downed half of it and rested her head against the seat. One thing was for sure, the retreat had not been relaxing. Just the opposite. Her eyes grew heavy. She let them fall shut and drifted off to sleep.

When she woke up, they were descending into DCA. The plane banked along the curves of the Potomac River and glided over Washington, DC. From her window, the Washington Monument, the White House, and the golden dome of the Capitol all came into view. A warmth washed over her. She was home. Although she'd been in Arizona for only a few days, it felt like she'd been gone at least a month.

She hopped the Metro from the airport, riding it to the Dupont Circle station. As she dragged her wheelie suitcase nearly three-quarters of a mile uphill to her apartment, she vowed to someday move closer to a Metro station.

When she approached her building, she winced. Her lovely, but incredibly chatty neighbor was out in her garden. After enduring the intensity of the retreat, the last thing Lydia had energy for was a chat with Mrs. I-could-talk-to-a-wall-for-an-hour. With a pang of guilt, she swiftly made a sharp left turn, the wheels of her suitcase clacking over the brick-lined alley that ran behind her building.

A group of her neighbors were congregated around two uniformed officers. *What's going on?* Lydia cautiously approached them. Her friend and downstairs neighbor, Callie, leaned over and whispered in her ear, "Last night, like ten people on our block had their tires slashed."

Lydia's hand went to her mouth. "Oh, that's awful. I always considered this neighborhood so safe." She scanned the alley. Although she hadn't noticed it at first, she now spotted multiple cars with flat tires including Callie's red Volvo station wagon. She turned back toward her friend. "Oh, no. They got your car too."

Callie shook her head. "Afraid so. I have the dubious honor of being the only person who had all four tires slashed."

"Oh, Callie, I'm so sorry. Do you need help covering the cost of getting them fixed?" Whenever Lydia borrowed Callie's car, she always returned it with a full tank of gas. Still, contributing toward repairing the tires seemed like the least she could do.

"It's nice of you to offer," Callie said. "But insurance should foot the bill."

Lydia gestured toward one of the cops. "Do they have any leads on who slashed the tires?"

"Not yet, but I overheard some of the neighbors talking. Apparently, Grayson, the guy who lives in the house on the corner, caught someone on one of his surveillance cameras. You know he has like seven of them."

Lydia nodded. Grayson had quite a reputation for being overly paranoid. "Do they believe this was a random act, or are the cops thinking the vandals targeted someone in particular?"

"I'm not entirely sure, but Doug," Callie said, referring to another one of their neighbors, "hinted that the culprits appeared to search for a specific license plate. He speculated that they slashed a few more tires on their way out just to make it appear like a random attack."

Lydia's eyes widened. "Whose car do they think the vandals were after?"

Callie wrapped her arms around herself. "Mine."

"But why?"

Callie shook her head. "I have absolutely no idea."

As soon as Lydia got to her apartment, her cell phone rang. It was Jen, wanting to FaceTime with her, something they rarely did. Jen had bombarded her with texts since she'd landed in DC, eagerly awaiting details about the retreat.

The second Lydia answered the call, Jen launched into a parade of questions. "So, how was the retreat? Did you introspect and all that shit?"

Lydia went to the fridge and pulled out a bottle of Sauvignon Blanc. "Honestly, I'm not sure where to start."

Jen leaned closer to the screen. "Was it gorgeous? Were your digs swank? Did you chant?"

"The setting was beautiful," Lydia said as she poured herself a healthy glass of wine. "The Arizona desert is stunning. Red and gold sand as far as the eye can see, towering rock formations, cacti everywhere, some of them massive. Oh, and the sunsets paint the sky with hues of orange and purple."

Jen nodded approvingly. "Sounds nice."

Lydia sank into her couch and propped her phone up on a cushion. "It was. And all the activities were incredible. We went on a few breathtaking hikes, did heaps of yoga—I even got into the chanting. It was oddly liberating."

Jen got up and started walking around her apartment. "What about the workshops? Were they like mind-blowing?"

"Can you sit back down? You're jiggling your phone so much it's making me dizzy."

"Yeah, sure, hold on a sec."

"Anyway, mind-blowing might not be the right description, but they were good. And there was something comforting about being surrounded by people who were all on the quest for self-discovery."

"Ah, the quest for self-discovery, huh? So deep."

"Bite me, Jen."

"Okay, okay, I'm sorry. In all seriousness, I hope you found what you were looking for and that it was all worthwhile."

Lydia's response came out slowly. "It was definitely worth it, but in a different way than I expected."

"What do you mean?"

"There was this woman—"

"At the retreat?"

Lydia nodded. "Yes, at the retreat."

"I knew it," Jen said. "I was right. You went to Arizona to find a woman."

"I didn't, I swear to God. I went there with the best intentions, I really did." Lydia went on to tell Jen about Vanessa. "For much of the retreat I berated myself for getting caught up on a woman instead of focusing on the reason I was there."

"That's too bad."

Lydia shifted on the couch and sat cross-legged. "Yes, it is. However, I kind of had this epiphany on the plane ride home. The whole experience at the retreat sparked me to introspect in a way I never have. It got me to think hard about some of the reasons I am the way I am. It got me to think about Melody."

Jen groaned at the mention of Lydia's stepmother.

"You know how much I hated all the stupid beauty pageants she towed me to."

Jen nodded.

"Well, I don't think I've ever stopped to think about the impact those pageants had on me—or, more aptly, Melody's reaction each time I was passed over. I never lived up to her expectations. Maybe that's why I practically kill myself trying to live up to what I perceive are other people's expectations of me. Maybe that's why I worked so hard to be the person Carrie wanted me to be."

"Wow, I think you're onto something. Melody was so awful to you. It's no surprise it left lasting scars."

They talked through Lydia's "Melody issues" for a while longer. Eventually, Lydia smiled at her friend. "Thanks for listening to me ramble on about this."

"Anytime."

Lydia stared up at the ceiling and then looked back at her phone. "Do I feel like I fully understand who I am? No, definitely not. But at least I've begun to pull back the banana peel. I don't think I need any more introspection retreats. I'll keep listening to my podcasts and I'll read all those self-help books I ordered. Talking with a therapist would probably help too. I don't think Melody is the root of all my issues, but she certainly was a contributing factor to some of my insecurities. And unfortunately, her effect on me didn't disappear when she died."

Jen leaned toward her screen and drew her arms wide. "Virtual hug. I am really proud of you, Lydia."

Lydia's heart swelled. "Thanks, that means a lot. I'm kind of proud of me too."

"I'm glad you're back home safe and sound."

Lydia bolted upright. "Oh, gosh, I almost forgot to tell you. You know my neighbor Callie, the one whose car I borrow sometimes?"

"Yeah, of course."

"Her tires got slashed, and a few other people's too."

"Why would someone do that?"

Lydia shook her head. "I don't know, but it might not have been random. It's possible Callie was targeted."

Jen's eyes widened. "That's creepy."

"I know," Lydia agreed. I feel super bad for her."

CHAPTER ELEVEN

The following Saturday morning, Lydia arrived at the WEC a little before eleven a.m. Today she had the field trip with her students and Sofia. The addition of Sofia to the outing had Lydia looking especially forward to it. She was eager to learn more about the remarkable student turned teacher.

Four of Lydia's students had signed up for the field trip, but two of them were carpooling in from Maryland, and their car wouldn't start. That left Bea and Nadia, and Lydia was okay with that. It meant the two women would get a more private, tutor-like experience.

Lydia waved when she reached the school and found Bea and Nadia standing outside with Sofia. She gave Sofia a one-armed hug and gestured down the sidewalk. "Is everybody ready to go?"

Although Bea and Nadia spoke very little English, they appeared to understand the question and both nodded. Sofia patted her shoulder bag and slid her sunglasses down over her beautiful brown eyes. "Yep, I'm ready."

They made their way down the hill and began to wander through the large farmers' market in Dupont Circle. The market was generally mobbed during the early morning hours, but by the time they arrived, the crowds had thinned out considerably.

Even with their limited English, Bea and Nadia didn't hesitate to approach the first stall they reached, peppering the vendor with questions about his wares. In Lydia's experience, many people, herself included, were reluctant to engage people in a foreign country when they didn't speak the language with at least some fluency. The few times Lydia had been fortunate enough to venture abroad, she'd always been nervous to speak the native tongue for fear of messing up or being laughed at.

As they continued through the market, Bea paused outside at a large tent.

"Do you want to go in there?" Lydia asked.

Bea nodded.

Inside the tent, table after table was piled high with fresh fruits and vegetables. Bea pointed to a wooden crate. "Eples."

"Yes," Lydia said. "Apples."

Bea picked up a bundle of green stalks off another table and gave Lydia a questioning look.

"It's similar to the Spanish word," Lydia said. "Asparagus."

"I like espárragos."

"Me too." Lydia picked up a neighboring bundle and handed it to Bea. "Guess the name of this."

"Brócoli," Bea said.

"Yes. Broccoli." Lydia scanned the tent and went to a table with carrots. "This is harder. Carrots."

Bea repeated the word and then pointed to her face. "Good for eyes."

Lydia laughed. "Yes, you're right."

After the vegetable stand, they moved through the rest of the market, stopping at one stand that sold honey and fresh baked bread and another that sold chicken, beef, and eggs.

"You are both very brave. Great job," Lydia said when they reached the last stall.

Both women beamed. "Thank you."

After the farmers' market, they walked a few blocks to a small women's clothing boutique where Lydia's friend Jessie worked. Jessie arranged a few outfits and accessories out on a table and together she, Lydia, and Sofia helped Bea and Nadia with the words for the various items.

When they left the boutique, Lydia rubbed her belly. "Are you hungry?"

Sofia replied first. "Yes, very. I forgot to eat breakfast."

Lydia spotted the bright red and yellow sign for Ben's Chili Bowl down the street, one of her favorite places to eat in the city. She hadn't been there in ages—Carrie thought the food was too greasy. She pointed toward the restaurant. "We could have lunch there."

Bea pointed to herself. "Work."

"You need to go to work?" Lydia asked.

"Yes."

Nadia seemed hesitant to stay for lunch without Bea and Lydia certainly didn't want to push her to stay if she wasn't comfortable. Rather than walk all the way back to WEC, Sofia and Lydia helped Bea and Nadia navigate to a bus stop, ensuring they both knew how to get home.

Once the two women boarded the bus, Sofia and Lydia wandered back in the direction of Ben's Chili Bowl. Lydia welcomed the chance to enjoy lunch alone with Sofia. This surprised her. While she wasn't an introvert, per se, Lydia generally shied away from one-on-one interactions with people, especially in nonbusiness settings. Jen, of course, was an exception, and now, inexplicably, Sofia appeared to be too. Sofia's strength and courage inspired Lydia. Despite being soft-spoken and sedate compared to the rest of the WEC teachers, Sofia managed to light up a room with her infectious smile.

After they'd ordered—a chili cheeseburger for Lydia and a bowl of chili con carne for Sofia—they settled into a booth near the front of the restaurant, both sipping from their sodas as they waited for their food. The silence didn't feel awkward at all. Lydia was remarkably comfortable in Sofia's presence even though they were practically strangers.

Sofia leaned against the wall and rubbed her eyes.

Had Lydia been presumptuous in assuming she wanted to stay for lunch? While Sofia had indicated that she was hungry, she hadn't expressly communicated a preference to have lunch at Ben's. "I hope you don't mind having lunch with me," Lydia ventured, a twinge of uncertainty in her tone. "I'm sorry, I should have checked with you first."

Sofia responded with an affirming smile. "Yes, I'm happy to be here with you," she said, stifling a yawn. "I had an early morning, but I'll be fine after a little food."

"What had you up so early on a Saturday morning?" Lydia asked.

"Work."

Lydia winced inwardly at her unwitting oversight. *You noob. Not everyone gets the weekend off.* "It speaks volumes about your dedication to WEC, joining the field trip even when you had to work today."

"Not a problem at all. I'm glad I was able to do it. Like I told you before, I really want to do a similar outing with my students."

"Where do you work?" Lydia asked.

Sofia took a long pull from her soda before responding. "My main job is as a customer service rep for Logan Airlines, but I only landed that position recently. For the last few years, I've worked in the kitchen at Chevy Chase Country Club. That's where I was this morning. Occasionally, I pick up shifts there to help my friends."

"That's really kind of you."

"It's the least I can do. My friends have helped me through some very difficult times."

Lydia had heard through the grapevine at WEC that Sofia had lost her husband, but she didn't know under what circumstances, and she didn't want to pry. She simply said, "Good friends are very important."

Sofia nodded. "Yes, they are." She hesitated for a moment as if considering if she should say more. Just when she opened her mouth to speak, the man behind the counter called out their order.

As they ate, they discussed the morning they'd spent at the farmers' market with Nadia and Bea.

"Do you have any tips for leading an outing like that?" Sofia asked.

Lydia imparted what wisdom she could before adding, "Getting a chance to practice English outside the classroom is so important. Clearly, some students are more comfortable out in the wild than others. Never push a student to do something they don't want to do. It will only backfire. Talking to real live people in a foreign language can be scary." Lydia paused and caught Sofia's eye. "Sorry, obviously you're well aware of that. I know it wasn't long ago that you were in the same boat as Bea and Nadia—beginning to learn English."

"Yes, I was." Sofia pushed her near-empty bowl of chili con carne aside. "I'm volunteering at WEC as a teacher because the school means so much to me. It helped me so much. I feel I must give back. You see, I came to the school after my husband, Diego, was killed. I was a bit desperate."

Lydia could see the pain in Sofia's eyes as she spoke her husband's name. "I am so sorry about Diego. If you don't mind me asking, how was he killed?"

Sofia shook her head. "No, I don't mind. He went to the corner market to buy milk…" Her bottom lip trembled, and she took two deep breaths before continuing, "There was a robbery. Diego herded the other patrons into a storeroom and then tried to wrestle the man to the ground. That's when he was shot."

"Wow," Lydia said as she brought both hands to her chest. "Diego was a hero."

"He was a very good man." Sofia took the paper napkin from her lap and folded it neatly on the table. "He spoke English well, and I relied on him for everything. After he died, I had only myself to depend on. I learned to speak English to support myself. I only got the job at Logan Airlines because I speak English very well and Spanish fluently. I'm lucky. My new job there pays me enough to cover all my bills. I'm now even able to save a little."

"I'd say it's more than luck. You're a very strong and brave woman."

Sofia briefly diverted her gaze before responding. "I didn't have a choice but to be brave."

Lydia eyed the beautiful and kind woman sitting across the table from her. Many people in Sofia's position would be mad at the world, they would retreat into themselves, but not Sofia. She refused to be beaten down. It was incredibly inspiring. Her story, while not quite as tragic, was somewhat like that of Ana, the woman who had written to Dear Birdie. "May I ask you a favor?"

"Of course."

"I have a student in my class. Her name is Ana, and like you, she's from Venezuela. I'm not certain, but I believe she recently lost her husband in a terrible accident. As a result, she may be in a situation like the one you faced after Diego died." Lydia didn't divulge that she speculated Ana was the woman who had written in to Dear Birdie. That fact didn't seem important. "Anyway, maybe I could introduce you two. If nothing else, you would be an incredible mentor for her. Going from student to teacher like you did is nothing short of amazing. It might show Ana that, if you put your mind to something, anything is possible."

Sofia placed her hand over Lydia's. "I'd be honored to meet her."

Lydia cupped Sofia's hand in both of hers. "Thank you."

CHAPTER TWELVE

On the walk to work the following Tuesday morning, the mere thought of teaching at the English Center that night brought a smile to Lydia's face. An image of Sofia flickered in her mind, and she thought back to their time together during the field trip on Saturday.

But surely, Sofia wasn't the only reason Lydia was excited to go to the school that night. Lydia adored her students and the two precious hours she spent with them offered refuge from the outside world, a sanctuary where she could momentarily shed the weight of trying to be the best darn Dear Birdie. That, and the stress that came with her new status as "single." As frustrating as it was, Lydia could not push past the belief that being single was a bad thing.

A ping-pong game played in her head. On one side of the table, a voice urged her to plunge headlong into the search for true love, as if time were slipping through her fingers like sand. Each time the ball volleyed to its side it yelled out, *"Oh my God, you're single! Hurry, find your soulmate before it's too late…"*

On the other side of the table, a gentler, yet equally persistent voice, begged her to exercise caution, to take a breath and embark on a journey of self-discovery. *"Slow down,"* it whispered. *"Take some time to discover who you are and what makes you tick."* No doubt it would be a tight match—both sides were quite persuasive and eager to have their voice heard.

While Lydia battled with the internal ping-pong game, she had another equally loud voice to contend with: that of Cherie, the woman who hosted the Arizona retreat and "The New You" podcast. Although Cherie's relentless peppiness had begun to grate on her nerves, Lydia remained resolute and listened to every last episode. If she didn't, how could she possibly fathom understanding who she really was? And how on Earth would she navigate the path toward becoming the new and improved Lydia Swann without the peppy podcaster there to guide her?

She briefly questioned whether perhaps she could find a balance between all the voices swirling around in her brain. What if the ping-pong opponents called a draw and met in the middle? What if Lydia didn't follow all Cherie's teachings—more like preachings—to a T? Everything in life didn't need to be black-and-white. Who said she couldn't seek out true love while simultaneously continuing her journey to self-discovery?

For a minute she grew excited about this parallel approach, but the elation was short-lived. Jen's words echoed in her mind—Lydia had to first understand herself before she could develop a deep and authentic connection with another person. Deep down Lydia knew Jen was right, but what if sometimes things worked the other way around? What if she had to find her soulmate *first* because only through them could she crack the code and determine who she was? *You know that's utter nonsense, Lydia. Give it a rest.*

One thing was for certain, at this rate, Lydia was going to drive herself insane. Thankfully, she'd arrived at her office building. All this soul-searching stuff would have to wait.

Hardly two minutes after she settled at her desk, Tisha appeared at her door, her expression etched with concern. "He's sent another letter."

Lydia feigned ignorance. "Who?"

Tisha's eyes narrowed and she pointed to Lydia's computer screen. "The menacing ex-boyfriend, Now Single Joe. I forwarded you an email that came in late last night."

Tisha crossed her arms over her chest and waited while Lydia read the letter.

Dear Birdie,

Did you get my last letter? I bet you did. Why haven't you written back to me yet?

Apparently, you're not only a busybody, poking around in everyone else's lives, but you're also an inconsiderate wench. I write you to say I'm sad about losing my girlfriend and it's radio silence. Thanks a lot, you dumb bitch.

You better smarten up and write back. I'm still in a real bad spot. If I don't get my girlfriend back, I promise you, I will go mad. Right now, she's totally avoiding me. It's not only rude but also cruel. I'm here hurting, and she won't even answer my fucking texts. I'm so damn angry I can't see straight.

To makes things worse, being forced to sleep on my buddy's couch really sucks.

What's a guy to do?

I hope to hear from you soon,

Now Single Joe

Lydia swiveled back and forth in her chair and met Tisha's gaze. "Well at least he sounds a tiny bit less angry than he did in his first letter."

Tisha's brow furrowed. "I don't know about that. Look at some of the words he uses…like he's forced to live on his friend's couch. It shows he's not willing to take any responsibility for his current circumstances. You don't have to be a rocket scientist to tell that the guy is seriously bad news."

Lydia waved a hand at her computer. "What am I supposed to do, respond to him?"

Tisha shook her head. "No, I don't think so. Like last time, I'd share it with Dr. Fern the psychiatrist and I think we should definitely forward it to our security people too. My gut, though is that replying to the letters will only encourage Now Single Joe."

Lydia's eyes grew wide. "Encourage him to do what?" she asked although she wasn't sure she wanted to hear the answer. There was no telling what a guy like Now Single Joe might be capable of.

"Heck if I know," Tisha said. "But I have zero interest in finding out."

"I think you're right though. Responding to Joe might give him false hope." Lydia spun one of the silver rings on her finger. "It seems to me like he's desperate for someone to talk to and in his demented mind, he thinks he and I are going to become pen pals."

"I think you're spot on. Joe does seem kinda lonely, but Lydia, you're currently his number one enemy. He believes you're the reason his girlfriend dumped him." Tisha sat down and rested a hand on Lydia's desk. "We need to take this seriously. A guy like this...let's just say, things could escalate, and fast. And, I hate to sound alarmist, but make sure you keep your wits about you when you're out and about. A quick Google search for 'Who is Dear Birdie?' and bam, the name Lydia Swann would pop up."

Lydia felt a lump form in her throat. This conversation about Joe was freaking her out. Was there a chance...could Joe have been the person who slashed Callie's tires? Maybe he thought it was Lydia's car. She did borrow it a lot and had recently driven it to work. *Nah, now she was just being paranoid.* She glanced at Tisha. "Did any wackos harass Maudie Zeller when she oversaw the *Dear Birdie* column?"

Tisha put both hands in her lap. "No, not anything quite like this."

"Hmm," Lydia said. "I don't know if that's good or bad."

"There were, of course, cases where people didn't like the advice that Dear Birdie dispensed. They'd write Maudie nasty notes, call her a quack, or say that she was out of touch with reality." Tisha paused for a moment before continuing, "But I don't recall any letters from a third party—someone like Now Single Joe—who was impacted by, and unhappy with, advice Dear Birdie had doled out to someone else."

Lydia drummed her fingers on the desk. "If Joe is this hostile to me, presumably, it's fair to assume he's also pretty furious with his ex-girlfriend. Do you think she might be in any kind of danger?"

"It's certainly a possibility," Tisha said.

"Maybe we should check in with her and make sure she's okay."

"I can pull up the original email we received from Gainfully Employed Girlfriend, or more aptly, Gainfully Employed Now Ex-girlfriend. Maybe we could reply to her."

"Okay. Is that something we can do right now? My spidey sense is sending me powerful signals. Either something bad has already happened to Gainfully Employed Girlfriend or it's about to."

"Do you mind if I hop on your computer?" Tisha asked.

Lydia stood and shook her head. "No, not at all. Help yourself."

Tisha managed all the incoming communication Dear Birdie received, regardless of whether it came in via snail mail, email, direct message on social media or via *The Washington Post* website, and she kept everything organized in a portal that only she understood.

Once all this business with Joe blew over, Lydia made a mental note to get a tutorial from Tisha on how the *Dear Birdie* database functioned and how best to query it. Not to be morbid, but if Tisha got hit by a bus tomorrow, the whole *Dear Birdie* enterprise would be up shit creek without a paddle.

Tisha sat down at Lydia's desk, and after a few clicks of the mouse, she said, "Hmm, exactly as I thought."

"What is it? Did you find the letter we got from Gainfully Employed Girlfriend?"

"Yes, but, as is often typical, the girlfriend didn't give her real name and her Gmail address is a series of letters and numbers. That may indicate that it was a temporary email account she set up. We can reply to her message, but if it bounces, our only other option is probably to get the IT department involved. They might be able to trace the IP address her email was sent from or something like that."

"Let's at least try to reply to her email," Lydia said. "We can reach out to IT later if we need to. Right now, I'm not sure the

situation warrants that kind of escalation. I mean assuming IT could even trace the IP address."

Tisha opened the girlfriend's email, hit reply, and typed off a brief email inquiring whether she was in any kind of danger. "Okay, I'm going to hit send."

"Go for it. What do we have to lose?" After Tisha sent the email, Lydia checked her watch. They still had a little time before the ten a.m. meeting and Lydia had one more thing she wanted to discuss with Tisha. She gestured toward the door of her office. "Would you mind closing that. I have something else I want to discuss with you."

Both Tisha's eyebrows rose, and she got up and closed the door.

When she was seated again, Lydia said, "I'm not really sure how best to broach this topic so I'm just going to come out and ask...Do you have any hard feelings about the fact that I was tapped to take over from Maudie?"

"No, I have no hard feelings at all."

Tisha's response was immediate, almost as if it was rehearsed. *Other people have probably asked her the same question.* Lydia gave her a sympathetic smile. "Okay, I just wanted to make sure."

Tisha's eyes widened theatrically. "Oh, my, gosh, have I given you that impression?"

"No, not in the slightest. It's only...It hasn't escaped me that you're excellent at your job. So good in fact, that I can't figure out why you weren't named the new Dear Birdie. Because I believe transparency and openness are vital to a healthy working environment, I wanted to bring the issue up with you."

Tisha winked. "I appreciate where you're coming from, but trust me, it's all good. I like the role I'm in. Weeding through all the letters is the fun part and I don't have any of the stress. If Dear Birdie loses followers, no one will point fingers at me." Tisha paused for a moment. "And to be brutally honest, if Maudie had tapped me for the role, a part of me wonders if I would have been accepted by the powers that be."

"What do you mean?" Lydia asked, although she suspected she knew the answer.

"I don't have a college degree from a fancy institution," Tisha said flatly.

Lydia was about to respond that surely the *Post*'s leadership would have been able to look past that, especially given Tisha's long track record at the paper, though, it was probably true. "Please know that I respect you immensely and I'm so thankful to have you on my team. I don't even think I could do this job without you."

"Thank you for your kind words." Tisha winked. "You're doing great, kid. I have no doubt you'd manage just fine on your own." She stood and opened the door to Lydia's office. "I'm going to hit the ladies' and grab some coffee. I'll see you in the conference room at ten."

Lydia gathered her notebook and pen and filed out the door behind her.

Today, they'd decided to let Sally, the intern, take a shot at curating letters for the morning review sessions.

While they scanned the last letter Sally had for them to review, Tisha tapped Lydia's arm. "You know that email we sent to Gainfully Employed Girlfriend earlier?"

"Yeah."

"Well, I just got weird response. I think it's some sort of error message."

"What does it say?"

Tisha held up her phone for Lydia to see and she squinted to read the message. It said: *Improper forwarding causing mail loop.* Lydia looked back at Tisha. "What does that mean?"

Tisha shrugged. "Heck if I know. Hopefully the email reaches Gainfully Employed Girlfriend."

"Yeah, let's hope," Lydia replied. "Although, would you mind checking with IT? I bet they know what that error means and maybe they can determine if the email was delivered."

* * *

When Lydia woke up the next morning, she instinctively picked up her phone and opened the news feed. Her stomach

sank. There'd been another horrible murder. This time, the victim was a twenty-something woman, her life snuffed out in a car outside a Costco Superstore in suburban Virginia near Dulles airport. Although the women's throat had not been slit like all the other victims—the initial report was that she'd been strangled—a red scarf had been tightly tied around her neck. This led the police to believe that the serial killer had struck yet again. Either that, or a copycat murderer had surfaced.

Lydia shivered. Having one serial killer plague the region was bad enough. The notion that a second one might be prowling around the DMV was too much to even contemplate.

The news report delivered yet another disheartening revelation. If the woman in the Costco parking lot had indeed fallen victim to the Red Scarf Murderer, it would signify the first murder unfolding in a crowded public space—a disturbing prospect, suggesting the murderer might be growing bolder.

Because she was a glutton for punishment and because of the collective obsession everyone in the DC region had about the serial killer in their midst, Lydia couldn't resist the morbid temptation to delve deeper into the details of the most recent murder.

She navigated to the website for one of the local news stations. Not surprisingly, their lead article was about the Costco murder. It identified the victim as Claudia Spiess and offered some additional details about the crime scene including a few photos. When Lydia reached the last image, her heart pounded in her chest and another shiver shot down her spine. Spray-painted on the pavement beside the victim's car were the words *Dumb Bitch*.

While the cruel use of derogatory language was, sadly, not uncommon, the words struck Lydia to the core. In both letters Joe had written to Dear Birdie, he'd referred to her as a dumb bitch. A sense of unease settled over her. Was it a coincidence?

"It has to be," Lydia assured herself out loud. She was being paranoid. But what if…What if Joe was somehow connected to the serial killer roaming the DMV. Lydia sat up in bed. Or, God forbid, what if Joe was the killer!

Lydia gripped her phone. Should she call Tisha? Aside from Dr. Fern and the *Post*'s security team, Tisha was the only other person who'd read the menacing letters from Joe. When Lydia located Tisha in her contacts, her finger hovered over the call button. Was she being an alarmist? She tossed her phone aside with a heavy sigh and climbed out of bed.

As she paced around her apartment, Lydia took a series of deep breaths. Joe was nothing more than a poor loser who'd lost his girlfriend. Okay, he'd sent a few threatening letters, but that was a far cry from being a serial killer. She was losing her mind and needed to get a grip.

CHAPTER THIRTEEN

On Saturday, Lydia met Jen for a morning run in Rock Creek Park and they followed the bike path north toward the National Zoo.

After running in silence for the first quarter mile, Lydia casually mentioned the letter Dear Birdie had received from Gainfully Employed Girlfriend a few weeks earlier. "The woman wrote in to ask if she should dump her unemployed, video game playing boyfriend," she explained.

"Oh, yeah. I remember that letter. Your advice was spot on. That woman totally needed to dump her lazy-ass boyfriend, ASAP."

"I'm glad to hear you agree with Dear Birdie's advice." Lydia grinned. "And I'm touched to hear you read my column."

Jen's eyebrows rose up her forehead. "Are you kidding me? Of course, I read *Dear Birdie*. I love it. I mean who doesn't like reading all the wild stuff people write in about?".

Once they'd started back in the other direction, Lydia turned toward Jen. "Um, the reason I brought up the letter from Gainfully Employed Girlfriend was because—and please don't share this with anyone—it appears that the woman who wrote that letter did in fact dump her boyfriend."

Jen raised both hands in the air. "Hallelujah!"

"Yes, I agree. Unfortunately, though, the boyfriend in question does not share our enthusiasm."

Jen laughed. "No, I suppose he wouldn't." She wiped a bead of sweat off her forehead. "Hold up, how do you know all of this? Did Gainfully Employed Girlfriend write back and give you an update or something?"

"No," Lydia said. "However, I have gotten a few letters from Joe, the boyfriend in question. In Joe's not-so-kind correspondence, he's basically told Dear Birdie to fuck off."

Jen gritted her teeth. "Oh, wow, that's more than a little frightening." She clasped onto Lydia's arm. "Wait, he hasn't threatened you or anything like that, has he?"

"No, not directly. Although it's obvious the guy is angry. In each of his letters, he's referred to me as a dumb bitch. Which is why…Oh, forget it. It was just my mind going berserk."

"No, tell me. Why what?"

"It's stupid, but the Red Scarf Murderer spray-painted 'Dumb Bitch' on the pavement next to his most recent victim, the one they found in the Costco parking lot. So, of course I—"

"Jumped to the conclusion that Joe and the RSM are one and the same."

"Yeah. Like I said, it was stupid."

"Stupid or not," Jen replied. "I don't blame your brain from going there."

"I guess I'm a little more on edge than I thought." Lydia clutched her side. "I've got a cramp. Do you mind if we walk the rest of the way back?"

Jen came to an abrupt stop and gave Lydia a wide-eyed stare. "Do you think Joe slashed Callie's tires? I mean you're always borrowing her car. Maybe he thought it was yours."

"I actually wondered the same thing myself," Lydia admitted. "I suppose it's possible, but honestly it wigs me out to even think about it."

"Fuck, it would wig me out too." Jen threw her arm over Lydia's shoulder. "You're always welcome to come stay with me and Eric if you want."

"Thanks, Jen. If things escalate, I may take you up on that offer."

When they reached the bottom of the hill where they'd started, Lydia propped her foot up on a bench to stretch her leg and looked over at Jen. "Since I got my sorry butt out of bed to run four miles, don't you think I deserve pancakes?"

Jen patted her on the back. "I think you do."

Over breakfast at a greasy spoon not too far from the park, Lydia once again bemoaned not having a girlfriend. "What if this journey of self-discovery takes me ten years? No way I can be single that long. I'll wilt away and die."

"I doubt that. And while I realize that I've been in a relationship with Eric since college, I really don't get why you're completely freaked out about the single thing. Lots of people, normal balanced people, are single and it's A-okay."

"Can I blame it on my stepmother?"

"Sure, if you want, but I think you still need to dig a little deeper into the driving force behind your single phobia."

Lydia swiped a forkful of pancakes through a puddle of syrup. When she finished chewing, she asked, "Do you remember that one year in high school when Melody forbade me from going to the prom, all because I didn't have a date?"

"Yeah, I remember. A bunch of us girls went together as a pack, but Melody insisted you needed a proper date."

"Righto."

Jen winced. "She was such a bitch."

"You know," Lydia said, "I often wonder what my life would have been like if my parents had never divorced."

"It's obviously impossible to know, but it probably wouldn't have been peaches and cream. You said that, on the rare occasion that your mother made an appearance during your childhood, she and your dad fought like cats and dogs."

"They did."

"And not to be harsh or anything, but your mom has always had some serious issues. Who knows what it would have been like had she been more present during your childhood?"

"Yeah, who knows? Although, I'm darn certain she wouldn't have dragged me around the beauty pageant circuit."

"Probably not. That was Melody's special gift."

Lydia grunted out a laugh. "I wonder why my mother has never remarried. I mean, she was still in her twenties when she and my dad divorced."

"Beats me, but honestly that might be part of your problem?"

"What do you mean?"

"Well, we both know she's always struggled with money, and perhaps part of the reason she suffered from depression was because she was lonely."

"Maybe."

Jen cupped her hands and set them on the table. "Do you think you're so paranoid of being single because you're afraid you'll end up like your mother?"

"Maybe, but I mean, come on, I am absolutely nothing like my mother."

"I think I've met your mother a grand total of twice. I don't know much about her except what you've told me." Jen rested her elbows on the table. "If nothing else, talk it through when you meet with your new therapist. They love talking about mommy issues."

Lydia laughed. "I bet they do. Although in my case, it might be more about step-mommy issues." She blew out a breath. "Anyway, thanks for listening."

"Sure thing."

Lydia glanced down at her phone. "We should probably get the check. I plan to take a few of my WEC students on a field trip this afternoon and I need to get home to shower."

Jen motioned to the waiter and then asked, "Didn't you take your students on a field trip last Saturday?"

"Yes, but a lot of them couldn't make it so I offered to do another field trip this weekend. Doing everyday errands is an excellent way for them to practice their English."

"Hmmm, I guess that makes sense."

"This semester I'm teaching level 1B so the students have pretty limited English, but I take all my classes on a field trip like this, regardless of their level. Not only so they can learn new words, but also so they can gain confidence speaking the language outside the classroom."

"Do all the teachers at WEC do field trips like this with their students?"

Lydia shrugged. "Most don't, but that isn't going to stop me from doing it. You know how much my students mean to me. Many of them have faced such adversity and I'm constantly in awe of their courage to learn a new language from practically scratch. The least I can do is go the extra mile to help them succeed."

Jen patted her hand. "I've said it before and I'll say it again, you're a good egg, Lyd."

Lydia gave her a small smile. "This week I'm joining forces with Sofia, another teacher at WEC. She and I both plan to bring a few students from our class."

"That's cool."

"Yeah, I'm excited." They both stood and made their way to the front counter to settle their bill. When they stepped outside into the sunshine, Jen pulled Lydia into a hug. "You're amazing, Lydia, don't ever forget that."

Lydia stepped back. "Thanks." She gave Jen a wave goodbye.

Walking home, Lydia made a conscious effort to shove aside any lingering negative thoughts. Jen was solid gold and she thought Lydia was amazing. Maybe, it was time for Lydia to start believing it too.

CHAPTER FOURTEEN

As Lydia made her way up to the Washington English Center, her mind drifted to Sofia. Spending more time with her made Lydia downright giddy, a detail that she was not quite ready to unpack. And even if she was, she didn't have time to dwell on it now. She'd almost reached the school.

Sofia stood with a group of students in the sunshine out in front of the church that housed WEC. Today she wore her silky black hair pulled back in a tight ponytail. A flowy orange dress hung out beneath her coat.

"Good morning," Lydia said as she approached. Sofia and a few of the students waved hello.

Three students from Lydia's class and three from Sofia's class had signed up for today's field trip. The group included Ana, the woman from Venezuela, Ahmed, a soft-spoken engineer from Egypt, Li, an accountant from China, Pedro, a chef from Brazil, and Chantou and Davi, a mother-daughter duo from Cambodia.

Although Lydia was excited to take the students out into the real world, she selfishly wished she could spend the afternoon alone with Sofia. She pushed that thought from her mind and addressed the whole group. "Is everybody ready to go?"

Everyone nodded and they took off single file down the street.

Li came up beside Lydia as they walked. "Where do we go?"

"First, we will go to a neighborhood grocery store, only a few blocks from here. It's a place that sells food."

"Good," Pedro said from ahead of them. He rubbed his large belly. "I am hungry."

When they got to the store, Lydia and Sofia handed each student a fake shopping list, explaining that they must wander the aisles of the store to locate the items written on the slip of paper. Each person had a different list and the items on them were everyday staples, making the task hard, but not overwhelmingly difficult.

All the students eyed their lists skeptically.

"You can ask store employees or other shoppers for help," Sofia assured them.

"Do not worry," Lydia said. "If you have questions, Sofia and I will be here to answer them too. And it is only practice. It is okay if you do not find everything on your list."

"Or if you bring back the wrong thing," Sofia added.

Pedro and Ahmed both headed off down an aisle with breakfast cereal and coffee and the rest of the group wandered toward the deli and produce section.

Lydia smiled with pride as she watched them go. Grocery shopping was generally a simple task when you were in familiar surroundings and spoke the language. However, when neither of these things were true, the task could be daunting. Lydia also smiled because she'd done this exercise with her previous students, and it could be amusing to see what items they returned with.

Once all the students had ventured out of sight, Lydia roamed the store to keep an eye on them. She caught a glimpse of Sofia in the produce section. Her face lit up with enthusiasm as she helped Ana engage with one of the clerks. Not wanting to disturb them, Lydia ducked behind a bin piled high with lemons and limes.

Apparently, Ana got the information she was looking for. Her face broke into a broad smile, and she uttered an enthusiastic thank-you to the clerk. Watching the interaction warmed Lydia's heart.

Once Ana headed off to a different section of the store, Lydia watched Sofia circle the produce department, presumably searching for any other students who needed help. She was so damn earnest... And so damn beautiful. *Whoa, tamp it down, Swann.*

Lydia shook her head to clear her mind and zipped off in the opposite direction. After observing Li in the frozen food aisle and Pedro talking to the butcher, she made her way to the front of the store to wait for her students to finish "shopping" for the items on their lists.

One by one they came up beside her, their baskets overflowing with groceries. Lydia examined their items. She picked a box of wax paper out of Li's basket. "What is this?"

"Diapers," Li said.

Lydia had no idea how wax paper had gotten confused for diapers, but translations and cultural differences were tricky. She pulled a package of diapers out of Ahmed's basket and held it up. "Diapers."

Li blushed. Lydia gave her an encouraging smile and patted her on the shoulder. "It's okay. This is not easy."

Ahmed had the only other incorrect item. Instead of a loaf of bread, he'd come back with a Hungry-Man frozen meatloaf dinner.

After they'd successfully returned all the items to their proper place in the grocery store, they ventured to the post office. Without prompting, Ana confidently approached the counter and inquired about how to send a package internationally. It was still early in the day and the post office was otherwise deserted. The sole postal worker, a young Black woman, patiently guided Ana through the steps of sending a parcel, helping her with the vocabulary along the way.

When Ana was done, Li approached the counter. In broken English she explained to the clerk what she needed. "My friend moved to a new city. I want to write her a letter."

It took a little back and forth, but Li successfully procured a book of stamps to mail a letter both domestically and internationally.

After a stroll through the clothing store where Lydia had taken Sofia, Bea, and Nadia the previous weekend, the group headed to a local café.

In the classroom, both Li and Ahmed rarely spoke up and generally kept to themselves, but not today. They both laughed and talked with their fellow students. It was wonderful to see them come out of their shells.

Occasionally, Lydia or Sofia provided gentle grammar corrections or helped with vocabulary, but otherwise they sat back and let the students talk amongst themselves. One of the many wonderful things about WEC was that the students came from such diverse backgrounds, and as a result, often did not have the same native tongue. This forced them to speak the shared language of English rather than resorting to their native language.

As they made their way back up the hill toward WEC, Lydia thought that each of the students stood taller than they had at the beginning of the day. When they said their goodbyes, everyone shared a round of high fives and thanked Lydia and Sofia profusely for taking them on the field trip to practice their English.

Once the students had gone their separate ways, Lydia's stomach grumbled. Apparently, the three saucer-size pancakes she'd inhaled at breakfast had not been enough to offset the energy she'd expended on the run with Jen.

She turned toward Sofia. "Would you like to grab lunch?"

Sofia didn't respond right away and Lydia worried that she'd overstepped. "It's okay if not. I understand if you need to go home or to work."

"No, no," Sofia said. "I'd love to have lunch with you. Thank you for the invitation."

"Fantastic. There's a deli not far from here that I love. Does that work?"

Sofia cocked her head. "Work?"

Lydia bit her lip. While Sofia's English was darn near perfect, it was still a relatively new language for her. Although she knew a lot of idioms and slang, there were obviously many phrases she was not yet familiar with. "Um, 'Does that work?' is sort of the same as saying, 'Are you cool with that?'"

Sofia smiled. "Yes, I'm cool with that."

Lydia had an extra bounce in her step as they walked a few blocks to the deli. Being in Sofia's presence appeared to have a peculiar effect on her.

The aroma of freshly brewed coffee and baked goods filled the air of the small restaurant. At the counter, Lydia ordered her favorite sandwich and Sofia opted for a spinach salad. Food and sparkling waters in hand, they crossed the street to a small park and grabbed one of the last available spots, a cylindrical concrete slab with two metal stools sprouting out of the ground on either side of it.

They each dug into their meals and ate in silence. When Lydia finished her sandwich, she balled up her wrapper and shot it toward the garbage can about ten feet from their table. In hit the rim and fell into the can.

Sofia clapped. "Excellent!" She then proceeded to stuff her salad container back into the paper bag it had come in, launched it into the air like a volleyball, and swatted it toward the garbage can. When it came up a few feet short, they both laughed.

Sofia got up from the table to toss her paper bag in the garbage. When she sat back down, she reached over and gently touched Lydia's hand with her delicate fingers. "Thank you for doing the second field trip today. You're so kind to give your time to the students at WEC. It's such important work."

Lydia blushed slightly. "Thank you, Sofia."

"To me it's so incredible to see the transformation in the students. Did you see Li today at the coffee shop? She was so confident with her English."

"Yes, I noticed that too."

"It's because of you."

"Oh, I don't know about that."

"Oh, yes. You're the best teacher at the school," Sofia said.

Lydia laughed. "You're very sweet to say that, but there are many teachers who are much more talented and have a lot more experience than me."

"Well, you may not be the most experienced teacher, but you have the most passion, and according to the students I've talked to, you're everyone's favorite. They all love you."

This made Lydia's heart swell. "I love them all too."

"That is very obvious," Sofia said with a smile.

"Did you get much time to talk to Ana today?"

The expression on Sofia's face grew serious. "A little. I asked her why she enrolled at WEC, aside from the obvious reason, to learn English." She paused for a moment before continuing, "As you believed, Ana recently lost both her husband and daughter."

The muscles in Lydia's chest tightened and she hung her head. So, she'd been right. Ana, the student in her class, was the same Ana who had written the handwritten letter to Dear Birdie. Knowing this made her happy because it meant Ana was strong—she'd taken Dear Birdie's advice and enrolled at WEC—but this news was also unsettling. It meant the sweet woman in her class had to be experiencing unfathomable grief. It also meant putting a face to the horrendous story of loss that Lydia had read on paper.

Sofia clenched her fists and crossed them over her chest. As if reading Lydia's mind, she said, "I know, her story is a lot to take."

Lydia just nodded in response.

A sad smile crossed Sofia's face. "I offered to tutor Ana each week after class. I know it's not much, but I want to do anything I can to help her. She's taken such an important step—showing up at the school—but she still has a long road to become fluent in English."

"From the little I know about her, she at least has a strong support network of friends."

"Well, that is very good to hear."

Lydia nodded slowly. "Yes, it is. Having friends and family to buoy you is crucial."

"Buoy?"

Lydia laughed. "Ah, sorry." She explained what a buoy was. "I grew up on a lake and I sometimes weave boating terms in everyday conversation."

"Growing up on a lake must have been nice."

"Yes, it was beautiful. During the summers, I think I spent half my life in the water." *When Melody wasn't chaperoning me to beauty pageants…*

Sofia took a long sip from her can of sparkling water and set it back on the concrete table. Her brown eyes sought out Lydia's. "So, Miss Lydia, tell me more about yourself. Do you have a family?"

"I'm single—my girlfriend and I recently broke up—and I don't have kids," Lydia blurted. The question had caught her off guard and she felt silly for her knee-jerk answer. She tried again. "I mean, I hope to one day have kids."

"There is time," Sofia said, giving Lydia a reassuring smile.

If Sofia was alarmed that Lydia mentioned having a girlfriend instead of a boyfriend, she didn't let it show. "Maybe so, but time's ticking, and I can't deny there's a bit of pressure."

"Pressure from your parents?"

Lydia blew out a breath and shook her head. "No, not from my parents, from myself. My father died years ago and my mother…Let's just say she doesn't hassle me about having kids."

"Does your mother live nearby?"

"Last I heard, she lived in Oregon. But, um, we're not close." Lydia shifted on the metal stool. "What about you? What do you like to do for fun?"

The normal thing would've been to ask about Sofia's family, but Lydia hesitated. She sensed it could be a difficult topic. Sofia had lost her husband, and if her other relatives were back in Venezuela, that might be a sore spot too.

A hint of sadness crossed Sofia's face before she sat up straighter and smiled. "For fun, I like to cook." Sofia poked Lydia's arm. "Do you like to cook?"

Lydia buried her face in her hands. "I'm a terrible cook." She peeked over her fingers. "I keep promising myself I'll learn, but I haven't done it yet."

Sofia's face lit up. "Come to dinner at my house. My neighbor Marta and I will teach you how to cook. We'll show you some of our special Venezuelan recipes."

Lydia loved the way Sofia's eyes crinkled at the corners when she smiled and the pure joy on her face... How could Lydia possibly say no to her offer. "I would love to."

Sofia reached across the table and gently clasped Lydia's hand. "Soon, Lydia, you'll be an excellent cook."

How was it that being with Sofia was so effortless? The sun glistened on her dark hair and Lydia had this intense urge to reach up and let her fingers play through Sofia's silky hair. The connection between them was undeniable, like a jolt of life coursing through Lydia. Whenever they were together, a spark flared up within her. Their eyes locked, and Lydia held onto Sofia's gaze, a comforting warmth spreading through her entire body.

Sofia's eyes dropped to her watch. "I'm sorry. I need to go."

Lydia sprang to her feet, feeling terrible for keeping her for so long. Of course, Sofia had other places to be. "Thank you for joining me for lunch. I enjoyed your company."

"Thank you for inviting me. Soon you will come to dinner at my apartment."

"Yes, soon. I can't wait," Lydia said, and she meant it. Anything to spend more time with Sofia.

They walked to the edge of the park and exchanged a brief hug before parting ways.

After she'd taken a few steps away from the park, Lydia glanced back over her shoulder. She caught Sofia glancing back toward her, a tender expression in her eyes. Lydia gave her a wave and quickly turned away. Was it possible that Sofia felt the same pull Lydia did? Was it possible she also sensed a growing connection between them?

CHAPTER FIFTEEN

The late October sun sat low in the sky as Sofia made her way up the block toward home. She burst through the front door of her squat brick building and headed straight for her friend Marta's apartment, eager to tell her every detail of the day's outing.

Marta greeted her with a warm hug and before they'd even settled around the small table in her kitchen, Sofia launched into a description of the field trip with her class. In rapid-fire Spanish, she described their visit to the grocery store, telling Marta how incredibly brave all her students were. After she finished, she took a deep breath before sharing the most important part about her day. "But, Marta, there is something else…"

Marta raised an eyebrow. "Your expression tells me you've got some beans to spill. What is it?"

"I don't know how to explain it." Sofia looked down at the table and then back at her friend. "Just like last weekend, another teacher from WEC led today's field trip. Her name is Lydia. After all our students left, she invited me to lunch. We had a very nice time."

"And?"

Sofia's face broke into a smile and her leg began to bounce beneath the table. "I'm very drawn to her."

"Drawn to who?"

"Lydia. Being around her feels good. I find myself wanting to spend more time with her."

Marta chuckled and fell back in her chair. "Are you trying to tell me that you have a crush on this teacher, Lydia?"

"Maybe," Sofia said. Blood rushed to her cheeks. "I've never...I've never had a crush on a woman before."

"There's a first time for everything."

"You don't find it surprising?"

"Perhaps a little, but I'm not alarmed or bothered, if that's what you're asking."

"I don't know what I'm asking." Sofia crossed and then uncrossed her legs. "I feel confused. Does this mean I'm gay?"

"I don't think having a crush on a woman makes you gay, but even if you figure out you are, it's good with me. You'll always be the same old Sofia to me."

Sofia playfully punched Marta's arm. "Thanks, I'd feel the same if you came out to me. Nothing would change. Back in Venezuela, things might have been different. I mean, I wouldn't have known any better. But here in the US, we've got friends who are gay, and my cousin Iris has dated women for ages. They're all amazing people. I don't care who they love."

"Growing up, Catholic views on gays definitely loomed large," Marta said with a laugh. "I'm happy we're now surrounded by people who are more open-minded."

Sofia nodded in agreement. "Getting back to Lydia...It's completely possible that I'm making something out of nothing. You know how much I love WEC, how exciting it is now that I'm a teacher there. Maybe I'm equating some of that excitement with Lydia? She's the best teacher at the school. Maybe I don't have a crush on her. Maybe...instead...I have a crush on everything that's related to WEC, and it's gotten me confused. It's got me thinking I have a crush on her when I really don't."

Marta laughed again.

"What's so funny?"

"Talking in circles like that won't do you any good."

"What do you mean?"

"Your face lights up like a Christmas tree when you say Lydia's name. If you ask me, you like this woman very much."

Sofia shrugged. "What am I going to do about it? I'm supposed to be focused on my students, not another teacher."

"Do you think Lydia feels the same way about you?" Marta asked.

"I don't know."

Sofia picked a wooden napkin ring off the table and swirled it on her finger as she thought back to her interactions with Lydia. Had their eyes locked a few times? Perhaps. Had Lydia's hand brushed against hers on more than one occasion? Yes, but maybe it had been by accident. There was a distinct possibility Sofia was imagining something that wasn't there.

Marta patted her hand. "You're only getting to know this woman. Give it some time."

Sofia set the napkin ring back on the table and pushed it around like a soccer ball. "I guess I can do that, just try to enjoy our time together both in and out of school." She blew out a breath. "Geez, the last thing I want to do is make things awkward between us."

"Perhaps someday soon I will get to meet this Lydia," Marta said.

Sofia smiled over at her friend. "You will. I invited her to dinner. I told her you and I would teach her to cook."

Marta winked. "I see."

CHAPTER SIXTEEN

"I've got a few updates for you," Tisha said when Lydia arrived at work Monday morning.

Lydia hung her coat on the back of her door. "Okay, shoot."

"Well, first, IT got back to me about that weird mail loop error we got in response to our email last week."

"Oh, great. What did they say?"

"The guy I talked to used a lot of techno-speak, but from what I understood, the error occurs when the recipient creates rules to auto-forward emails from one account to another. Problems can arise with mail clients that generate auto-replies. If one autoreply triggers another autoreply on the other side, an email loop is created."

"I guess that makes sense," Lydia said. "So, does that mean our email to Gainfully Employed Girlfriend didn't go through?"

"Probably not. The loop error basically means the email bounced. Still, the guy said there's a chance the issue eventually resolved itself and the email will be successfully delivered."

Lydia pinched the bridge of her nose and took a seat behind her desk. "Okay, what else do you have for me?"

Tisha gave her a grave look. "We got another letter from our buddy Joe. A rambling handwritten one. If you ask me, it doesn't make any sense. It came into the mailroom Friday afternoon. They brought it up to me about twenty minutes ago."

"May I see it?"

Tisha pulled two sheets of yellow legal-size paper out of a long manila envelope and spread them out on the desk. The letter was double-spaced and written in sharp block letters. Seeing Joe's actual handwriting made him seem more real—and scarier.

Dear Birdie,

I hope this letter finds you well. (Not really, but it's the polite thing to say.)

You still haven't responded to me. Why not?

I'm going old school, hoping that if I mail you a fucking handwritten letter, it'll spur you to pay attention to me. I'm running seriously low on cash, and I need to figure something out fast. Got any bright ideas?

Once upon a time, I used to like to paint. Should I brush up my painting skills? Ha ha, get it? Brush up! Maybe I could sell some of my shit. What do you think? It may not work, but my next best idea is to rob a bank. Do you advise that? Risky, but a quick reward.

I like beer, just like Justice Kavanaugh. Especially a good Lager. To me, Lager is much better than those hoppy IPAs that are so trendy right now. Lager, Lager, Lager. Not to be confused with a Logger. Ha ha.

It seems you're a very busy woman. Maybe you don't have time to drink beer. That would be a shame.

Do you know that all equestrians are alike? It's true.

They spend countless hours riding a fucking horse around in circles. Sometimes they gallop across fields and jump over shit.

When they aren't riding their beloved animals, they like to talk about them, incessantly. Either that or they're grooming them or talking about someone else grooming them.

Have you ever heard of dressage? I bet you have. What a pretentious word. You must stick your nose in the air when you say it. Equestrians think they're better than everybody else, a trait they all have in common.

I mean, look at their outfits. Those fucking helmets and tall shiny boots. God forbid they get muddy.

Keep a firm grip on those reins, Birdie. You never know what's coming down the pike. Watch your back. Pack a snack. Let the—

A blaring siren echoed through Lydia's office and a white light flashed brightly over her desk.

"Fire alarm," Tisha said.

Lydia slipped the letter back into the envelope, tucked it under her arm, and followed Tisha out of her office to join the throngs of people streaming down the stairwell.

When they got outside, Lydia pulled out the letter and finished reading it. It only got more scattered as it went on, making brief references to commodity prices and pink flowers, seemingly with no context. She peered up at Tisha. "I'm with you. This guy is whacked."

Tisha nodded in agreement. "I'll make a few copies of it when we're allowed back inside and run the original down to security. They can decide whether to loop in Dr. Fern."

Thirty minutes later, the fire department gave the all-clear and everyone was allowed back in the building. When Lydia and Tisha got back upstairs, they had another surprise awaiting them, yet another unexpected letter to Dear Birdie. This time though, it wasn't from Joe, it was from his now ex-girlfriend, Gainfully Employed Girlfriend.

Dear Birdie,

I wanted to express my deepest gratitude to you for your invaluable advice that empowered me to make a difficult decision. It's been a journey, but I finally summoned the courage to end things with my now-ex-boyfriend, Joe. Your words were a beacon of light in my darkest moments, guiding me toward a path of self-respect and liberation. For that, I am truly thankful.

However, as the dust settles and reality sets in, I find myself grappling with conflicting emotions. While I know deep down that breaking up was the right choice for me, I can't shake off this lingering guilt. Joe isn't taking the breakup well, to say the least. His reactions have been unpredictable, ranging from desperate pleas for reconciliation to moments of anger and resentment. It's a storm of emotions I never anticipated.

In moments of weakness, I catch myself wondering if I made the right decision. Should I have stayed and tried harder to make things work? Did I give up too easily? These doubts gnaw at me like a groundhog.

I know, logically, that I can't blame you or anyone else for Joe's reaction. He's responsible for his own emotions and actions, just as I'm responsible for mine. Yet, in the quiet corners of my mind, there's a voice whispering, "If only I hadn't listened to Dear Birdie…"

Best,

Gainfully Employed Girlfriend

Lydia let out a long sigh after she'd read the email. "I don't get it."

Tisha shook her head. "I don't either. She starts out by thanking you for giving her the courage to dump her boyfriend—"

"But by the end of the letter, she kinda blames me because Joe isn't taking the breakup well."

Lydia tapped her pointer finger on her chin. "And it's strange. She didn't mention the email we sent her and this doesn't appear to be in response to it."

"That is odd," Tisha replied. "Maybe this confirms she never got our message, you know, because of that loop error thing."

"Maybe, but either way, I wish the message today indicated whether she's okay. With Joe's letters growing increasingly bizarre, I'm even more anxious about her than I was last week."

"It couldn't hurt to try and reach out to her again," Tisha suggested. "Why don't we respond to the email she sent us today?"

Together, Lydia and Tisha composed another email to Gainfully Employed Girlfriend, who they agreed, they'd refer to as GEG going forward. About three minutes after they sent it, a strange reply came back. *This email address is not private.*

Lydia jolted back in her chair and stared over at Tisha. "Jesus, that's kind of freaky."

Tisha nodded in response.

"Do you think that's an auto-generated message, kinda like the error loop message we got last time we wrote to her?"

"I don't think so."

"Would you mind checking with IT on this too?" Lydia asked.

"Not at all." Tisha paused before adding, "Given all the angry letters from Joe, and now this...I'm kind of wishing Dear Birdie had never replied to GEG."

"I know, me too."

CHAPTER SEVENTEEN

Lydia stepped into Sofia's cozy apartment and a smile spread across her face. Despite its petite size, it was warm and inviting—bookshelves lined with paperbacks and magazines, and windowsills peppered with photographs. Art of all different shapes and sizes adorned the walls, giving the space a distinctive feel.

"Welcome to my home," Sofia said. "May I take your coat?"

Lydia set her shoulder bag on the table near the door and wriggled out of her snug, fleece-lined leather jacket.

A petite woman with waist-length hair emerged from the kitchen. She greeted Lydia with an affectionate hug and introduced herself in flawless English as Marta, Sofia's neighbor.

"Welcome, welcome, we're so happy you're here." Marta gestured toward Sofia with a playful grin. "We've both lived in this building for many years, and from the moment we met, we've bonded over food—cooking it, and of course, eating it."

Lydia laughed. "Thank you for having me."

Marta placed a hand on Sofia's shoulder. "We cannot wait to share our food with you."

Lydia pulled a bottle of red wine out of her bag and handed it to Sofia.

"You are very thoughtful," Sofia said. "It wasn't necessary to bring anything."

"Come, come," Marta said. "We shall begin to cook."

Lydia trailed them into the kitchen. Marta stationed her at the round wooden table nestled in the corner. As soon as Lydia took her seat, a streetlight outside flickered to life, drawing her attention to the window. She caught a glimpse of a figure standing on the sidewalk. The glow of a cell phone screen outlined their silhouette. After swiftly pocketing the phone, they melted into the shadows.

Lydia returned her attention to the small kitchen. It already buzzed with activity and the sound of clinking utensils.

Sofia stood at the stove, stirring a pot of traditional Venezuelan black beans. She held up a large wooden spoon full of her concoction. "I make them with both red and green peppers, onions, garlic, brown sugar, and cumin." She dropped the spoon back into the beans and pointed to another pot on the back burner. "That's pork shoulder. I stewed it for many hours with garlic and onions, and by now it should be very tender."

Lydia licked her lips. "Yum. I can't wait to try it."

Sofia briefly held Lydia's gaze before Lydia looked away. A small butterfly took flight in her stomach. She inhaled deeply and shifted in her chair. It was high time she reined in her growing feelings for Sofia—pronto. She moved her attention to Marta. Her small brown hands skillfully molded arepas—golden pancake-size patties crafted from corn flour and water. "These are a cornerstone of Venezuelan cuisine," she explained to Lydia.

Lydia briefly closed her eyes and savored the aroma of spices that filled the air. "It all smells so wonderful. What can I do to help?"

"When it comes time, you can help with the arepas," Sofia said. "For now, please sit and relax."

"Okay, but only if you promise to let me help with the dishes."

Both women waved her off and returned to cooking. Lydia couldn't help but smile as she watched them gracefully move around the tight quarters. Whenever Marta needed an ingredient from the fridge or a bowl from the cupboard, she glided around Sofia as she bustled between the stove and the sink. It was as if they'd rehearsed this perfectly choreographed dance a thousand times before, which, perhaps they had. Every now and then, they'd poke fun at each other and break into infectious bouts of laughter.

Lydia felt a cozy glow spread through her chest as she took in the entire scene, prompting her to pepper the two women with questions about their childhoods in Venezuela and how they'd each learned to cook.

"I grew up in a small city," Sofia said, "and I learned to cook by helping my mother and my grandmother prepare meals for our extended family. Food holds immense significance in Venezuelan culture, and many of the dishes I make are secret family recipes that have been handed down through generations."

Sofia wiped away a tear before she returned her focus to the pot of beans on the stove.

"I also learned to cook from my grandmother," Marta said. "When I was still very small, she put me to work chopping vegetables." She laughed. "Probably much too young to be wielding a sharp knife."

"Did you also grow up in an urban environment?" Lydia asked her.

Marta gave Lydia another of her infectious smiles. "Yes and no. My family lived in a small city, much smaller than Caracas, but I spent every summer on my grandparents' farm. That's where I learned to grow vegetables—everything from tomatoes to lettuce to cabbage, carrots, and eggplant." Her face fell slightly. "But farming in Venezuela is not like it once was."

Lydia had some knowledge about what had happened in Venezuela under Hugo Chávez's government and wanted to ask both women more about it, but she sensed now was not the time. That, and politics was never a good topic of conversation with people you'd only just met.

Marta's hands returned to work and she showed Lydia how to shape the remaining dough into perfect arepas, patiently guiding her as she tried her hand at the traditional technique.

Compared to Marta's perfect arepas, Lydia's looked like they'd been made by a small child.

"It takes practice," Marta said.

Lydia glanced over at Sofia. "I told you I was a terrible cook."

Sofia turned from the stove, and when their eyes met, Lydia's cheeks flushed. She forced herself to look away and cleared her throat. After a moment, she said, "I find cooking so daunting. For instance, last weekend, I went to the farmers' market and bought a bunch of fresh vegetables, vowing to cook a fancy, nutritious meal. But when I got home and laid everything out, all I could do was stare at it. I had no idea where to start."

"Please tell me you did not throw the food away," Marta said.

Lydia stood and leaned against the doorway. "Oh, no, of course not. It's still in my fridge, begging to be made into something."

Sofia came up beside her and curled an arm around Lydia's waist. "Cooking should be easy and fun, and a meal doesn't have to be fancy to be nutritious."

It was wonderful to be tucked up next to Sofia and Lydia suppressed a whimper when she withdrew her arm and returned to the stove. "I know food doesn't have to be fancy," she said. "But in magazines and on Instagram, all the meals people make are so perfect and I—"

Marta held up her hand. "Stop looking at those things. Just cook. Don't dwell on it, and definitely don't attempt to make something that's Instagrammable. Those pictures online may be fabulous, but the food probably doesn't taste any good."

Sofia nodded. "Marta's right. The food you see in magazines has no flavor, no spice. All they care about is presentation. Who wants to eat a pretty picture?"

Marta reached for Lydia's hand. "The point is, cooking is not a beauty pageant."

"Good, because I've never liked beauty pageants," Lydia said, chuckling to herself about the apt analogy. She nodded toward Sofia as she plated their arepas. "Although, you've got to admit, this meal is gorgeous. The way the golden exterior of the arepas contrasts with all the assorted fillings. They look like they belong in a magazine."

Marta patted her stomach. "No, the arepas belong in our bellies."

Lydia and Sofia both laughed as they took their seats around the kitchen table. Over dinner, Sofia and Marta encouraged Lydia to start a small herb garden on the balcony off the kitchen at her apartment.

"You will have to wait until spring, though," Sofia said. "Winter is around the corner and the plants won't like that."

After Lydia cleaned her plate, she leaned back in her chair. "That was probably one of the best meals I've ever had in my life. The combination of textures and flavors...It was truly delicious." She brought her fingers to her lips and kissed them.

"Did you save room for dessert?" Sofia asked.

Lydia laughed. "I suppose I could squeeze in a few more bites."

They moved to the living room and Sofia brought out a caramel flan that Marta had made. It was silky and sweet and even though she was stuffed from dinner, Lydia managed to devour it.

Eventually Marta stood and excused herself, saying she needed to say goodnight to her daughters before they went to sleep. She gave Lydia a hug goodbye and said she hoped to see her again soon. After she left, Lydia stayed behind to help Sofia with the dishes.

Sofia rinsed the final plate, and when she set it on the dishcloth, her hand brushed the soft skin on Lydia's arm. The light touch was enough to send a spark through her body. She busied herself draining the dishwater from the sink, fearing the expression on her face would give her away, give away the fact that standing side by side with Lydia in her small kitchen made her tingle and feel all warm inside. If only Marta was still here. Being alone with Lydia forced Sofia to examine feelings she wasn't fully ready to confront.

After they dried and put away the last of the dishes, Sofia bent to hang the dishcloth on its hook. She turned away from the sink, bringing her face-to-face with Lydia. They both froze. Sofia ached to run her fingers over Lydia's cheek, to trace the gold chain that hung around her neck. Instead, she took a step back, moving to a safer distance.

Desperate to prolong their time together, Sofia invited Lydia to stay for a glass of wine, her voice cracking as she spoke.

Lydia hesitated before she answered.

"I understand if you need to go," Sofia said.

"A glass of wine sounds wonderful."

"Shall we open the bottle you brought?"

When Lydia nodded, Sofia scrounged in a drawer for a wine opener.

"It's a twist off."

The temperature in the room felt like it had gone up about twenty degrees and Sofia's brain was all jumbled. She contorted her mouth into a lopsided grin and tossed the opener back in the drawer.

Once she finally succeeded in getting the wine bottle open, she poured them each a glass, and handed one to Lydia. "Let's sit in the living room."

They settled side by side on the couch, and Sofia lit the cluster of stout, round candles on the coffee table in front of them. The only other light in the room was from two table lamps and the candlelight cast gentle shadows across their faces.

"This room is incredibly cozy," Lydia said. Her eyes moved to the photographs scattered on the table below the window.

Sofia's gaze instinctively drifted to the photograph on the table beside her. It was a picture of her with Diego when they'd taken a trip to Ocean City, Maryland.

Lydia eyes followed Sofia's. "Is that Diego in the photo with you?"

Sofia reached for the photograph and held it up for Lydia to see. Although she and Lydia hadn't known each other for long, Sofia had no hesitation in opening up and sharing the profound grief she carried. "Yes. He surprised me with a trip to the beach."

Lydia accepted the photograph, studying it for a moment before handing it back.

Sofia gently returned it to its spot on the table. "At the beach, Diego and I played soccer on the sand for hours and took long swims in the ocean. Little did I know it would be our last trip together. He was killed a few weeks later." Sofia's voice quivered. "I miss him so much. It's hard to believe he's been gone for almost three years."

Lydia's face crinkled up as if she were in pain. Tears welled up in her eyes and she wiped them with the sleeve of her shirt.

Seeing the emotional reaction from Lydia, made Sofia start to cry. Without uttering a word, Lydia wrapped her arms around Sofia, holding her tightly as she wept into her shoulder.

"The ache in my chest," Sofia choked out, "it never fades."

When Sofia's tears began to subside, she sat back and brushed Lydia's arm. "I hope I did not ruin your sweater."

Lydia took Sofia's hand and gave it a reassuring squeeze. "I don't care about my sweater. I care about you. The pain you must feel after what you've been through."

Sofia dabbed her eyes. "I've struggled so hard to find meaning in all of it, Lydia. To comprehend why Diego was torn away from me."

"I wish I had an answer for you," Lydia said and gave Sofia a sad smile.

One of the candles on the table hissed and burned out. Sofia pushed it to the side and drew the remaining candles into a tighter circle. She leaned back against the couch. "Thank you for comforting me."

"I'm here anytime you need to talk."

"Talking about Diego always helps. It helps to keep my memories of him alive and eases the pain a little bit."

"It's never good to keep pain and sadness bottled up inside."

Sofia shifted on the couch. "That reminds me, I forgot to tell you, I tutored Ana after class last night."

Lydia's face immediately brightened. "That's wonderful. How did it go?"

"Good, but not much actual tutoring took place. We mostly talked. Such tragedy has befallen her, but she is so strong. I think it helped us both to share our grief."

Lydia inched closer to Sofia. They sat nestled together on the couch until another of the candles burned out.

By the time Lydia left for her own apartment, the sun had long since dipped below the horizon. Although the quickest route home entailed weaving through the residential streets of Sofia's neighborhood, Lydia was emotionally drained and didn't have her wits about her. It was a weeknight and the quietness of the streets added to her unease. While she generally felt safe strolling through the neighborhoods in Northwest DC, she was a woman alone at night. It, therefore, seemed prudent to cut over to the main drag and follow it home.

As she made her way back to her apartment, her mind was consumed with thoughts of Sofia and Ana and the immense burden they both carried. Lydia remained in awe of their strength, facing each day without their loved ones by their side while also being thrust into providing for themselves. Having the guts to walk into a classroom of strangers and learn a new language practically from scratch.

Maybe Lydia could convince one of the writers at the *Post* to do a story on the two women—assuming Ana and Sofia agreed, of course. An inspiring story about Ana and Sofia would certainly be a welcome change from the depressing stories in the news and the constant reminders that a serial killer was in their midst.

A strong gust of wind came up behind her as she turned off Columbia and onto her own narrow, tree-lined street. An empty Coke can rattled down the sidewalk and dry leaves swirled around her feet. It was otherwise eerily silent, and an unsettling feeling washed over her. She picked up her pace and tugged the zipper on her leather coat to her chin.

A car door clicked shut nearby, accompanied by the faint sound of someone whistling. She paused, her senses tingling as she scanned her surroundings. A shadow drifted under the streetlight on the far side of the street and came to a halt. Clad entirely in black, Lydia couldn't discern if it was a man or a woman from her vantage point. Instinctively, she reached into her coat pocket, curled her fingers around her phone, and clutched it tightly.

"Hello," she called out. There was no answer, but the shadow resumed its path.

It was probably one of her neighbors returning home late from work or out walking their dog.

She started walking again. The sound of her boots hitting the pavement echoed through the empty street. A car horn honked in the distance. When she was about three doors down from her apartment, she thought she detected movement out of the corner of her eye. Was she being followed? Joe's veiled threats echoed in her mind. *Keep a firm grip on those reins, Birdie. You never know what's coming down the pike. Watch your back...*

She hurried under the light over the front entry of her building and slipped inside. Once the door clicked securely behind her, she climbed the stairs to her apartment and dug out her keys. Only after she had double-bolted the door behind her, did her heart rate begin to slow.

CHAPTER EIGHTEEN

Lydia needed to get going. Her class at WEC started in less than an hour and she'd promised Arleen she'd get there a few minutes early to finalize their lesson plan. But as she went to log off her computer, a new email came in. It was from Joe. How could she not read it? The hair on Lydia's arms stood up as she skimmed his latest musings.

Dear Birdie,

I've begun to question my own instincts and there is no telling what I might do!

The damage is done.

A labyrinth of thoughts is swirling through my head. You cannot fathom the convolution of my notions. I shall forge ahead with even more conviction than before. I shall feed off the hypnotic symphony of chaos rather than be dragged down by it.

Are you familiar with the term hidden in plain sight? Well, that's the case now. The puzzle pieces appear scattered, but they are not. Listen, Birdie. The whispering winds carry faint echoes of a name.

People will never be the same.

Ha, I'm a poet and I didn't even know it.

Listen to the music, everything's gonna be all right.

The right lane is turn only.

In the language of symbols lies a glimmer of hope. It is said that the constellation of Orion holds within its celestial embrace a cosmic arrangement that mirrors a terrestrial truth. Seek the heavenly constellation on the darkest of nights.

Brace yourself for it's time to embark on a twisted journey.

As autumn's chilling breath descends upon us, the trees shed their vibrant attire, whispering secrets of transformation and decay. In this season of metamorphosis, hidden signs writhe and slither before you.

A figure dances on the fringes of normalcy, wielding a brush as an extension of their soul. Their canvas is life's platter, transcending the bounds of convention.

There's a leak, drip, drip, drip. Do you hear it?

The mob never knows the answer. Don't follow them to the white tent. Red, always red.

The train is safer than driving especially on Lee Hwy. Take the 5:05 to the third stop. If you have time, stop for ice cream, but don't forget the cherry on top. Trust me, it will be so much fun.

May your days...

Lydia didn't have time for this mumbo jumbo right now. She could finish reading the email tomorrow morning. First, though, she should make sure Tisha had forwarded it on to security. She opened her messenger app and shot Tisha a quick note. *Did you send Joe's latest letter to security?*

Lydia stabbed the button on her keyboard to log out of her computer, pulled on her coat, and rushed out of the office. On her way down on the elevator, a reply came in from Tisha. *Yep, I shared Joe's latest with security.*

Lydia threw her phone in her shoulder bag and hurried across the lobby to the revolving doors. She sucked in the cold November air when she hit the sidewalk. These letters from Joe were going to drive her insane. Maybe the security crew would be able to make sense of them.

Lydia briskly maneuvered through the bustling halls of WEC, making it to class in the nick of time. The room was already alive with the usual whirlwind of activity that Arleen fondly referred to as "chaotic fun."

Each student brought their unique energy, creating a dynamic atmosphere that kept Lydia on her toes. While she strived not to play favorites, working hard to treat all students the same and give them equal attention, there was one shining exception that tugged at her heart—Ana.

Ana's sharp intellect and the sheer dedication she poured into her studies set her apart. Then of course there was her tragic backstory. Despite Lydia's commitment to treat all the students equally, she couldn't help but dote on her. Ana had been a student at the school for barely a month and the strides she'd made mastering English were nothing short of impressive. Although Ana had done all the heavy lifting—practicing and studying for hours—Lydia still felt a sense of pride at the tangible progress she'd made. She was so grateful Ana had written to Dear Birdie and taken her advice to enroll in the school.

Yet, beneath Ana's academic prowess, a shadow of grief lingered in her gaze. Lydia yearned to be more than just a teacher to her. She also hoped to be a source of support as Ana weathered her grief and learned to stand on her own two feet without her husband by her side. If there was any way she could uplift Ana, Lydia wanted to do it.

After class let out, Lydia strolled down the hallway, her eyes casting over the large windowless room that housed the school library. As she was about to breeze past, she spotted Sofia seated at one of the tables. Her glorious brown eyes fixated on the pages of a book like it held the secrets of the universe. A few wisps of hair had escaped her ponytail, and a pencil was tucked behind her ear. Spoiler alert: Sofia was adorable as heck.

Unable to resist saying hello, Lydia pushed the library door open and nearly tripped over her own feet as she waved hello. "Hey, Sofia," she said as nonchalantly as she could, although the high pitch of her voice probably gave her away. Being within ten feet of Sofia had her heart doing the cha-cha. "Um, how'd teaching go tonight?"

Sofia raised her head, a warm smile spreading across her face as she closed the textbook and set it on the table. "Hi, Lydia. Class went well. Thanks for asking. How about for you?"

"Mildly chaotic—Arleen and I have an energetic bunch this semester—but good." Lydia let her heavy bag slip off her shoulder and drop down onto the table, knocking over a small stack of books in the process. She quickly righted the books and said, "Ana is such a treat to teach. So smart and eager to learn."

"She's an incredible woman, no doubt about it." Sofia checked her watch. "Actually, I'm waiting on her now."

"For a tutoring session."

"Yep."

Lydia gestured toward the hallway. "I saw her talking to another student. I'm sure she'll be along any minute."

Sofia leaned forward and rested her elbows on the table. "May I ask your advice on something?"

"Of course." Lydia pulled out a chair. "What is it?"

"As you know, I'm teaching one of the intermediate classes this semester."

Lydia nodded.

"Well, one of my students, Margo, is really struggling." Sofia's eyes reflected a mix of empathy and concern. "I hate to send her back a class level. I think it would be a blow to her confidence, but at the same time, she's having such a tough time keeping up with the rest of the class. I can tell she's frustrated. So much so that I'm afraid she'll give up and quit, which of course, is the last thing I want."

"That's tough. I've definitely had students like that. You're caught between the desire to support her growth and fear of denting her confidence."

"Right," Sofia said, leaning closer to Lydia. "So, what should I do?"

The proximity to Sofia muddled Lydia's brain. She ached to reach up and stroke her cheek. Not trusting that she could keep her hands to herself, she clenched them like she was praying for divine intervention. "Obviously," she croaked, "each situation is different, but I can share some of the strategies that have worked for me in similar circumstances. The key is to find the approach that resonates with the individual student."

"What do you mean?"

"Well, it might be worth having a one-on-one conversation with Margo," Lydia suggested. "Understanding her specific challenges and goals will help you tailor your approach. And don't be afraid to tap some extra resources. Show her how to find online tutorials. Talk to Guy in the computer lab. He can help if Margo doesn't have good access to the Internet at home."

Sofia jotted something in her notebook and then turned her gorgeous eyes on Lydia. "Okay, I'll track Guy down tonight after my tutoring session with Ana."

Lydia diverted her gaze and stared intently at a pencil on the table as she spoke. "You should also make sure Margo has a tutor. If she doesn't, help her get one. As you know, there are a slew of volunteer tutors like yourself. Oh, and one other thing," Lydia said, braving a glance at Sofia. "Is there another student in your class—maybe one that's a bit stronger than the others— who you think would be willing to mentor Margo during class each week?"

"Oh, yeah, definitely," Sofia said. "Everyone in the class is super supportive of each other."

"Excellent. Pick a student and assign them as Margo's buddy. Have them work through the exercises together during class." Lydia shifted in her seat and gave Sofia an encouraging smile. "You've got this. Teaching is as much an art as it is a science. Trust your instincts."

Sofia rested a hand on Lydia's thigh. "Thank you so much. You've given me some great ideas."

Cue internal meltdown. How was Lydia supposed to maintain her composure with the warmth of Sofia's hand on her leg? She bit her bottom lip and focused on the large world map hanging on the wall. The only sound in the room was her shallow breathing and the hum of the overhead lights. When she felt able to speak, her voice came out huskier than a saxophone solo. "Um," she said, trying to avoid eye contact with Sofia. "It's always a delicate balance between nurturing a student's confidence and addressing their struggles head-on." She took a risk and shifted her gaze from the map to Sofia. Bad idea. Sofia's eyes were like lasers that bore into her. Her lips curved into a soft knowing smile.

Lydia was now almost certain. There was definitely something there, something more between them. What had started as a simmer was approaching a full boil. The question was, what was Lydia going to do about it?

Ana burst into the room, disrupting the tension hanging in the air. "Sorry I am late. Other students talk a lot."

Sofia laughed and patted the chair on the far side of her. "It's okay. Have a seat and we'll get started."

Lydia stood. "I'll leave you two alone." As the library door closed behind her, Lydia blew out a long breath. *Oh, Sofia Soto, what have you done to me? Why do you drive me so crazy?* She strode down the hallway toward the exit. By now, the echo of student chatter had faded, and the school seemed to exhale.

Lydia got home from WEC a little before nine p.m., changed into sweats, made a plate of cheese and crackers for dinner, and promptly called Jen.

As soon as Jen picked up, Lydia said, "I've got an issue."

"Okay," Jen said. "What is it?"

"I think I'm developing a crush on someone."

"Who?"

Lydia slid onto one of the stools at her kitchen counter and ran a hand through her hair. "Remember how I told you I joined forces with another teacher on that shopping field trip with my students?"

"Yeah, I think you said the other teacher's name was Sophie or something like that?"

"Close, Sofia."

"And she's the one you're crushing on?"

"Yeah, I think so. No, scratch that. I totally am. I saw her tonight at WEC, and I got all flustered and tongue-tied. If it hadn't been so embarrassing, it would've been comical."

"Do you sense the feeling is mutual?" Jen asked.

"I don't know. I feel like something is there, but I can't tell for sure. I'm terrible at reading the signs…or whatever." Lydia drummed her fingers on the kitchen island. "The thing is, I'm pretty sure she's straight. Sofia used to be married to a man." Lydia gave Jen a quick overview of Sofia's backstory, explaining how her husband had been killed during a robbery.

"Oh, gosh," Jen said. "That's terrible about her husband."

"Yeah, I know. Sofia had me over for dinner last week. She and her neighbor Marta made this amazing Venezuelan meal. Anyway, Sofia showed me a photo of her and her husband. It was so incredibly sad."

"How long ago was he killed?"

"About three years. And the incredible thing is, rather than wilt under the grief, she showed unbelievable resilience. In the span of only three years, Sofia went from newbie student to teacher at WEC."

"Geez, talk about inspiring."

"I know. I'm blown away by her fortitude. To endure all that hardship and to carry on with such grace and determination… It's beyond remarkable. *She's* truly remarkable. So smart and driven, but kind and sweet at the same time."

"I hope I get to meet her sometime," Jen said.

"Yeah, me too."

Lydia leaned over the counter and propped her chin on her hand. "I know this will sound super cheesy, but from the moment I met her, I've felt this almost odd comfort in her presence. I'm not sure how to explain it. It's just there." Lydia shrugged. "We're strictly friends, though, and I'm not sure we'll ever be more than that. I have to accept that and try not to act like a complete idiot when I'm around her."

"Having a new friend who inspires you and who you enjoy spending time with is not a bad thing."

"I know. I need to suppress that growing part of me that wants something more with her. I think Sofia kinda sees me as a mentor, at least as far as being an ELL teacher is concerned. She's put her trust in me, and I'd hate for her to think I have an ulterior motive. I mean, I don't really, and I certainly didn't when we first started spending time together. I have so much respect for her and I don't want to do anything to jeopardize the friendship we've started to build. Plus, she might be the straightest person on the planet."

"I hear what you're saying," Jen said. "You two are still getting to know each other. Wait and see how things play out. Don't overthink it."

Lydia laughed. "Yeah, I'm so good at that."

CHAPTER NINETEEN

The following Monday morning Sofia texted Lydia to say she'd had a productive conversation with her struggling student, Margo, and had arranged for her to have a tutor.

Lydia texted her back. *That's great to hear. I'm glad the conversation went well.*

Me too. Thanks for the suggestion to talk to Margo.

Lydia began to craft a response, but paused when three dots appeared on her screen, indicating that Sofia was typing.

In other news, I was also promoted to supervisor this morning. A red-letter day. Sofia's text ended with a series of emojis.

Lydia smiled at Sofia's use of "red-letter day." It was an idiom in the WEC curriculum that most students were taught. She hammered off a response. *Congratulations on the promotion. That's awesome. I'm sure it was well deserved.* Her fingers hovered over her phone. Should she invite Sofia out for a drink to celebrate? That's what a friend would do, right? Or would that be weird? "Oh, what the heck," Lydia muttered and typed out a quick message to Sofia. *Could I take you out for a celebratory drink after class tomorrow night?* She added, *I mean just as friends*, but then erased it. Why would Sofia think it would be anything else?

A few moments after Lydia hit send, a response came back from Sofia. *I'd love to go out for a drink. Thank you for the invitation.*

A smile crept across Lydia's face, and she pumped her hand in to the air. Hot damn. *No, no, no. This is not a date. You must remember that.*

After class the next evening, Lydia briskly walked down the long corridor and poked her head into Sofia's classroom. There was only one occupant inside, Sofia. The mere sight of her filled Lydia's heart with joy.

Sofia stood from behind the big desk at the front of the room and greeted Lydia with one of her exquisite smiles.

Without thinking, Lydia stepped forward and wrapped her arms around Sofia. "Congratulations again on your promotion. I'm so proud of you." She released Sofia and squeezed her hand.

"Thank you. I'm excited but I worry. It's a big step up."

"I have full faith in you. You'll excel in the new position at Logan, I'm sure of it." Lydia caught Sofia's eye. "Ready for the celebratory drink I promised you? I mean if you still want to go."

Another smile crossed Sofia's face. "You are very kind. Yes, I'd still like to go, very much."

In the cozy neighborhood bar, a stone's throw from the school, Lydia felt the stress of the day slip away. Once she and Sofia both had a glass of wine and had toasted Sofia's promotion, she rested her elbow on the weathered wooden bar. With her eyes focused intently on Sofia, she asked, "Did things go better with Margo in class tonight?"

"They did," Sofia responded, a note of satisfaction evident in her voice. "I assigned another student as her buddy and Margo didn't seem to struggle as much to follow the lesson."

"That's fantastic. I'm sure things will get even better once she starts to work with a tutor."

Sofia nudged Lydia playfully. "I wish you were my coteacher. My coteacher, Rose, is very sweet but not half as good as you."

Lydia rolled her eyes in mock disbelief. "You're only saying that because I bought you a glass of wine."

"Okay, yeah, you're right. Rose is much better than you."

Lydia couldn't tell if Sofia was telling the truth or not. "I'm, um, glad to hear that."

Sofia nudged her again. "I'm kidding, Lydia. Although Rose is very competent, she doesn't have an ounce of your passion and she doesn't engage with the students the way you do."

Sofia's voice held a layer of genuine admiration that stirred something within Lydia. "Thank you. That means a lot coming from you."

"And one thing is for certain, Rose is not nearly as beautiful as you are," Sofia said with a wink.

Although Sofia's words were delivered in a teasing tone, Lydia's cheeks burned. A mixture of happiness and surprise washed over her. The compliment had, without a doubt, been unexpected, and its implications lingered in the air between them. Lydia opted to keep things lighthearted. "Flattery will get you everywhere, you know?"

"Oh, is that a fact?" The subtle twinkle in Sofia's eyes spoke volumes.

The flutter in Lydia's stomach was a potent indication that, in an instant, the dynamics between them had shifted. Their relationship now had a new realm of possibility, one that Lydia welcomed but hadn't quite anticipated, not tonight anyway, and maybe not ever. She found Sofia's eyes, and for a moment, the gentle hum of conversations around them disappeared.

"Another glass of wine, ladies?" the bartender asked.

Lydia lifted her empty glass. "Yes, please."

When he gestured toward Sofia, she nodded yes. Lydia couldn't tell if the look on her face was one of relief or disappointment at the bartender's interruption.

"Perhaps I should have asked for a glass of water instead," Sofia said after the bartender was out of earshot. "Apparently, the wine has already lowered my inhibitions."

Lydia just grinned back at the genuine, compassionate, warm, graceful woman sitting next to her.

After the bartender delivered their fresh glasses of wine, Sofia took a sip before asking, "So, how did you become an advice columnist?"

Lydia welcomed the shift to a safer topic. "Sort of by accident," she replied and told Sofia about her educational background and the years she'd spent at *Forté*. "I only became the advice columnist at the *Post* a little less than two months ago."

"It's a big and very well-regarded newspaper," Sofia said. "I'm impressed that you work there."

"Thanks. It's all still so new and I've got to admit, I regularly question whether I have what it takes to do the job."

Sofia's eyebrows inched up her forehead. "That's difficult for me to believe. From the outside, you appear so strong and confident."

Lydia chuckled. "If only that were the case. Unfortunately, nothing could be further from the truth."

Sofia ran a finger along the grain of the bar's rail, her gaze thoughtful. "I guess I have a lot to learn about you."

"And I about you." Lydia rested a hand on Sofia's leg. "How did you come to work at Logan Airlines?"

"I have a friend who has worked in the customer service department for many years. She helped me get an interview."

Lydia reluctantly pulled her hand back and placed it in her lap. "Do you like the job?"

"I do," Sofia said. "Well, I should say, I like working for Logan, some days working in customer service, not so much. People are not always nice."

"I bet. People can be such jerks. I can't even imagine some of the stuff you have to put up with. I don't think I'd last a day in that job. I'd get fired for telling someone off."

Sofia laughed. "It can be hard. You need a thick skin and must remember that people's screaming and yelling is not personal." Sofia swirled the wine in her glass. "Someday, I hope to move to Logan's pricing department. I'm good at math. I've had an affinity for numbers since I was a child and I think a job in airline pricing would be fascinating."

Lydia snorted. "I'm the complete opposite. Ever since I was a kid, I've been allergic to math."

"Allergic, huh?" Sofia asked with a smirk.

"I'm serious. I got hives during an algebra test once." Lydia gave Sofia a sideways glance. "I don't think I've ever admitted that to anyone, I mean aside from the school nurse. It was super embarrassing."

Sofia gave her a gentle smile. "Thank you for telling me. I promise never to make you take an algebra test."

"Ha, thanks. That's very kind of you."

Lydia was surprised how comfortable it was to be with Sofia. For once, she felt free to cast off any pretense and just be who she was. It was refreshing and liberating. There was never any awkwardness when she was with Sofia, which was a rarity, especially with someone she'd only recently met. As they neared the end of their second glass of wine, Lydia's heart felt lighter than it had in months. It wasn't only Sofia's intellect or her ambition that drew her in, it was the way she listened intently, the way her laughter filled the air, and maybe more than anything, her authenticity.

"Is everything all right over there?" Sofia asked. "You've become awfully quiet. Did I say the wrong thing?"

Sofia's eyes were wide with concern. God, she was so darn adorable. There it was again, the flutter in Lydia's belly. She looked down at the bar and then back at Sofia. "No, no, not at all. I was…It's nothing."

"Okay, if you're sure?"

"Yeah, yeah, I'm sure." Lydia took the last sip from her wineglass and an idea came to her. "Hey, Sofia?"

"Yes?"

"If you're not busy next Thursday—it's Thanksgiving, that American holiday where everyone eats way too much food and then falls asleep. Anyway, my friend Jen is hosting a Friendsgiving. Would you like to come with me?"

"Friendsgiving?"

"It's Thanksgiving, but with friends rather than family. Folks who can't spend the holiday with family, for whatever reason, gather with friends instead."

"Oh, what a nice concept." Sofia cleared her throat, her gaze dropping for a moment. "I would love to come with you, but I have to ask, what time does Friendsgiving start?"

"Let me double-check." Lydia picked up her phone and opened her calendar. "The invite says four p.m."

A smile played at Sofia's lips. "That should work perfectly. I asked about the time because I've agreed to cover some shifts in the kitchen at Chevy Chase Country Club. The Thanksgiving buffet is very popular with the members and there's a lot of prep work to do on Thanksgiving morning. They asked me to help, and because it's a holiday, I'll get paid time and a half…"

A pang of guilt shot through Lydia. She hadn't even considered that Sofia might have to work on Thanksgiving. "I totally get that you need to be at the club that day. If you can't make it to Friendsgiving, I'll understand."

Sofia gave her a reassuring smile. "Like I said, I'd love to come with you. The timing should work well." She paused for a moment. "Can I cook a dish to bring?"

"That would be wonderful, I mean assuming you have the time."

"I will make time," Sofia said.

"Well, given that we're in DC, there'll be people at Friendsgiving from lots of different countries. Jen and her boyfriend will whip up the traditional fare, like turkey and stuffing, but the potluck element is the best part. People bring such a variety of dishes. I bet your arepas would steal the show."

"Okay, then I will make them. What dish do you plan to bring?"

Lydia gave Sofia a sheepish grin. "The same dish I bring every year, a can of cream of mushroom soup mixed with green beans."

"Perhaps I could help you prepare something, um, more interesting."

"You would do that?" Lydia asked.

"Of course. It would be my pleasure."

"Okay then, this year I'll up my game." Lydia pushed her empty wineglass to the far side of the bar. "Well, I guess we should head out."

They walked to the corner together and when it came time to part ways, they stared awkwardly at each other. Eventually, Sofia leaned in and gave Lydia a gentle, but lingering hug, and brushed her cheek with a kiss. "Goodnight, Lydia. Thank you for the wine." With that, she turned and started up the sidewalk.

Lydia resisted the impulse to chase after her. The touch of Sofia's lips against her skin had left her craving more, even if it was only to embrace Sofia for a few more precious moments. When Sofia disappeared around the corner, Lydia sighed and turned to head toward her own apartment.

As she walked, she couldn't deny the warmth that had seeped into her heart during the evening. However, she was also left grappling with a tightly packed suitcase of conflicting emotions. Elation mingled with tentative joy but also trepidation. Her heart had been through so much in the two months since her relationship with Carrie had ended. An underlying sense of fragility warred with her desire to charge full speed ahead.

Her instinct was to throw caution to the wind. After tonight, she felt more certain that there was something between her and Sofia. Their connection was both natural and exceptional and Lydia sensed that Sofia felt it too. They were like two puzzle pieces that snapped easily together. Was there a possibility that they could become more than friends? Lydia sure hoped so, although she needed to be careful not to get ahead of herself, as she often tended to do.

Lost in thoughts of Sofia, Lydia absentmindedly stepped into the crosswalk. A black sedan with tinted windows careened through the stop sign, narrowly avoiding her. Startled, she was jolted back to the world around her. *Be more careful, Lydia. Don't let your guard down.*

CHAPTER TWENTY

The night before Thanksgiving, Sofia scrambled around her kitchen. Marta and her daughter Alana sat at the table sipping from mugs of tea.

"When are you going over to give Lydia her cooking lesson?" Marta asked.

"Tomorrow," Sofia said, "after I finish at the country club. Friendsgiving doesn't start until four so we should have plenty of time."

"Try to stick to a simple recipe," Marta warned. "If you overwhelm her, she'll swear off cooking for good."

"I won't overwhelm her, I promise." Sofia pressed her hand against her forehead and groaned. She hadn't seen Lydia since they'd gone out to celebrate Sofia's promotion a week earlier and Sofia harbored some serious anxiety about seeing her again. "I still can't believe I told her she was beautiful. I didn't intend to. The words just came out of my mouth. I mean, I think she is beautiful, but why did I have to go ahead and say it out loud?"

Marta laughed. "My dear sweet Sofia, perhaps it was a good thing you said it. From what you've told me, Lydia was, how shall I say it, receptive to the compliment?"

"I think she was, yes."

"Well, consider this. If you hadn't said anything, you two would have danced around each other for who knows how long, both of you too afraid to admit how you feel. At least now you've opened the door to something."

"But what exactly is that?" Sofia asked.

Marta winked. "Time will tell, Sofia, time will tell."

"I didn't confess this to you earlier," Sofia said, avoiding eye contact with Marta. "But, the other night, when Lydia and I said goodbye to each other, I brushed my lips on her cheek. Her skin was so soft. It made me want to properly kiss her on the lips. And, I must admit, I nearly did." Sofia groaned again. "Thank goodness I had the restraint not to. I'd be utterly mortified if I'd actually kissed her! What in God's name has gotten into me, going around wanting to kiss a woman?"

"You better turn the heat down under those beans," Marta said. "You don't want them to burn."

"Oh, gosh, thank you." Sofia grabbed a spoon off the counter and turned the knob on the stove. She was making arepas to bring to Friendsgiving and she wanted them to be perfect.

Marta shot her a curious glance. "Before you told me you'd never had a crush on a woman. Are you positive about that?"

"Well," Sofia said. "Funny you should ask. I've been mulling over this whole Lydia situation quite a bit. Looking back, I think I might have had feelings for a few women along the way. There was this one woman I used to play soccer with who stands out in particular. Back then though, I wasn't even aware that having feelings for a woman was a possibility, so it didn't register with me."

"But it does now," Marta said.

Sofia nodded. "Yes, it does now."

* * *

Lydia swung open the door to her apartment and instantly smiled at the sight of Sofia. She greeted her with a hesitant hug, mindful not to cross any boundaries as much as she desired to. "Come on in."

Sofia's eyes swept the space. "Your apartment is beautiful. So much natural light and I love how open it is."

"Thanks. It's a rental. I don't own it." Lydia bit her lip. Why had she said that? Sofia probably didn't care one way or another.

Sofia held up the large tin foil-covered serving dish she carried. "Do you have a place where I could set the arepas?"

"Oh, gosh, yeah, I'm sorry." Lydia took the dish from Sofia. It was still warm, and the aroma of chili, onion, and cilantro wafted to her nose. Placing the arepas on the kitchen island, Lydia returned her attention to Sofia. "I think I got all the ingredients on the list you sent me."

"Great, let's get started," Sofia said.

"We probably should." Lydia eyed the clock on her microwave. "We're due at Jen's at four." She met Sofia's gaze, her brown eyes holding a hint of warmth. "I can't tell you how appreciative I am that you're willing to help me."

Under Sofia's tutelage, she was going to attempt to make Brussels sprouts and kale sauté. When Lydia was a kid, her grandparents had always hosted Thanksgiving and every year, Brussels sprouts were on the menu. When she'd shared this tidbit, Sofia had suggested the sauté they were about to make. Apparently, it had been something Sofia often made for her husband, Diego.

Sofia surveyed all the ingredients Lydia had set out on the counter and nodded approvingly. "Everything looks fresh." She rested a hand on Lydia's shoulder. "Where do you keep your pots and pans?"

Lydia pointed toward a cupboard next to the oven. "In there." She laughed. "Most of them have never been used."

Once Sofia had selected the vessel she wanted, she assessed the knives in the butcher block on the counter. "Are any of these sharp?"

"Try the one with the green handle," Lydia said. "It's a fancy one. I bought it a while ago, hoping it would spur me to cook."

The smile on Sofia's face was both inviting and teasing. "Don't tell me, it's never been used either."

Lydia grabbed a dishtowel off the counter and gently snapped it in Sofia's direction. "Busted." At that moment, it once again struck Lydia. When she was with Sofia, she was honest and candid, not the fake persona she'd often been with Carrie and not the person in the ridiculous profile she'd created for Sapphire.

They stood side by side, slicing and dicing salami, Brussels sprouts, and kale, their knives rhythmically hitting the cutting board. Sofia's chop, chop, chop to Lydia's thud, thud, thud.

When they were done, Sofia picked up a large onion. "Would you like me to conquer this?"

"Yes, please. I almost lost a finger the last time I attempted to slice an onion."

Lydia stood back and watched as Sofia wielded the knife. In what had to be less than a minute, she deftly transformed the onion into a pile of neat little chunks. Next, she moved on to a clove of garlic, mincing it with her blade.

Lydia put her hand on her hip. "Okay, I'm impressed."

Sofia laughed. "I'm happy to hear that." She gestured to the stove. "Now it's time to cook."

"I'm on it," Lydia said as she hoisted the bowl of salami slices and ceremoniously dumped them into the pot, causing the oil to hiss.

They both jumped back.

Sofia curled her arm around Lydia's waist. "Maybe we should turn the heat down a little bit."

Lydia stifled a laugh. With their bodies pressed together, it wasn't only the heat on the stove that needed to be turned down.

When Sofia deemed the salami done, she playfully nudged Lydia aside with her hip and tossed the remaining ingredients into the pot. After she gave them a quick stir, she sprinkled in a few pinches of kosher salt and cayenne pepper.

Lydia had never seen anyone cook like that, adding spices willy-nilly. "I have measuring spoons if you need them?"

Sofia winked. "Measuring is for amateurs."

"Whatever you say, Top Chef."

"You must be Sofia." Jen's raspy voice greeted them at the door. "Lydia's told me so much about you. It's great to finally meet you."

"Thank you very much for including me in your Friendsgiving, Jen," Sofia replied. She glanced over at Lydia. "Lydia has told me much about you too."

Jen's boyfriend, Eric, came to the door, taking the serving dishes both Lydia and Sofia held. "I'll get these on warming plates with the rest of the food."

They added their coats to an already large pile of garments on the bed in the guest room. Sofia stayed close to Lydia, their hands occasionally brushing, as they wandered into Jen's living room. Friendsgiving was already in full swing, and a melting pot of people filled the apartment.

Although the wind whipped through the trees outside, a fire crackled in the small stone fireplace. Jen added a log to the fire and meandered over to them when she was done. She pointed toward the abundance of food in the dining room. "I hope you both brought your appetites."

Sofia's eyes widened as she scanned the array of serving dishes that adorned the table and the sideboard. "That's a lot of food."

Lydia laughed. "It sure is. We're very fortunate." Per the tradition of Jen's Friendsgiving, everyone had brought a dish, something that held meaning to them or had been part of their own family traditions. She nodded her head toward a tall man in the corner of the room. "I'm happy to see that Joop is here. His bitterballen are my absolute favorite." She turned to Sofia. "I don't know if you've ever had bitterballen but they're a delectable Dutch treat. You absolutely must try one."

"And don't worry," Jen said, "we've also got all the traditional American fixings. Turkey, mashed potatoes, green beans, cabbage, and gravy made with my family's secret recipe."

Before dinner everyone crammed into the living room to hear two of Jen's friends, both of whom moonlighted as musicians, play a violin concerto. Even though it was blustery outside, the room quickly grew warm, and Eric had to crack a few windows.

When it came time to eat, people piled their plates high with food and sat around one of the many folding tables Jen and Eric had set up. When the chairs filled, people simply huddled together on the floor. Lydia and Sofia found a spot in the corner of the living room, not far from the fire, and sat cross-legged beside each other.

Jen stood near a table at the far end of the room and held up her glass. "To friendship and gratitude. May this Friendsgiving celebration remind us of the power of coming together, celebrating our differences, and finding joy in the shared experience of breaking bread."

The apartment erupted into cheers and the sound of glasses clinking. Once everyone quieted, they all dug in. The only sound in the apartment was the clatter of forks against plates.

After Lydia inhaled an empanada and a mound of mashed potatoes soaked in gravy, she came up for air and took a long sip of water. "I think my eyes were bigger than my stomach," she whispered to Sofia.

Sofia rubbed her belly. "Not me. After I finish this, I'm going back for seconds. I worked up quite an appetite earlier today."

"How early did you have to get to the country club this morning?" Lydia asked.

"Five a.m."

"You must be exhausted."

Sofia smiled. "I think it's fair to say I will sleep well tonight."

"How many people do they expect for the Thanksgiving buffet at the club?"

"Three hundred and fifty. Not all at once, of course," Sofia said with a laugh. "They'll have two or three seatings. First families with small children, then families with older kids, and a final seating for adults only."

"I can't imagine what it must be like to make turkey and mashed potatoes for that many people. I bet the kitchen was crazy."

"Yeah, it was a total whirlwind." Sofia gave Lydia a half-smile, her lips parting slightly. "And there was a little mishap with the cranberry sauce."

"Uh-oh."

"Yeah, a big uh-oh. After it had cooled, I helped my friend Bonnie transfer it from the big soup pot into a storage container. Let's just say more cranberry sauce ended up on Bonnie than it did in the container." Sofia giggled. "And the fact that we were both laughing hysterically didn't help matters."

"Oh, my God, that's absolutely hilarious."

"Yeah, it was pretty funny. Fortunately, the head chef has a sense of humor. I caught him laughing too. This year, the buffet will be a little light on cranberry sauce. Nothing the kitchen staff can do about that at this point. I hope none of the members complain."

Lydia rolled her eyes. "Oh, I'm sure they will." She poked Sofia's arm. "Because you know the world might end if one of them doesn't have cranberry sauce to accompany their turkey."

"I know, right? Not having the perfect ratio could knock the Earth off its axis."

Lydia stabbed the last bitterballen on her plate and held it up. "Have you tried the bitterballen yet?"

"Not yet. I didn't have enough room on my plate."

"Here, you can try one of mine." Lydia leaned forward, hoisted her fork, and fed the bitterballen to Sofia.

Jen came up beside them and gave Lydia a knowing smile. "You two doing okay over here?"

"Yes," Sofia said. "Everything is delicious." She turned toward Lydia. "I may need to learn how to cook bitterballen. It's so good. In fact, I think I need to get myself some more." She got to her feet. "Be right back."

After she disappeared into the dining room, Jen mouthed, "I really like her."

Lydia blushed. "Yeah, she's pretty great."

Jen nodded. "Her smile is radiant, and she seems so real and down-to-earth. When you talk to her, she looks you in the eye. You can tell you have her full attention. Unlike some people

I know—a.k.a Carrie—you never get the sense that Sofia's scanning the room, looking for somebody more important or more interesting to talk to." She nudged Lydia with her hip. "And Sofia's totally into you."

"What makes you think that?"

"Trust me. She looks at you the same way you look at her, with big ole googly eyes." Jen winked. "You should totally make a move. Sofia's a catch, don't let her get away."

CHAPTER TWENTY-ONE

Tisha knocked on Lydia's door late Monday afternoon and said, "Breaking story out of the newsroom. The Red Scarf Murderer has claimed yet another victim."

Bile threatened to rise up Lydia's throat. She swallowed hard to keep it down. "I'm almost afraid to ask. Where was the murder this time?"

"Alexandria."

Lydia leaned back in her chair, closed her eyes, and massaged her temples. "This is getting ridiculous. Why can't they catch this guy already?"

Tisha shrugged. "Beats me, but it's about darn time. My nerves can't take much more of this. The police have got to put a stop to these murders. Every day I wake up and wonder, who will it be next?" She stepped into Lydia's office and slumped into one of the spare chairs.

Lydia wheeled her chair around the edge of her desk to face Tisha directly. "Have they released any information about the victim in Alexandria?"

"Nothing more from the police, but the deceased has some chatty neighbors who, apparently, have no qualms about yakking to the press."

"Oh really? What did they have to say?"

"Well," Tisha said, "according to the woman who lives next door, the victim was male, late sixties, and in his later years, was a total recluse. She told a reporter that he was a retired psychiatrist who spent his days cultivating award-winning bonsai trees and dabbling in taxidermy."

"Taxidermy?" Lydia asked.

"Yeah, you know, preserving an animal and crafting—"

"I know what taxidermy is, Tisha." Lydia's lips twisted into a wry smile. "I'm not a total noob. It's just a peculiar hobby for an urban-dwelling psychiatrist."

Tisha grunted out a laugh. "People are weird. But wait, it gets even stranger. Evidently, the guy's specialty was woodchucks."

Lydia couldn't help but laugh. "Now you're messing with me."

Tisha threw up her arms. "I'm not, I swear. Go ahead and Google the murder—the *Post* already has an article up about it. It sounds like over the last few years, the chatty neighbor lady has filed a bunch of complaints about the taxidermist. In them, she claimed that the victim's house emitted strong chemical smells."

Lydia chuckled. "Yeah, and I bet having a bunch of dead woodchucks laying around wasn't exactly roses either." She wheeled back around behind her computer to search for more details about the murder in Alexandria. "You're right, woodchucks." She read on. "Oh, God," she muttered under her breath, her gaze glued to the screen as she read a description of the gruesome crime scene. "They think the taxidermist had been dead for at least a week when his body was found."

Tisha let out a whistle. "Oh God, it must have smelled like high heaven."

"No joke, but the article says that the stench didn't raise a red flag with the neighbors right away—"

"No surprise there. Because of the dead woodchucks, they were accustomed to his house emitting offensive smells."

"Righto." Lydia clicked on another article about the crime scene. "Holy shit."

"What is it?" Tisha asked.

"Greg West has a piece about the murder too," Lydia said referring to one of the *Post*'s investigative reporters. "Greg writes that he interviewed the man who discovered the taxidermist's body. He quotes the guy as saying the victim was splayed out on his bed over a white sheet. Blood, potentially mixed in with red paint, was splattered everywhere."

Tisha gave her a wide-eyed stare. "How bizarre. Like now the murderer has become some kind of twisted artist?"

It was Lydia's turn to shrug. "Who the hell knows? What a sick bastard."

"You can say that again," Tisha replied. "I also read somewhere that the Red Scarf Murderer has begun to leave meticulously arranged objects at the crime scenes. As if he has a newfound obsession with symmetry and order. It's like the killer is becoming more deranged and demented every darn day."

"Such a comforting thought."

"I know, right? But you know what really wigs me out?"

Lydia rested her elbows on the desk and looked over at Tisha. "What?"

"The fact that the cops haven't been able to establish any connection at all between the victims. It's like this bastard is picking victims at random. I mean who on Earth would murder Mr. Taxidermy, a guy who likes to hibernate in his basement and didn't bother anybody?"

"Except for the lady next door who filed complaints about him," Lydia pointed out.

"True," Tisha conceded. "Maybe she's the murderer?"

"Maybe. Only one problem with that theory. What about all the other victims? What was her beef with each of them?"

"Good point." Tisha laughed. "I guess I wouldn't make the best police detective."

"On the contrary," Lydia said. "You have such a knack for sifting through the letters Dear Birdie receives. You always weed out the best ones. Tisha, you understand the human mind much better than most people."

"Maybe so, but this Red Scarf Murderer sure has me stumped."

That evening, Lydia got about three blocks from the office and stopped dead in her tracks. Her heart sunk and a pit formed in her stomach. Tisha's comment about the Red Scarf Murderer cycled through her brain. "...*now the murderer has become some kind of twisted artist.*"

The last email from Joe, the one he sent a week or two before Thanksgiving...In it, he'd made some reference to art; Lydia was sure of it. She turned on her heels and raced back to her office.

The security guard gave her a raised eyebrow when she burst back into the *Post*'s building and stabbed at the elevator button. "Come on, come on," she mumbled. Eventually, she gave up, cut across the lobby, and took the stairs two at a time to the seventh floor.

Her hands trembled as she logged in to her computer. It took her three tries to get the password right. She scrolled frantically through her inbox. What day had that email come in from Joe?

When she finally found it, her chest clenched like someone had sucker-punched her. All Joe's previous letters had gone to the *Dear Birdie* general email account. Tisha had then forwarded them along to Lydia. But not this time. Instead, Joe had sent his last email directly to Lydia.Swann@washingtonpost.com. How on Earth had she missed that detail when she'd first opened the email? She thought back to the day she'd received the letter. She remembered being in a rush to leave work, but still, she should have been more observant.

The fact that the last letter from Joe had come straight to Lydia meant...only Lydia had seen it, not Tisha, and certainly not the *Post*'s security squad. Tisha was blissfully unaware a fourth letter even existed.

After Lydia had received the email from Joe, and before she'd rushed out of the office, she recalled messaging Tisha. She'd asked her if she'd forwarded Joe's latest letter to security. Tisha had said yes. But Tisha didn't know about the fourth letter. She must have assumed Lydia was inquiring about the third letter, the one that Joe had handwritten. There was no reason for Tisha to think otherwise.

Lydia jumped to her feet and immediately sat back down. Before she went ringing alarm bells, maybe she should reread that fourth letter from Joe again. Perhaps she was wrong. Perhaps he didn't make a reference to art. After all, it had been two weeks since the letter had landed in her inbox. Since she'd presumed the letter had been scrutinized by the security folks, Lydia had practically forgotten about it, and she hadn't reread it since.

She clicked on her desk lamp, took a deep breath, and forced herself to read the letter slowly, line by line.

Joe rambled on about the convolution of his notions, puzzle pieces, and the constellation of Orion...But then, near the end, there it was, the reference to art. Lydia had been right after all.

A figure dances on the fringes of normalcy, wielding a brush as an extension of their soul. Their canvas is life's platter, transcending the bounds of convention.

There's a leak, drip, drip, drip. Do you hear it?

She pounded her fist on the desk. What the hell did it mean?

A Google search for "canvas drip artist" returned a picture of Jackson Pollock along with images of a few of his most famous pieces. Lydia had of course heard of him. In recent years, several of his paintings, each with his signature paint-splattered canvas, had sold at auction for exorbitant sums.

In her mind, Lydia tried to recall the description she'd read about the taxidermist's murder. The guy Greg West had interviewed...What had he said? She pulled up Greg's article again. "*...the victim was splayed out on his bed over a white sheet. Blood, potentially mixed with red paint, was splattered everywhere.*"

Was it a coincidence that Joe's letter echoed parallels to the most recent Red Scarf murder? Of course it was. It had to be.

Lydia was reading way too much into it. Joe was a rambling lunatic, that was it...*But what if there was more to his madness? What if Joe...*Every hair on Lydia's arms stood up.

For a moment, she considered calling the police but decided against it. Before she'd met Carrie, Lydia had briefly dated one of DC's finest, a detective named Daphne in the DC Metropolitan Police Department. Daphne had some control issues and things hadn't ended well. After they'd broken up, Lydia misplaced her grandmother's diamond earrings. She'd blamed Daphne, who in Lydia's defense, did tend to have sticky fingers. At any rate, Lydia made a big stink about it, including filing a report with the police.

A few weeks later, Lydia had opened a small wooden box where she stored various knickknacks. And there were the earrings. The whole incident was ugly—and not Lydia's finest moment. Not surprisingly, she was now a little wary about reporting anything to the police, especially when she didn't have solid evidence—like now. While she had a strong premonition that Joe was somehow linked to the RSM, it was, at this point, pure speculation.

So, instead of calling the police, she picked up her phone and did something she really didn't want to do. She called Carrie.

"Hey, babe," Carrie said when she answered the phone. "What a lovely surprise. I've gotta admit, I didn't expect to hear from you ever—"

"I need to talk to a curator at the Phillips Collection, ASAP."

"Um, okay. You're finally taking an interest in the arts, I see."

Lydia ignored her comment. "Can you help me or not?"

"I don't understand. Are you in trouble or something?"

"No, nothing like that. It's imperative that I talk to a curator, ideally one with expertise in Jackson Pollock."

"Um, okay. Let me see what I can do. Oooh, is this by chance for an article in the *Post*?"

"No, it's not. Listen, Carrie, I don't have time to explain. It's kind of an emergency. I need to know whether you can help me."

Carrie laughed. "What kind of emergency requires a museum curator?"

Lydia pinched the bridge of her nose. "This is serious, Carrie. I'm not messing around."

"Okay, okay," Carrie said, a hint of indignation in her voice. "Give me thirty minutes. I'll make some calls. You know, ever since I joined the museum's contemporary's group, I've become very well-connected."

Lydia gritted her teeth. Good old Carrie, sneaking in any opportunity to tout herself. "Thank you. Like I said, time is of the essence."

"Fine, I'll call you back in fifteen minutes," Carrie said and ended the call.

Lydia paced around her office. There was little doubt in her mind that Carrie would come through for her. After all, Lydia had served up the perfect opportunity—a chance for Carrie to show off how well-connected she was. And, true to her word, Lydia's phone rang exactly fifteen minutes later.

Carrie got right to the point. "Archibald McQueen, a renowned curator at the Phillips, is available to meet with you in an hour."

Lydia huffed out a breath. "Thank you, Carrie. You're a lifesaver."

"Are you going to tell me what exactly your little emergency is?"

"At some point maybe, but not right now. I've got to get to the Phillips. Thanks again, bye."

After she printed out a copy of Joe's rambling email, Lydia tugged on her coat, pulled her bag up over her shoulder, and bolted from her office.

This time she didn't even bother with the elevator and instead made a beeline for the stairs, flying down them until she popped out into the ground floor lobby. The security guard gave her another raised eyebrow as she tore across the atrium and spun through the revolving door.

Archibald McQueen was a tall thin man with leathered skin, as if he spent his days at the beach rather than confined to a museum warehouse, no doubt monitored by a hygrothermograph—the little cylindrical machine that measures humidity and temperature.

"What is it I can do for you, Ms. Swann?" His voice was soft, but deep.

He listened quietly as Lydia laid out the situation as calmly as she could, telling him about the latest letter from Joe and the parallels it had to the taxidermist's murder. When she finished, she said, "Basically, I need an expert to read the letter from this guy, Joe. I want to determine if it contains any additional clues that point toward Jackson Pollock."

Archibald's eyes grew big. "Okay," he said slowly, as if Lydia had just told him she was visiting from Mars.

Lydia ran a hand through her curls. "It's obviously too late to save the poor taxidermist in Alexandria, but if there's a chance that the person who wrote this letter is in any way connected to the Red Scarf Murderer, I want to know. If the letter does indeed hold clues to one murder, who's to say it doesn't offer clues about other murders, possibly including murders that maybe we could help prevent?"

Archibald scratched his nearly bald head. "May I see the letter in question?"

"Yes, yes, of course."

He led her to a long metal table in the center of the room. Lydia withdrew Joe's letter from her bag—three pages, stapled at the top—and handed it to the curator.

He carefully laid it on the table, smoothed it with his hand, and pulled a pencil from behind his ear. "Is it okay if I mark on the paper?"

Lydia nodded. "Go right ahead, it's just a printout."

As Archibald read the letter, he tapped the eraser end of the pencil on the table. Eventually he muttered, "Quite intriguing."

Lydia practically lurched at him. "What is it?"

Archibald patted the stool beside him and indicated that she should sit. Lydia took off her coat, wrapped it over the little round stool, and sat on top of it. Using his pencil, Archibald deliberately circled a handful of words in the letter. Lydia's leg bounced like the needle on a sewing machine as she waited for him to explain what he saw.

"As you mentioned, the letter references a canvas followed by the words drip, drip, drip. That plainly appears to hint at Pollock and his infamous 'drip technique,' but there's more…"

Lydia really appreciated the guy's help, but she wished he'd get to the point. Why did all the academic types talk so darn slow?

He pointed to the words inside one of the wide circles he'd drawn on the letter. *A figure dances on the fringes of normalcy, wielding a brush as an extension of their soul. Their canvas is life's platter, transcending the bounds of convention.* "Here, in the second sentence, if you take the 's' from the word *life's* and slide it in front of *platter*, you get the word *splatter*. Pollock was most well known for producing art using splatters of paint."

"You think that's a coincidence?"

"I don't know for sure, but hold on, let me show you what else I see." Archibald slid his bony finger down to another sentence in the letter.

The train is safer than driving especially on Lee Hwy.

"That doesn't seem to have anything to do with Pollock," Lydia said.

"To the contrary." Archibald peered at Lydia. "You may not be aware of this, but Pollock died in a car crash."

"Oh, gosh, no, I didn't know that. That's terrible. How old was he?"

"Forty-four. He was drunk."

"Wow, that's even more tragic."

"Yes, it was. The crash was so massive, Pollock was decapitated," Archibald said matter-of-factly.

Lydia's hand went to her mouth. She didn't have a response to that.

"Anyway, back to the letter. Another thing I observed, is the reference to Lee Highway. Pollock was married to Lenore Krasner, but she went by the name Lee." Archibald put the pencil back behind his ear. "That's all that jumps out at me right now, but do you mind if I keep this copy of the letter? I'd like to examine it a bit more."

"Yes, of course, it's all yours."

"If I uncover anything else, I'll contact you immediately," he said.

Lydia stood and gathered her coat. "Okay, please do. I really appreciate your help."

"I like puzzles," Archibald said and turned back to the letter.

Lydia took that as her cue to leave.

As soon as she got outside, Lydia burst into tears. It was well after eight p.m. and the temperature hung in the forties, but she was too numb to even try to button up her coat. In her mind, there was now little doubt that the last letter from Joe—letter number four—alluded to Jackson Pollock. Couple that with the fact that the taxidermist's murder also appeared to bear eerie echoes of Pollock, and to her, the threads between the letter and the taxidermist's killing were too compelling to dismiss.

Stepping out of the biting wind, Lydia found refuge in the alleyway beside the museum. After wiping the tears from her face, she pulled out her phone, desperate to talk this through with Jen.

As soon as Jen picked up, Lydia began to sob again.

"Lyd, what's wrong."

Lydia took a few deep breaths to calm herself down. "I could have stopped a murder."

"What do you mean?"

"The taxidermist."

"The man who was killed in Alexandria?" Jen asked.

"Yes...I think Now Single Joe...The last menacing letter he sent..."

"What about it?"

"Both his letter and the taxidermist's murder had indications of the artist Jackson Pollock. I can't help but wonder, is Joe the Red Scarf Murderer?"

"That seems like a bit of a stretch to me," Jen said.

Lydia wasn't convinced. "I can't shake it. When I got Joe's last letter, I didn't even realize he'd sent it to my personal email. I'm such an idiot. I should have done something, alerted someone. Instead, what did I do? I let his letter fester in my email inbox. Heck, I didn't even notice until today that he sent it directly to me rather than to Dear Birdie. When I originally got his email, I was rushing to get out of the office. I totally brushed it off, thinking it was his usual rambling bullshit." Her voice trembled. "If only I had paid closer attention…The taxidermist might still be alive."

Jen's voice was gentle. "Lydia, please don't blame yourself. The parallels between the letter and the murder might seem obvious now, in hindsight, but there's no way you could have predicted it was foreshadowing a murder, I mean, assuming it even was. There's still a strong possibility the Jackson Pollock link is nothing more than a bizarre coincidence."

"I suppose you could be right," Lydia said although her fear persisted.

"I am right."

"But what if you're wrong? What if Joe is the murderer and he's using me as his pawn, believing I'm too dense or too preoccupied to see through his games?"

"Lydia."

"Yeah."

"Your analytical mind is going on overdrive. What you need is sleep. Go home and go to bed."

"Fine, but just hear me out. Even if I'm going overboard, elevating Joe to serial killer status, he believes I'm to blame for his girlfriend dumping him. He's taunting me because he wants to punish me. And now he's doubly pissed because I'm ignoring him, not giving him the attention he obviously craves." Lydia's eyes darted up and down the alley. "I mean Jesus fucking Christ, Joe knows where I work. I'm pretty sure he knows where I live. I've got this feeling someone's been following me. I'm freaking out. I think it's about time I talk to the police."

"Where are you?" Jen asked.

"In the alley right outside the Phillips."

"Go stand in front of the building where it's well-lit. I'm sending Eric over to get you. I'll tell him to escort you up to your apartment and to ensure you're safely locked inside before he leaves."

Lydia sighed into the phone. "Okay."

CHAPTER TWENTY-TWO

Lydia spent the entire night tossing and turning, berating herself for not sounding the alarm earlier about Joe's eerie "Jackson Pollock" letter, as she referred to it now. Before dawn, she abandoned any hope of sleep and got out of bed.

The blurry-eyed security guard finishing up the night shift gave her a wave when she stepped into her office building just before seven a.m. As she waited for Tisha and the *Post*'s security team to arrive at work, she mapped out the connections between Joe and the RSM on the whiteboard in her office.

When Tisha emerged from the elevator, Lydia hurried over and briefed her on the meeting with Archibald McQueen the night before.

Tisha stabbed the button for the elevator. "Sounds like we need to pay a visit to the security folks."

Lydia nodded. "My thoughts exactly. And I'm inclined to call the police too."

Discussions with Tisha and a few members of the *Post*'s security team offered Lydia some reassurance about her inaction on the "Jackson Pollock" letter from Joe. Their opinions echoed

Jen's—the Pollock-esque similarities between Joe's letter and the taxidermist's murder were likely only a strange coincidence. They also reminded her that, even if the letter had contained clues to the actual murder, hindsight was always twenty-twenty. Any one of them could have read the letter prior to the taxidermist demise and none of them would have grasped the letter's significance.

Nevertheless, the security team agreed that the latest letter from Joe should be shared with the police. They also called in Paul Gibbons, the lead investigative reporter at the paper.

The cops didn't exactly jump up and down when presented with the "Jackson Pollock" letter, but they promised to dig into it and touch base with the curator at the Phillips. Lydia figured they'd follow through. The murder of the taxidermist seemed to be a tipping point for a lot of people. A mounting body count and law enforcement's lack of leads had pushed anxiety levels to a fever pitch. Describing the police as eager to crack the case would be the understatement of the century. At the very least, Lydia hoped they'd uncover Joe's true identity. Having a face to put behind the letters might soothe her nerves about Now Single Joe.

Lydia's frustration mounted as two days passed with no word from the cops and no public updates on their investigation into the RSM case. Late morning, Lydia went into the office kitchen to refill her coffee. A group of her coworkers were huddled in the corner. As Lydia approached the coffee machine, one of the men turned toward her and said, "We're talking about the latest murder."

"The taxidermist," one of the women whispered. Her shoulders were hunched, and her eyes darted around the room like an animal sensing a predator. "I'm to the point where I'm afraid to come to work." She shivered. "But I don't feel safe at home either."

A few of the other women nodded in agreement. Both men tried to appear stoic, but one picked incessantly at a hang nail and the other rocked from foot to foot.

"It makes sense that we're all on edge," Lydia said. "The volume of letters Dear Birdie has received on the topic of RSM has skyrocketed in the last few days."

Tisha ran into the kitchen and held her phone in the air. "The Red Scarf Murder case...The police..." She paused to suck in a breath. "They have a suspect!"

Everyone's eyes went wide, and they peppered Tisha with questions.

"Who is it?"

"Are they certain they've caught the murderer?"

"Do they have someone in custody?"

Tisha pointed at her phone. "The *Post* just dropped an article on our website. It's all in there."

Everyone scattered from the room like a flock of startled pigeons, and in a matter of moments, only Lydia and Tisha were left standing in the kitchen.

Although Lydia was as eager as her coworkers to read the article, it was as if her feet were stuck in concrete. While a million questions swirled through her mind, one sat at the forefront—Was Joe, whoever he was, the suspect? Lydia was almost afraid to learn the answer. She forced one foot in front of the other and slowly followed Tisha back to her office. Rather than log in to her computer, Lydia grabbed her *Post*-issued iPad. She and Tisha huddled together at the small conference table in Lydia's office and read the article.

Law Enforcement Questions Local Teens in RSM Serial Murder Investigation

Two teenagers are being questioned by police in connection with the Red Scarf Murder investigation. A license plate matching one of their vehicles was captured on a Ring doorbell camera near the time authorities believe the most recent murder occurred.

Earlier on the same evening, the teenagers drew the attention of local law enforcement after being stopped for running a stoplight. During the routine stop, the officer noticed open liquor bottles in the car, prompting a thorough search of the vehicle. According to the official police report, the officer discovered a trunk filled with cans of red and black paint, a detail that has become a focal point for investigators.

When questioned about their unusual cargo, the teenagers claimed to be aspiring graffiti artists. However, authorities are actively exploring the possibility that the paint may be connected to the crime scene. As previously disclosed, red paint was splattered around the body of the most recent murder victim, identified as retired psychiatrist Albert Moss of Alexandria, Virginia.

As the investigation unfolds, residents are left speculating about the potential link between the teenagers and the RSM serial murder case. While the police have not officially designated them as suspects, the proximity of their vehicle to the crime scene and the presence of paint in their vehicle has heightened interest in their possible role in the murder of Mr. Moss.

Authorities are now delving deeper into the backgrounds of the teens, exploring any connections they may have to the previous victims of the RSM. The community remains on edge, eagerly awaiting further developments in the case of the RSM, a case which, to date, has perplexed law enforcement.

The article went on to summarize the spate of recent murders believed to be connected to the RSM. After Lydia finished reading it, she crossed her arms and turned toward Tisha. "Well, maybe you and everybody else was right. I read too much into Joe's letters and the Jackson Pollock connection. It seems unlikely that he's one of the kids they're questioning. I have no idea how old Joe is, but given what we do know about him, I doubt Now Single Joe is a teenager."

"I'm with you there," Tisha said. "The original letter we got from Gainfully Employed Girlfriend indicated she and her boyfriend lived together. The two teenagers in question probably live with their parents."

News of the teenagers eased Lydia's mind. Joe might be a wacko, but he wasn't a murderous wacko.

CHAPTER TWENTY-THREE

When Saturday rolled around, Lydia was downright giddy. It was the night of the annual progressive dinner in her apartment building, and she was determined to put Joe out of her mind and have a good time. Each course would be hosted by a different neighbor, and Lydia had invited Sofia to be her plus-one. The previous year, Lydia had hosted one of the courses. This year, though, she hadn't raised her hand to volunteer, though now she wished she had. It would have been the perfect opportunity to invite Sofia over for another cooking lesson.

She whistled to herself as she wandered to her closet to pick out an outfit. The attire at the progressive dinners tended to be all over the map, from jeans and T-shirts to blazers and pressed slacks. Lydia wasn't in the mood to wear a dress and jeans were too ordinary. She tried on multiple outfits but discarded each one on the bed in frustration. She wanted to look nice for Sofia and nothing seemed right.

When her eyes settled on a pair of hunter-green corduroy overalls in the back of her closet, she snapped her fingers. They'd be perfect. Lydia had honestly forgotten all about them. It was early December, and the corduroys struck the right balance between festive and comfortable without going overboard like wearing an ugly Christmas sweater.

Ten minutes later, when the intercom by her front door buzzed to announce a visitor, Lydia's heart rate sped up. She waved a quick hello to Sofia on the little video monitor and buzzed her into the building. While she waited for Sofia to come up to her apartment, Lydia grabbed a bottle of rosé from her fridge and hunted for a reusable gift bag in her pantry. Just as she located one, there was a brisk knock on her door. Sofia must have practically sprinted up the stairs. There was no way the building's antiquated elevator could have gotten her up here that quickly.

Lydia greeted Sofia with a warm hug and welcomed her inside. She hung up her coat and gestured to the bottle of rosé. "Let me grab that and we can head out."

Sofia shifted from one foot to the other. "Can I ask you something before we go?"

"Of course. What's your mind?" Lydia set the wine on the counter and gave Sofia her full attention.

Sofia pointed at herself and then at Lydia. "Marta and I went for a walk together this morning, and she asked me if this is a date. She thinks it is, and I told her I didn't know, and she said I should just come out and ask you if it was because…" She grinned sheepishly. "Okay, I'll stop rambling now."

Lydia gazed into Sofia's expressive brown eyes. "Do you want it to be a date?"

Sofia hesitated, her eyes darting to the floor. "Kind of. I mean, assuming you want it to be a date."

Lydia closed the distance between them and slipped a hand around Sofia's waist. "Nothing would make me happier. If it were a date, I mean."

Sofia's face broke into a smile that took Lydia's breath away. Without thinking, Lydia leaned in and gently kissed her on the lips before pulling back. Sofia's eyes were as wide as saucers. Apparently, the kiss had caught them both off guard.

"Sorry," Lydia mumbled. "You were standing there looking all beautiful, and I guess it made me forget my manners. I shouldn't have kissed you without asking permission."

"Maybe we should try it one more time."

Lydia furrowed her brows and tilted her head. "Try what again?"

"The kiss," Sofia clarified.

Lydia felt her cheeks burn. "Oh, right. That's a good idea."

This time, Sofia took the initiative, cupping Lydia's cheeks with her hands and running her fingers through Lydia's curls. Their eyes locked for a brief moment before their lips met in a tentative kiss. A warm shiver spread through Lydia's body. The kiss was over in an instant and she whimpered when Sofia stepped back.

"Perhaps more later?" Sofia whispered, her eyes full of warmth and affection.

Lydia smiled down at her. "Yes, please."

Wanda, one of Lydia's quirky neighbors, played host for the first course, and her apartment was already bustling with activity when Sofia and Lydia arrived. The dining room table and kitchen island were laden with platters of deviled eggs, shrimp cocktail, stuffed mushrooms, an assortment of chips and dips, and a colossal cutting board piled high with fruit and cheese.

Sofia surveyed the obscene spread of hors d'oeuvres. "Is Wanda expecting an army?"

Lydia shook her head. "She always hosts the first course, and she tends to go a bit overboard. Tomorrow morning, she'll undoubtedly show up at each of our doors with leftovers neatly bundled in tinfoil."

"At least the food won't go to waste," Sofia said as they made their way to the makeshift bar set up in the corner.

Wineglasses in hand, they began mingling with the other guests. Horace, the man who lived in the penthouse apartment, pulled Lydia into a conversation about the city's proposal for a new bike lane in their neighborhood. She tried to extricate herself politely, but Horace didn't get the hint. Not that Lydia wasn't interested in the topic, she was, but she didn't want to leave Sofia alone in a sea of strangers. After all, they were on a date. The thought brought a smile to her face, and even as Horace droned on, her gaze kept returning to her gorgeous date across the room.

Lydia's concerns about leaving Sofia on her own appeared to be unfounded. Sofia was handling herself just fine. She was engaged in an animated conversation with Carmen, one of Lydia's neighbors who also hailed from Venezuela. Each time Sofia cast a glance in her direction, Lydia's heart fluttered.

When Horace declared that he absolutely had to sample the pork wontons and trotted off into the kitchen, Lydia sidled up next to Sofia and Carmen. Soon, Carmen excused herself to grab another glass of wine.

"Finally, a moment alone with you," Lydia whispered.

Sofia ran her fingers down Lydia's arm and curled them around her hand.

Lydia's eyes dropped to Sofia's lips. "I'm dying to kiss you again."

"Me too," Sofia replied. She glanced down at their intertwined fingers. "Can I tell you a secret?"

"Of course."

"I've never kissed a woman before."

Lydia wasn't entirely surprised, but it left her curious about what had spurred Sofia to even consider changing teams.

"I am very drawn to you, Lydia." Sofia's eyes sparkled. "And your lips are incredibly soft."

Lydia returned the compliment with a warm smile. "I'm also drawn to you, Sofia." *Oh, God, more than you can imagine.* "Perhaps, soon, we can go on a proper date, just the two of us."

"I'd like that very much."

Callie came up beside them with a tray of hors d'oeuvres. Lydia introduced Callie to Sofia and reluctantly released Sofia's hand to take a stuffed mushrooms from the platter.

Callie looked Lydia up and down. "Love the overalls. They're totally you."

"Um, thanks," Lydia replied. "I should wear them more often." Lydia couldn't shake the terrible feeling about Callie's car tires getting slashed. She wanted to share her suspicion with Callie—that Joe believed the car was Lydia's and slashed the tires to punish her. But no sense in opening that can of worms tonight.

"I'm hosting the final course this evening," Callie said. "I can't wait for you both to taste the desserts I've prepared."

"Callie is a forensic accountant," Lydia explained to Sofia, "but she could easily have a career as a pastry chef."

"I can't wait to try your treats," Sofia said.

After Callie moved on with her mushrooms, both Sofia and Lydia reached for a cocktail napkin on the table beside them. Their hands brushed, sending an electric shock through Lydia. When their eyes met, they shared a knowing look.

Soon, it was time to move to the next apartment for the second course. Lydia placed her hand on the small of Sofia's back as they joined the crowd heading out the door.

As they climbed the stairs, Sofia's phone rang. She pulled it from her back pocket and said, "I'm so sorry, Lydia. I have to take this. It's Marta. She knows I'm with you and she'd only call if something were wrong."

"No worries at all. Please, go ahead."

After a brief conversation with Marta, Sofia ended the call and returned the phone to her pocket. "I'm afraid I have to leave. Marta's older daughter, Alana, is very sick. I need to go home and watch the little one while she takes Alana to the emergency clinic."

"Oh, no," Lydia said. "Do you want me to come with you?"

"No, no. You stay here and enjoy the rest of the dinner. I'm so sorry to cut our date short."

"Helping Marta is more important," Lydia assured her. "And, I promise, soon I will take you on another date."

Lydia ran upstairs to retrieve Sofia's coat and accompanied her down to the lobby of the building.

Sofia brushed her lips over Lydia's cheek and whispered her goodbye.

"Text me to let me know how Alana is," Lydia called after Sofia as she disappeared through the front door of the building.

Later that evening, everyone converged in Callie's apartment for dessert, and true to form, she'd gone all out. Despite the crowd having devoured four prior courses, they managed to make a serious dent in Callie's spread—creamy cheesecake, gooey chocolate brownies, key lime pie, and zesty lemon bars.

"These fruit tarts are out of this world," Lydia said when Callie came up beside her.

"Thanks." Callie beamed with pride. "By the way, I'm really sorry Sofia had to leave early."

Lydia sighed. "Yeah, me too."

Callie playfully nudged Lydia's shoulder. "The chemistry between you two is off the charts."

Lydia feigned innocence. "Between me and Sofia?"

"Uh, duh. The air between you two tonight was positively electric."

Before Lydia could respond, Horace approached to bid his farewell. The clock inched toward eleven and most of the guests had already left. Only one other straggler remained—a forty-something graphic artist named Frank who lived next door. Despite Callie's and Lydia's not-so-subtle yawns, Frank was oblivious to the fact that it was past time for him to go home.

Although Lydia had planned to stay behind and help clean up, she first needed to help get Frank out of there. She winked at Callie and looped her arm through Frank's. "Come on, Frank. Let's head home and let Callie get some rest."

Fortunately, Frank didn't object, and once he disappeared behind his apartment door, Lydia tiptoed back to Callie's. As she lifted her hand to knock on Callie's door, a heavy weariness settled over her. The night had been fun but five courses and countless glasses of wine had sapped her energy. Still, no way would she leave her friend to clean up on her own.

As they loaded the dishwasher and wrapped up leftovers, Callie asked, "Will you stay for one episode of *Better Days to Come*?" She gave Lydia an exaggerated pout. "Just one. Then we'll go to bed, I promise."

Better Days to Come was a show on Netflix that Callie and Lydia occasionally binge-watched together. Lydia stifled a yawn. It was now past midnight and she longed to go to bed, but Callie had been through a bit of a rough patch lately and Lydia had been somewhat MIA as a friend. Being there for Callie trumped sleep. "Sure, I guess I can manage one episode."

Not long after they settled onto Callie's enormous sectional couch, Lydia's eyelids grew heavy. The gentle rhythm of the show and the cozy warmth of the room lulled her to sleep.

The next thing she knew, the rising sun painted the room with an orange glow. A soft cotton blanket was draped over her, presumably placed there by Callie when Lydia had dozed off the night before. A twinge of guilt pricked her. Some friend she was, falling asleep minutes into *Better Days to Come*. She swung her feet to the floor, folded the blanket, and scribbled a quick note to Callie before slipping out to head up three floors to her own apartment.

As she approached her door, she reached for her keys, but paused. Her door was slightly ajar. Had she left it unlocked in her haste to retrieve Sofia's coat the evening before? Improbable but her mind had been scattered lately and she'd done a few careless things.

Using her foot, she cautiously nudged the door open and stepped inside. Her heart pounded as her eyes darted around the apartment. Something was off and her apartment was freezing.

Edging into the living room, she halted to a stop. Her eyes locked onto an overturned bookcase obstructing the path to her bedroom. She whirled around to face the kitchen and screamed. A massive knife protruded from the wooden cutting board on the counter. A cold shiver raced down her spine. She lunged for the front door, her trembling fingers pushing it open.

At the sound of something crashing to the floor, she hesitated and turned around. The blue flowered curtains above her dining table billowed out from the window leading to the fire escape, and fragments of her grandmother's china vase littered the floor. Had the intruder entered through the window? She rushed across the room, slammed the window shut, making sure it was securely locked.

It was like she had dumbbells tied to her ankles as she stumbled back to the front door and spilled into the hallway. She paused briefly to steady herself against the wall before dashing back down the stairs to Callie's apartment.

She pounded on Callie's door.

Seconds later, the lock turned and when the door opened, she clung to her friend. "Someone broke into my apartment!" Lydia's voice quivered with panic.

Callie stepped back and locked eyes with her. "What?"

"Last night, while I was here, someone broke into my apartment. When I went home this morning, my door was unlocked. I thought maybe I'd forgotten to lock it, but my bookcase had been knocked over and..." Lydia covered her eyes and sucked in a breath. "There was a knife..."

"A knife?"

Between gasps, Lydia recounted the terrifying discovery of the knife in the cutting board.

Callie grabbed her phone off a nearby table and said, "I'm calling 911." She stabbed the numbers into her phone and put it on speaker.

"What's your emergency?" a calm voice on the other end inquired.

"There's been a break-in," Callie explained, detailing the discovery of the knife.

The dispatcher assured Callie that officers would arrive shortly.

"Shortly?" Callie asked, a hint of impatience in her voice. "Does that mean in like two minutes or an hour?"

"They'll be there as soon as they can, ma'am," the dispatcher replied patiently.

"My friend's life might be in danger! Did you catch the part about the knife in her cutting board?"

"Yes, ma'am. I've noted that."

Apparently satisfied with his answer, Callie thanked the dispatcher and ended the call. She turned toward Lydia. "They'll be here soon."

"Yes, I heard," Lydia replied in a monotone voice, concealing the pandemonium raging inside of her. She staggered to the sectional couch and sank into it. Next to her lay the cotton blanket she'd folded less than thirty minutes earlier.

Lydia hugged her arms around herself and rocked back and forth. A monsoon of questions swirled through her head. What if she hadn't fallen asleep on Callie's couch? What if she'd gone back to her apartment after watching an episode of *Better Days to Come*? Had the knife in the cutting board been intended for her or was it merely a warning? Would she ever feel safe sleeping in her apartment again?

Callie joined her on the couch and took her hand. "Any idea who would do this?"

Lydia shook her head and whispered, "No idea…Lately though, I've had this eerie feeling, like I'm being followed."

"By who?"

Lydia didn't have time to explain the whole saga with Now Single Joe. "A disgruntled reader of my column. It's a long story but I've started to wonder, it might explain why your tires were slashed. I borrow your car a lot. I could see how someone might think it belongs to me."

"I suppose. But my car was fixable. I'm worried about you." Callie glanced at her watch. "Speaking of which, we should probably go upstairs and wait for the cops to arrive."

"Okay," Lydia said and slowly got to her feet.

When they stepped into the hall outside Callie's apartment, they encountered Frank, the graphic designer. Callie quickly explained what had happened. "Did you see or hear anything out of the ordinary after you went home last night?"

Frank shook his head. "No, nothing at all."

Lydia followed Callie up the stairs to her apartment. They arrived at her door right as a gray-haired male and a fresh-faced female police officer emerged from the elevator. After they introduced themselves, Lydia recounted the events of the previous evening and described what she'd discovered when she'd returned to her apartment that morning.

The cops instructed them to stay outside while they searched her apartment. When they were done, they signaled for Lydia and Callie to enter.

Lydia stood frozen at the threshold of her apartment, her heart racing. She drew in a few deep breaths, attempting to steady herself, but her voice shook when she spoke. "I'm not sure if I can go in there again."

The male officer stepped beside her. "I know this is unnerving, but it would be helpful if you could tell us if anything is missing or otherwise looks amiss."

Eventually, flanked by both officers, she mustered the courage to step inside. Fear, anger, and vulnerability coursed through her veins.

Callie followed them into the apartment, and she recoiled when she saw the knife in the cutting board. "God, seeing it up close is much worse."

Lydia hazarded a glance at the knife and swiftly spun in the opposite direction. "It's terrifying!" She addressed the male officer. "You asked me to point out anything that was amiss. That knife. It most definitely wasn't like that when I left for the progressive dinner last night."

"What about when you came up to get Sofia's coat?" Callie asked.

"I don't know. I don't think so," Lydia replied. "But I rushed in and out so I can't be sure."

The female officer scribbled something in her leatherbound notebook and then gestured toward Lydia. "Do you feel up to checking out your bedroom area?"

Lydia nodded, though she wasn't entirely convinced she had the strength to walk back there. What if the intruder had gone through her things? A knot formed in her stomach as she followed the female officer. They stepped around the overturned bookcase and into her room.

Clothes were strewn across the floor and bed.

"Was your room like this when you left last evening?" the female officer asked.

"Yes," Lydia admitted. "I was in a rush to get ready last night, and I couldn't decide what to wear."

The officer gave her a reassuring smile. "I understand."

"I normally keep my apartment very tidy," Lydia said. It was silly under the circumstances, but she was embarrassed by the state of her bedroom and the neat freak in her itched to pick up the clothes and put them away.

The officer ignored her comment and opened the door to Lydia's closet. She flipped on the light and motioned toward the splintered mirror. "How about that? Was the mirror broken when you were last home?"

"Um, yeah," Lydia said sheepishly and opted to spare the officer the story about how'd she'd broken the mirror back in October when she'd hurled her high heel into the closet. At this point, had it not been for the knife in her cutting board, Lydia was sure the two cops would have dismissed the whole notion of the break-in and been on their merry way. If they knew Lydia's ex, Daphne the detective, they'd probably eventually reach the conclusion that Lydia had something to do with the knife in the cutting board too.

But Lydia knew she hadn't had anything to do with it. And as much as she wanted to, this was not the time to get hysterical. She clenched her fists, determined to hold herself together.

When they returned to the main room, the female officer nodded toward the knife and asked, "Do you have any idea who would do something like this? Perhaps a scorned ex-boyfriend?"

Lydia huffed out a laugh. "My girlfriend and I recently broke up, but she dumped me, not the other way around. Carrie has her faults, but I can't imagine her doing anything like this."

The officer didn't show any surprise or judgment at Lydia's revelation that she was queer. Did she know of Lydia's connection to Daphne the detective? *Please, please don't let that be the case.* She bowed her head and whispered, "It might have been Joe."

"Who's Joe?" Callie and the male officer asked in unison.

"I'm the advice columnist at *The Washington Post*." Lydia slowly began to recount the letters she'd received from Joe. "His girlfriend dumped him, and he blames me. His letters have become progressively more menacing and incoherent."

When they pressed her for more information, Lydia admitted that she didn't even know Joe's real name. "I recently raised the possibility with the police that Joe might somehow be connected to the Red Scarf Murderer," she added. "But that's all moot now I guess…I mean given the recent developments in the case, with the teenagers they have in custody and all that."

"Actually," the female officer said. "The teenagers were just released. It appears they were in the wrong place at the wrong time and don't have any connection to the murders."

"Oh, I didn't know that," Lydia said, shuddering at the thought that Joe remained a suspect. Lydia mentioned this to the officers.

They both shrugged. "If I had a dollar for every tip we get in the Red Scarf Murder case," the male officer said.

"We'll certainly look into this Joe guy concerning your break-in though, ma'am," the female officer added.

Lydia nodded her head in response. If the police weren't keen to sniff out possible links between Joe and the RSM, Lydia would don her detective hat and sift through Joe's letters for more clues. All his crazy riddles. Were there more breadcrumbs buried inside them? References she could latch onto to support her premonition about Joe.

CHAPTER TWENTY-FOUR

Once the crime scene team finished processing her apartment, Lydia randomly grabbed clothes, stuffed them in a large duffle, and got the hell out of there as fast as she could. Although she could've hunkered down in Callie's apartment, Lydia had no desire to be anywhere near her building. Instead, she went straight to Jen's house, and when Jen opened the door, Lydia launched into a frantic explanation about what had taken place.

Jen enveloped her in a hug. "Shh, shh. Calm down. Come inside and tell me exactly what happened."

Eric joined them at the door and together he and Jen guided Lydia to the couch in the living room. He muted the football game on the large-screen TV and went into the kitchen to get Lydia a glass of water.

When he returned, Lydia gulped down the water and then, her voice still trembling, began to slowly relay what she'd discovered at her apartment.

"Holy, fuck," Jen said. She wrapped her arms around Lydia again. "Oh, sweetie, thank God you weren't home."

"Are the cops going to try and find whoever it was that broke into your place?" Eric asked.

Lydia shook her head. "I hope so. I told them about Joe, and they took a few notes, but I'm not sure they took me seriously."

"I mean, break-ins happen," Jen said. "We live in a major city. It's a fact of life. But the knife in the cutting board...If you ask me, this was no run-of-the-mill robbery. It was personal." Jen's hand flew to her mouth. "Sorry, I shouldn't have said that. I'm supposed to be comforting you, not freaking you out."

"It's okay," Lydia said. "I think you're probably right." She shifted on the couch. "You've probably heard by now, but the cops released those two teenagers. Now they're back to square one regarding the Red Scarf Murderer."

Jen and Eric both nodded. "Yeah, we saw it in the news," Eric said.

"Well," Lydia said, "I know we've been through this, but now, after the break-in at my apartment, my spidey sense is flaring up again. I'm certain Joe is linked to the murders, although I know you all think I'm crazy."

"I don't think you're crazy," Jen said. "Based on what you've told me, Joe is definitely unhinged. But there still doesn't seem to be enough dots to connect him to the Red Scarf psycho."

"I agree with Jen," Eric chimed in.

"You're right, there isn't enough evidence to tie Joe to the murders," Lydia conceded. "Still, my gut tells me he's somehow connected to the RSM. Although, like I told the cops, I don't even know Joe's real name, let alone where he lives. For all I know, he could live in Antarctica. I mean, even though most of the *Post*'s readership is in the DMV, Dear Birdie gets letters from all over the world."

"Nonetheless," Jen said, "even if Joe isn't the Red Scarf Murderer, I don't like the idea of him lurking out there. You're welcome to stay here with us for as long as you want."

"Thank you. I appreciate that." Lydia got up and began to pace the small room. "While we're on the topic of Joe, there's something else about him that's been on my mind."

"What's that?" Jen asked.

"I'm worried about his ex-girlfriend, the one who originally wrote to Dear Birdie about her deadbeat boyfriend, Joe, the boyfriend she dumped because I advised her to. I mean, think about it. Joe's written me all the threatening letters and if he is indeed the person who broke into my apartment, there's no telling what else he might be capable of. If he's pissed off at me, he must be doubly pissed off at her."

"Good point," Eric said.

"Tisha and I have tried to reach out to the girlfriend, but I'm not even sure our emails reached her." Lydia began to explain about the weird autoresponses they got when they replied to GEG's emails, but the football game on TV suddenly disappeared, replaced by a flashing "Breaking News" banner.

Eric grabbed the remote off the coffee table and turned up the volume. The camera switched to a female news anchor and the banner at the bottom of the screen read "Another Murder Victim Believed to Be Tied to the RSM."

"Good afternoon, I'm Rae Reynolds, reporting live from Potomac, Maryland," the anchor said in a somber tone. "It appears the Red Scarf Murderer has struck again, this time at an equestrian center in Maryland, right outside DC." A picture of a large green-and-white horse barn appeared in the background.

"Earlier today," she continued, "authorities responded to a 911 call from the Regal Equestrian Center. Details are still emerging, but sources indicate that a deceased female was discovered in one of the horse stalls a little after eight a.m. this morning. It's been reported that the victim had a red scarf tied around her neck, although we have not yet been able to independently verify this. Investigators are on the scene and the victim has not been identified."

The screen transitioned to an image of multiple police vehicles parked outside the stable, yellow crime scene tape fluttering in the wind behind them. When the newscaster reappeared on the screen, she said, "We will bring you further updates as soon as additional information becomes available. In the meantime, we urge..."

Lydia didn't hear the rest of what the newscaster said. She collapsed onto the couch and put her head in her hands. Jen sat beside her and rubbed her back.

Eric flipped through the TV channels, stopping at another local broadcast from the stable in Maryland. This time, the newscaster was a white-haired man with bright white teeth. "Although the police have not released the name of the victim, we've learned that she boarded horses here at the Regal Equestrian Center."

Lydia sprang to her feet. "I have to go to the office."

"What? Are you nuts?" Jen asked.

Lydia ignored her and headed for the door. Both Jen and Eric rushed to her side, trying to dissuade her from leaving.

"Please," Lydia pleaded. "Let me go. One of the letters I got from Joe...It mentioned equestrians. I have to read it again, now! It might have what I've been looking for. It might have the proof I need to finally get the police to believe me."

"Can't you pull it up on your computer?" Eric asked.

"No," Lydia snapped. She pinched the bridge of her nose. "I'm sorry, Eric. I know you're only trying to help. I must go to the office because the letter I'm referring to was handwritten. There's a hard copy of it in one of my desk drawers."

Jen threw her hands in the air. "Fine, but I'm coming with you."

"Me too," Eric said. "We can take my car."

On the drive to the office, Lydia explained why she wanted to see the letter. "In it, Joe referenced me, and then wrote *all equestrians are alike*, or something like that."

"The equestrian link could be another bizarre fluke," Jen said. "Like with the whole Jackson Pollock thing."

Lydia slapped her hand on the car seat. "There's no way. This is all way too coincidental."

"Wait, hold on a second," Jen said. "Are you saying that Joe insinuated you're an equestrian?"

Lydia nodded. "Yeah, that's how I interpreted it anyway."

"What would make him do that? To my knowledge, you've never ridden a horse in your life." Jen turned around to look at the Lydia in the back seat. "Unless you've taken up a new hobby I'm unaware of."

"No, I haven't taken up a new hobby. And you're right, my only experience with horses was a pony ride at the county fair when I was five."

"Okay, so in that case, I definitely think you're reading too much into this. It's no wonder your brain is in freak-out mode. Mine would be too."

Lydia snapped her fingers. "Hold on." She pulled her phone from her bag, scrolled to *The Washington Post*'s Instagram account, and leaned forward to hand the phone to Jen. "If Joe saw this, he might have concluded that I'm into horses."

Jen took Lydia's phone and swiped through the photos in the Instagram post. "Where were these pictures taken?"

"At a polo match in Virginia. It was some charity event I went to with my colleagues from the *Post*."

"Huh, yeah, I guess this photo might cause Joe to deduce that you're some sort of equestrian." Jen held up the phone and zoomed in on one of the photos. In it, Lydia wore a riding helmet and stood beside a lean bay horse with a white blaze on its forehead.

Lydia put her phone away and stared out the window. They were now a few blocks from her office. "Anyway, now you can understand why I'm anxious to see that handwritten letter from Joe again. In it, he not only rambled on about equestrians and their horses but went off on a million other tangents. Maybe there are other clues hidden in his words. A hint that perhaps I didn't pick up on when I first read the letter but that will jump out at me now, in hindsight of the murder at the stable in Maryland."

Eric briefly took his eyes off the road and glanced toward Lydia in the back seat. "If there's even a hint of a clue, I say we take it to the police. For me, that'll be one coincidence too many."

Lydia leaned back against the seat and closed her eyes. "I'm with you, but the cops think I'm a total crackpot and I still don't have any concrete evidence to tie Joe to the murders."

"What's that James Bond quote about coincidences?" Jen asked. "Once is happenstance. Twice is coincidence. The third time it's enemy action…"

"That sounds right," Lydia said.

CHAPTER TWENTY-FIVE

The afternoon sun streamed through the windows of Lydia's office as she, Jen, and Eric gathered around the small conference table in the corner to read the handwritten letter from Joe. His cryptic words seemed to dance on the page, taunting them.

Lydia pinched her eyes shut. *Think, Lydia, think.* She opened her eyes and looked from Jen to Eric. "I know we're missing something. There's a message hidden in here somewhere. Even though Joe is demented as fuck, I sense that he's intelligent. He likes to play games, games he thinks no one else is smart enough to figure out, especially not me."

"Too bad we don't have a Rosetta Stone to help us decode his twisted mind," Eric said.

"What's the name of the stable where they found the woman's body?" Jen asked.

"Regal Equestrian Center."

"Okay, my mind may be playing tricks on me, but look at this." Jen ran a finger over a line of Joe's scribble.

I like beer, just like Justice Kavanaugh. Especially a good Lager. To me, Lager is much better than those hoppy IPAs that are so trendy right now. Lager, Lager, Lager. Not to be confused with a Logger. Ha ha.

"He likes Lager, so what?" Lydia's hand flew to her chest. "Oh, my, God, are you thinking…Lager is Regal backward."

"Yep," Jen said.

Eric tapped his pointer finger on his chin. "I want to say that you two are imagining things, but the way Joe stresses the word Lager over and over again in his letter…"

Lydia scooted over to her desk and sat down in front of her computer. "Something else just occurred to me. I remember watching an interview with the new police chief. When he was asked why they hadn't yet nabbed the Red Scarf Murderer, he replied that the investigation had been hampered by the fact that they hadn't gotten any hits on the DNA collected from the crime scenes." She did a Google search. "Yeah, that's exactly what he said, but, shoot, that interview was three weeks ago."

"There have been at least two more murders since then," Jen said.

Lydia grabbed her phone. "I've got an idea. I'm gonna call Paul Gibbons, one of the *Post*'s investigative reporters. He's been covering the RSM murder case in depth." She dialed his number and put her phone on speaker.

A gruff but friendly voice answered, "Hello?"

"Hey, Paul. It's Lydia, the advice columnist at the *Post*. Sorry to bother you, but I really need your help."

"Good to hear from you, Lydia. What can I do for you?"

"I've got a question about the Red Scarf Murder case."

"Okay, shoot."

"In the last two murders…Have the police gotten any DNA hits from the items they've collected at the crime scenes?" Lydia blew out a breath. "Sorry for my lack of proper crime scene lingo."

"No need to apologize, Lydia. The short answer to your question is no."

Lydia asked Paul a few more questions before thanking him for his time and ending the call. She turned to Jen and Eric. "We need to find Joe's ex-girlfriend."

"Why?" Jen asked.

"For two reasons. One, because like I said earlier, there's a possibility she may be in danger, and two, because she might have something with Joe's DNA on it." Lydia got up and began to pace. "The only issue is, I have no idea who his ex-girlfriend is or how to find her."

"At the house," Jen said, "you started to tell us about the weird auto responses you got when you tried to email her."

"Correct," Lydia said. "I have no way to know if she got the emails Tisha sent to her. Although, we did get a second email from her in early November, I think. It was kind of scattered and she gave no indication that she'd received our emails."

"What were the weird auto responses you got when you emailed her?" Eric asked.

"The first time we got a something about a mail loop, whatever that is. The second time a reply came back almost instantly. It said, *This email is not private.*"

Jen gritted her teeth. "Yikes. What the hell does that mean?"

Lydia shrugged. "I have no idea, but my first thought was that maybe Joe had access to her email or something. Anyway, Tisha and I haven't attempted to reach out to her since then."

Eric jumped to his feet. "Lydia, I think you're right. This GEG person is probably in danger. We've got to figure out a way to track her down that doesn't involve replying to her emails." He tapped his finger on his chin. "Do you think that investigative reporter guy you just called could help out?"

"Maybe," Lydia replied. "But hold up, I've got an idea." She searched for both emails Dear Birdie had received from Gainfully Employed Girlfriend. Once she found them, she turned her monitor so both Jen and Eric could see it. "Maybe these emails have some hidden clue about GEG, something Tisha and I missed before." A scan of the first email yielded nothing, but at the very bottom of the second email, a few lines below where GEG had signed off, there was a small logo of a sun and a moon.

Using a couple of AI tools, such as DALLE-E, along with Google, the three of them were able to link the logo in the email to a company called Sun & Moon Gifts, a seller on Etsy, the online marketplace where small businesses sell their wares. Armed with this information, it wasn't too hard to locate an address for Sun & Moon Gifts. Post office box #13555 in Bowie, Maryland, a suburb of DC. A quick review of Sun & Moon's profile on Etsy indicated that they were an active seller.

Jen sat back in her chair. "Okay, so what's the plan? Are you going to stake out this PO box in hopes that GEG makes an appearance?"

Lydia nodded. "Yes, that's exactly what I intend to do. If I can track this woman down, I can make sure she's okay, and with any luck, maybe she'll have something with Joe's DNA on it. If I'm able to locate some concrete evidence that ties Joe to the RSM murders, maybe the police will finally listen to me."

* * *

According to Google Maps, there were three posts offices in the vicinity of Bowie, Maryland. The next morning Lydia borrowed Callie's red Volvo, called in sick to work, and set out to find the post office in Bowie that housed PO box #13555.

Rush hour traffic headed into the city on New York Avenue was bumper to bumper, but the outbound lanes flowed smoothly from traffic light to traffic light. When Lydia reached the outskirts of Bowie, she drove to the post office that was furthest from DC, figuring she could work her way back home. Under the guise of wanting to rent a PO box, she entered the first post office and approached the attendant at the counter.

He slid an application across to her. "You need to fill this out."

"What if I want a PO box that begins with 1-3?"

He tapped the application with his finger. "You still need to fill this out. Then take it to the post office over on Point Ridge. They've got all the boxes that start with those numbers."

The post office on Point Ridge Place was bustling but small. The biggest challenge for Lydia was to stake out PO box

#13555 without appearing conspicuous. The sun was out but the temperature hung in the low forties. She'd brought a selection of coats, hats, and sunglasses. By changing her outfit frequently, she hoped to evade suspicion. She'd considered buying a wig but had dismissed the idea as being too over the top. But now that she'd seen the size of the post office on Point Ridge, she'd begun to think a wig would have been a good idea.

The other issue she confronted was that nearly three-quarters of the customers who visited this particular post office were Black. It made her question whether GEG, and possibly Joe, were Black. She was embarrassed to admit it, but all along, she'd assumed they were white. Ditto for the Red Scarf Murderer. She should have known better than to assume like that.

While she was busy chiding herself, she nearly missed a woman approach the bank of post office boxes and pause in front of #13555. Lydia held her breath, watching as the woman lifted her key. When she inserted it into box #13553 instead, Lydia let out a sigh of frustration. She'd been at the post office for almost three hours. How much longer would she have to wait before GEG showed up? *If she even showed up...*

Over the course of the next hour, and two costume changes later, two other patrons, a man and a woman, entered the post office and retrieved mail from the boxes above and below box #13555. By two p.m. Lydia was not only hungry—note to self, bring snacks on your next stakeout—but she'd also cycled through her collection of coats and hats. Perhaps this stakeout was the dumbest idea she ever had. What if Gainfully Employed Girlfriend only checked her mail once a week? And what if that day happened to be Friday? What was Lydia going to do, camp out here all week? The stern gray-haired postal worker behind the counter had already cast a few suspecting glances in her direction.

Another terrifying thought crossed her mind. What if Joe was staking out the same post office? Lydia inched toward the front door, slipped her sunglasses down on her nose, and eyed her fellow occupants. None of them fit her image of a potential serial killer. And anyway, why would Joe be here? Presumably he could track down his ex-girlfriend without staking out a freakin' post office.

Lydia shifted from foot to foot and tried to think rationally. If Joe was indeed lurking around somewhere, he would have come after her hours ago. After all, he most probably knew what she looked like, and Lydia's disguises were pretty pathetic.

At 2:47 p.m. the glass door to the post office swung open and a large-boned woman with long bleach-blond hair stepped inside the lobby. Lydia sucked in a breath and her skin pricked. Was this the woman she'd been waiting for? She got the answer a few moments later. The woman marched over to the bank of PO boxes and slid her key into box #13555. She emptied its contents, and with a box under one arm and a bundle of letters under the other, turned to leave.

Lydia snatched a discarded envelope from the garbage can near the door and followed her outside. "Excuse me, ma'am," she called as the woman crossed the parking lot.

The woman paused and glanced back over her shoulder.

Lydia waved the discarded envelope in the air. "I think you dropped this."

The woman turned and took a few steps toward Lydia. Her face was the opposite of warm and welcoming. Instead, it appeared to be in a perpetual scowl.

When they were face-to-face, Lydia whispered, "I'm Dear Birdie from *The Washington Post*. Are you Gainfully Employed Girlfriend?"

If the woman was surprised that Lydia was there, she didn't show it. She eyed Lydia up and down a few beats past before she responded, "Yes, I am."

"I'm worried you're in danger. Can we go somewhere and talk?"

The woman hesitated again before she answered, "Um, yeah, I guess."

"My car is right over there," Lydia said. "Maybe I could follow you to a spot that's more private?"

Without further prodding, the woman gestured toward a Suburban at the far end of the lot. "There's a high school about a mile away. Let's go there and talk."

"Sounds like a plan." Lydia paused before adding, "You know, I don't even know your real name."

Again, the woman paused before responding, "Britney."

"Britney, I got it. My name is Lydia Swann. Like I said, I write the *Dear Birdie* column for the *Post*."

"Happy to make your acquaintance, Lydia."

"You as well, Britney," Lydia said before she turned to walk to her own car.

She followed Britney to the high school and eased into the parking spot next to her. By now, it was after three p.m. School buses lined the curb in front of the school and packs of teenagers roamed around, their eyes glued to their phones. Britney and Lydia cut over to a neighboring soccer field and took a seat in a small set of bleachers.

"Let me start by saying that I'm sorry Joe hasn't taken the breakup well," Lydia said.

Britney waved her hand in the air. "It's no biggie. I guess I should have expected it."

This was a relief to hear. Lydia had been anxious that Britney, a.k.a Gainfully Employed Girlfriend, would have more than a little animosity toward her. Still, it was probably best to move on to the topic at hand. "A lot has happened since I received your original letter back in early October."

As Lydia began to detail the menacing ramblings Britney's ex-boyfriend, Joe, had sent Dear Birdie over the last two months, she spoke faster and faster. "Some of his letters have had bizarre parallels to the spate of recent killings attributed to the Red Scarf Murderer."

Britney's eyes had grown wide as Lydia talked but her lips were pursed, and her expression was hard to read. Was she shocked? Resigned? Regardless of what she was feeling, she remained quiet, perhaps eager to hear Lydia out before she piped in.

"Last but not least," Lydia continued. "My apartment was also broken into over the weekend. Thankfully, I wasn't home."

She explained about the knife in the cutting board. "I don't yet have proof, but I can't shake the feeling that Joe was the culprit."

Britney made brief eye contact with Lydia but stared out over the soccer field as she spoke. "Are you trying to tell me you think Joe—his real name is Macon, by the way—is in some way connected to the Red Scarf Murderer?"

"Well, I don't know for sure, but, yeah, that's my hunch. The patterns in Joe's, er, I mean, Macon's letters, the way they synch with some of the Red Scarf murders...It's a few too many coincidences for me."

Britney's eyes once again met Lydia's before she diverted her gaze to her lap. She clasped and then unclasped her hands. "Macon has his issues, for sure, and when he's in a real funk, his temper can flare up real bad." She blew out a breath. "Still, I'm not sure he's capable of murder." Her lips began to quiver. "I'm sorry, this is a lot to take in."

"Don't apologize," Lydia said. "I know this can't be easy to hear." She did a quick survey of their surroundings. "Possibly, Macon slipped over the edge. Perhaps his anger and frustration reached a boiling point, and then poof, he just exploded."

"Possibly," Britney said. "I haven't spoken to him in a little while, so I don't know his current state of mind." She rubbed her temples. "Um, have you gone to the police with all of this?"

Lydia nodded. "I have. I've also involved the *Post*'s investigative reporter who covers the RSM." She opted not to elaborate any more than that. "They say they'll follow up, but I don't know what they've uncovered, and in their defense, I haven't provided them with any solid evidence." She paused before adding, "Um, regarding the cops...They've collected DNA from each of the Red Scarf murder scenes. So far, though, they haven't been able to match the DNA to a suspect."

Britney nodded. "Yeah, I remember reading that somewhere. The police chief said that it's hampered their investigation."

"I read that too." Lydia carefully considered her next words. "That's one of the reasons I wanted to track you down. I was hoping...Do you by chance still have anything of Macon's? I know you two broke up but maybe he left something behind, like an old toothbrush or a comb, anything that would have his DNA on it?"

Britney's eyes fluttered a few times as if her brain was churning. "Um, I don't think there's anything of his at my place. He, um, took everything with him when he moved out..."

Lydia's heart sunk. "Oh, well, I thought it was worth a shot."

A small smile crept across Britney's face. "However, Macon has a big storage unit. I've stored some stuff there from time to time and I still have a key."

"Oh, wow. If you've got the key, maybe we could go and see if we can find any items that might contain his DNA? Only if you're okay with that, of course. If nothing else, it might help link him to the break-in at my apartment."

"Sure," Britney said without hesitating. "I'm happy to help you in any way that I can."

Lydia felt her heart pounding in her chest, momentarily uncertain if she'd correctly heard Britney. This meetup was going way better than she'd anticipated, but she had to play it cool. She couldn't blow it now. If she was too pushy, she might scare Britney away. "Where is the storage area located?" she asked gently.

"Only about ten miles from here." Britney dug around in her large leather handbag. "Unfortunately, I don't have the key with me. It's back at my apartment."

"Maybe we could head there now? I mean, assuming you have time."

"Yeah, no problem." Britney twirled her blond hair around her finger. "To be honest, I'm glad you tracked me down. Since our breakup, I've had some of my own concerns about Macon. I've spotted his car parked outside my apartment at all hours, or if I come out of the grocery store or something, suddenly, there he is."

"Interesting," Lydia said. "For the last month or so, I think someone has been stalking me too."

"Oh, really?" Britney leaned in closer. "Did you ever get a good look at them?"

"No. I just saw shadows, stuff like that."

"Okay," Britney said, settling back. "Well, I'm glad Macon never came after you."

"Me too," Lydia said. "Has he ever confronted you? You know, hurt you physically?"

"No, nothing like that. Whenever I catch him stalking me or whatever, he drives away. For all his faults, Macon has never laid a finger on me."

"Well, that's good to hear," Lydia said before they both stood.

They went back to the parking lot and Lydia followed Britney to her apartment. Britney got out of her Suburban and knocked on Lydia's car window. Lydia lowered it and asked, "Do you want me to wait here or come in with you?"

"Why don't you wait here? I'll be back in a jiffy." Britney turned and trotted across the parking lot toward a nondescript three-story gray building.

Lydia watched her climb the stairs and enter an apartment on the top floor. Five minutes passed, then ten. "Where the hell is she?" Lydia muttered under her breath. A terrifying thought crossed her mind. What if Macon had bugged Britney and knew what they were up to? Maybe he'd been hiding inside the apartment waiting for her? Maybe he was holding her hostage, or worse...*I better go check on her.* Lydia opened her car door, sprinted across the parking lot, and flew up the stairs to Britney's apartment.

When she reached the third floor, the door to Britney's apartment opened. Thinking it might be Macon, Lydia dove behind a vending machine. Only after Britney stepped outside alone and locked the door behind her, did Lydia emerge from her hiding spot. "What took you so long?"

Britney held up a small key. "Sorry," she said. "It took me forever to find this." She scanned the parking lot before focusing on Lydia. "I thought you were going to wait for me in the car."

"I was. It's just..." Lydia groaned internally. She was an idiot for overreacting and concocting the idea that Macon was holding Britney hostage. "Never mind, let's go."

They drove to the storage area and then weaved through a maze of squat concrete buildings until they reached unit #1813. It took a bit of jiggling, but Britney managed to get the padlock open. The metal garage door creaked as she pulled it up.

"Oh, gross," Lydia said. The stench of what smelled like a decaying rodent mixed with moldy gym clothes made her eyes water. They both stepped back and covered their noses.

Britney gagged. "I guess Macon hasn't been here in a while. God, it stinks."

Lydia didn't disagree, but she was so happy to see that the unit was full to the gills. And regardless of how bad it smelled; she wasn't leaving until she got what she came for.

It took some digging, but they eventually managed to turn up an array of potentially DNA rich items: an old baseball bat, helmet, and glove, a few soiled bandanas, an empty Coke can, and two combs.

"Do we need to put all this shit in a plastic bag or something?" Britney asked.

Lydia shook her head. "I don't think so. It's not evidence from a crime scene; it's stuff we hope has Macon's DNA on it."

"So, what now?" Britney asked. "Are you going to take all this to the cops?"

"Yes, but not directly."

"What does that mean? I helped you out. Don't get all wishy-washy on me now."

"You up for ride into the city?" Lydia asked.

Britney shrugged. "I guess, as long as you're driving. I find navigating the city overwhelming."

Lydia waved toward her car. "Come on, let's go."

Once they got on the Beltway, Lydia called Paul, the investigative reporter at the *Post*, and told him about the items she and Britney now had in their possession.

Paul's voice echoed through the car. "Let me make a quick call and I'll get right back to you."

"Who's he going to call?" Britney asked after the line went dead.

Lydia glanced over at her. "I have no idea, but hopefully one of his contacts at the police department."

As they were passing the National Arboretum on New York Avenue, Lydia's phone rang. It was Paul.

"Are you familiar with Montrose Park?" he asked.

Even though he couldn't see her, Lydia nodded. "Yeah. I walk on the trails near there a lot. It's in Georgetown."

"Correct. Can you meet me there in an hour?"

"On our way."

Lydia and Britney got there first. They waited back by the swing set in Montrose Park, away from the road.

"This is a seriously nice park," Britney said. "I had no idea DC had big green areas like this. I mean, I rarely come into the city, so I don't know it that well, but still."

"We're in Georgetown. It's pretty ritzy."

Lydia's words came out curter than she intended. Even though she was grateful for Britney's help, she didn't have a lot of patience for chitchat right now. Sweat slid down her back beneath her wool sweater. If Paul didn't show soon, she was going to lose her shit. The stress and lack of sleep over the last few days had taken its toll. She sat down on one of the swings and used her legs to propel her up and back. When she spotted Paul on the far side of the park, she dragged her feet on the cushy rubber surface below the swing and leapt off.

Paul wasn't alone. He had a very tall, very thin man with him. "Hello, Lydia," he said when they approached. He gestured to the man next to him. "This is Miller. He's a detective with the DC Police Department. I've given him the background on the situation."

Lydia shook Miller's hand and introduced Britney.

"Let's see what you've got," Paul said.

Lydia lifted the army duffle off the ground, set it on the picnic table next to them, and unzipped it to expose its contents.

"Where did you get these items?" Miller asked.

"From a storage unit that belongs to Macon Hardy," Lydia replied, explaining that Macon and Joe were one and the same.

"Macon has kept crap in that place for years," Britney said.

"How did you come to have access to this unit?" Miller asked.

"I had a key," Britney replied.

Miller looked toward Britney. "What is your relationship with Mr. Hardy?"

Britney looked irritated, and she answered his question curtly. "Macon is my boyfriend." Her eyebrows rose up her forehead. "Or rather, my ex-boyfriend."

Both Paul and Miller nodded, but neither of them spoke.

Lydia turned her attention to Miller. "As I'm sure Paul has told you, I'm convinced Macon has a connection to the Red Scarf Murderer. My hope it that the items in that bag"—she waved toward the duffle—"contain DNA that will match what you've gathered at the crime scenes."

After some more back-and-forth, Miller promised to speed through testing of the items in the duffle. It was also agreed that, if the DNA was a match, Paul would write an exclusive article in the *Post* about Lydia and Britney's role in solving the crime.

Before they parted ways, Miller gave them his card. "Please call me if you uncover any more information."

Lydia wasn't thrilled about the exclusive article part of the deal but felt she didn't have a choice. She needed to get the evidence in the hands of the police, and she needed them to prioritize its processing. So far, it seemed the best way to accomplish that was with Paul's help.

Paul and Miller bid them farewell, took the duffle, and walked back across the park.

"I can drive you back to Bowie now if you want," Lydia said to Britney.

"Thanks," Britney said, "but I'm good. I'll ride home with my sister. She works for the American Astronomical Society over on K Street."

Lydia was mildly taken back. When she'd proposed the idea of heading into DC to meet Paul, she sensed Britney was reluctant to visit the city. "Are you sure?"

"Yes. I wouldn't have mentioned it otherwise."

"Alrighty then." Lydia rested a hand on Britney's arm. "Thanks for all your help today."

Britney yanked her arm away. "It was my pleasure."

CHAPTER TWENTY-SIX

The next morning, Lydia could not get herself out of bed to go to work. Was she paralyzed from fear, exhaustion, a combination of both? Whatever it was, she had a queasy stomach, and her energy level was crazy low. Amidst the chaos-drama-excitement of tracking down Britney, it was possible she'd forgotten to eat the day before. That would explain why she felt like a car whose low fuel light had been flashing for miles.

In her entire life, Lydia had probably called in sick to work twice. The first time being when Daphne the detective goaded her into playing hooky and the second time being yesterday when she'd traipsed off to find Britney. Today would be day number three. Trying to track down a potential serial killer was not for the faint of heart.

Lydia sent Tisha a quick text saying she'd participate in the team's morning meeting virtually, but otherwise she would take the rest of the day off. She set her phone on the bedside table and promptly fell into a deep sleep, waking groggily when her alarm went off two hours later. After reviewing the day's letters with Tisha and the gang in the morning meeting, she dragged herself into the bathroom, splashed cold water on her face and brushed her teeth.

After sucking down two cups of coffee and forcing down a boiled egg and some dry toast, Lydia felt more human. In fact, she went from dragging her feet to bouncing with energy. It suddenly felt suffocating to be cooped up inside. She needed exercise, pronto.

According to the weather app on her phone, it was already fifty-five degrees outside, warm for DC in mid-December, and a peek out the window told her that it was a glorious sunny day.

Perhaps she should message Sofia. The nature of her customer service job meant she worked irregular hours, and if Lydia recalled correctly, typically she had Tuesdays off, at least until she had to teach at WEC in the evening.

Lydia hammered off a quick note to Sofia. *What are you up to today?*

A message came back a few minutes later. *Working on my lesson plan for tonight. I'm way behind.*

As badly as Lydia wanted to spend the day with Sofia, there was no way she'd distract her from prepping for class. Sofia took lesson planning very seriously, determined to make the most out of every class. Lydia had been teaching at WEC for years and had already outlined her lesson plan for that night. Her phone chimed with another message from Sofia. *Are you still staying at Jen's?*

Lydia replied in the affirmative. She'd told Sofia about the break-in at her apartment but had deliberately omitted certain specifics—such as the knife lodged in her cutting board and her growing suspicion that a crazy guy named Joe, who'd been sending Dear Birdie bizarre letters, might be the culprit. Sofia had been through enough in her own life, and the last thing Lydia wanted to do was add to her worries.

After exchanging a few more texts with Sofia, Lydia changed into her workout clothes. A brisk walk around the monuments sounded like a perfect idea. Before she left Jen and Eric's apartment, she filled a water bottle and scanned through email on her laptop. The email at the top of her inbox caused her to jump for joy. Jody, a coordinator at WEC, had sent a message to say that, due to a water main break, all WEC classes were cancelled for the next two days.

Lydia grabbed her phone to call Sofia. "Did you see the email from Jody? There's no class tonight."

Sofia's response came after a brief pause. "Oh, I see it now."

"Now that you don't have to teach class tonight, any chance I could interest you in a walk, or maybe a bike ride? It's a beautiful day and I'm dying to do something outside."

Sofia responded without hesitation. "A bike ride. But, uh, don't you have to work today?"

"Nope. I took the day off."

Forty-five minutes later, they met at the entrance to the Capital Crescent Trail at the edge of Georgetown.

Lydia greeted Sofia with a hug and quick kiss on the cheek. "You look adorable in your little bike outfit," she whispered into her ear.

Sofia stepped back and eyed Lydia. "So do you."

"Thanks. I borrowed it all from Jen." Lydia waved in the direction of the bike path. "How about we follow this to where it meets the C&O Canal path and then continue from there?"

"Works for me."

"If you want, maybe we can stop near Great Falls." Lydia patted her backpack. "I packed a thermos of hot tea and a sandwich for both of us."

Lydia was in decent shape, but she had to pedal like mad to keep up with Sofia, who sped along the flat gravel path like a competitor in the Tour de France.

Midway to Great Falls, at a spot where the canal path ran parallel to the Potomac River, Lydia pulled up alongside Sofia. "You up for a quick break?"

They rested their bikes against a weathered wooden bench and stepped through the bare bushes to reach a large rock on the edge of the river. Its jagged black surface had absorbed the warmth from the late morning sun. They perched themselves above a spot where the river swirled between massive boulders poking out of the water. Lydia pulled the thermos from her pack and poured them each a cup of tea. They sat in silence, staring at the river gushing past them. The sun was high in the sky, and it glistened on the water's surface. Occasionally, a plane bound for Washington National Airport buzzed overhead.

"How far is the airport from here?" Sofia asked.

Lydia shrugged. "I'm not exactly sure, but I'd guess about fifteen miles or so."

"I have only been on a plane once, when Diego and I came to the US. I barely remember it."

Lydia rested her hand on Sofia's leg. "That was a little over five years ago, right?"

Sofia gazed out over the water. "Yeah. It feels like a lifetime ago."

"Is Diego buried here in the US?"

"Yes." Sofia bit her lip and blew out a long breath before responding, "People in the community helped raise money for his funeral. I was deeply grateful for that. Now at least I have a gravestone to visit."

"I'd be happy to go there with you sometime."

Sofia scooted closer and rested her head on Lydia's shoulder. "Thank you. I'd like that."

By the time they reached Great Falls, the sun hung lower in the sky. They sat above the raging water of the falls and devoured the sandwiches Lydia had packed before hopping on their bikes to return to Georgetown.

However, about three-quarters of the way back, Lydia's back tire let out an ominous hiss. "Uh, oh, I think I have a flat." She did a quick calculation in her head. They'd left Great Falls about forty-five minutes ago, which meant they'd covered approximately nine miles. If that were the case, they had about five more miles to go before they reached Georgetown. That was a long way to walk a bike, not to mention the two or so miles Lydia had to go to get back to Jen's apartment.

Sofia pointed to a small grassy area ahead of them. "Let's pull over by Lock 5."

Although the C&O Canal was no Panama Canal, it had once been a vital waterway for transporting goods, and remnants of many of its old locks were still scattered along its path. Even some of the original lock masters' houses still stood intact, including the one at Lock 5. Lydia carefully steered her disabled bike to the old white stone structure and dismounted.

Instantly, Sofia sprang into action and began rummaging around in her pack. She pulled out a small canvas bag and held it up triumphantly. "Your tire will be as good as new in no time."

Lydia shot her an amused yet skeptical look.

Sofia emptied the contents of the canvas bag onto the grass, selected a few items, and knelt beside Lydia's bike. She set down her tools, stood, and in one swoop, flipped Lydia's bike upside down so it rested on the handlebars and seat.

Lydia watched in awe as Sofia swiftly disengaged her back tire, extracted the balloon-like inner tube, and replaced it with a new one. While she inflated the new tube with a hand pump, Lydia asked, "How in the world did you know how to do that?" She laughed. "And you happen to have a canvas bag full of bike tools?"

When Sofia finished pumping up the new tire, she reattached it to Lydia's bike and winked at her. "I'm full of surprises, huh?"

"You sure are."

"Diego and I used to bike a lot. Once we spent the money on our bikes, it was a free, fun activity and we loved to cycle around, exploring the different corners of the city. There are so many great trails around DC." Sofia picked up the canvas bag. "The bike shop where we bought our bikes even offered a free class on bike maintenance. I've had my fair share of flat tires and knowing how to fix them has come in handy."

"I'll say," Lydia said. "Thank you. You saved me a really long walk home." Without hesitation, she pulled Sofia into her arms and planted a quick kiss on the lips. "You're amazing."

Sofia stammered backward and gave Lydia a shy smile. "I like the way you say thank you."

Lydia gave her one more peck on the lips before they hopped back on their bikes.

As they cycled back to Georgetown, the sun dipped lower on the horizon, casting long shadows in their path. The temperature dropped rapidly, and Lydia zipped her coat up to her chin. They rode together into Rock Creek Park until they reached the P Street exit, the ramp Lydia had taken down into the park from Jen's apartment earlier that day.

Sofia stopped and straddled her bike, glancing down at the ground before meeting Lydia's gaze. "I had a really nice time today. Thank you."

Lydia returned the sentiment with a warm smile. "I did too. I feel bad about the water main break at WEC, but I'm sure glad I got to spend this glorious day with you."

"That bike ride made me very hungry," Sofia said. "I plan to go home and cook myself a big meal. Would you like to join me?"

Lydia's smile grew wider. "I'd love to. But remind me to text Jen to let her know where I am. I don't want her to worry."

As promised, Sofia prepared a delicious feast for them. After they finished the dishes, Lydia leaned back against the kitchen counter. "Well, I guess I should head out."

Sofia set her dishrag on the counter, closing the distance between them. Her hands rested on Lydia's hips, her eyes seeking out Lydia's. "Is there any way I could convince you to stay here tonight?" Without waiting for a response, Sofia gently cupped Lydia's cheek and leaned in for a tender kiss on the lips. "I just want to hold you," she whispered. "To fall asleep with you in my arms."

That sounded wonderful to Lydia. She grinned at Sofia. "Do you mind if I take a quick shower before we go to bed?"

Sofia shook her head. "Not at all. In fact, I'll jump in after you."

Lydia traced her fingers down Sofia's arm. "You're welcome to join me if you want." She laughed nervously. "I'd feel awful if I used up all the hot water before it was your turn."

Sofia took Lydia's hand and led her into the bathroom. They both shed their layers of bike clothes and stepped under the spray of warm water in the small shower. Lydia tried not to stare at Sofia's body, but she was only human. Breasts that would fit perfectly into the palm of her hand, perfect round nipples that Lydia ached to circle with her tongue, toned arms, a subtle ripple of muscles on her otherwise smooth stomach, legs that...

Sofia handed her a bottle of shampoo and Lydia feared she been caught drooling. "You're incredibly beautiful."

Sofia's eyes tentatively grazed Lydia's body. "So are you."

Lydia picked up the bar of soap and held it out. "May I?"

Sofia responded with a smile, and Lydia moved the soap slowly over her shoulders and down her neck. She could hear Sofia's breath catch when she gently slid the soap over her right breast, ensuring it was well lathered before moving to the left one.

"My turn," Sofia said, taking the soap into her own hand.

Lydia closed her eyes and let the warm water cascade over her as Sofia circled her breasts with the bar of soap. She tried to ignore the stirring desire between her legs and instead focused on the sensation of Sofia's touch. If the water hadn't begun to turn cold, she could have stayed in there forever.

Once they toweled off, Sofia fetched them each a pair of pajamas. Lydia would have been quite content to sleep naked beside Sofia, but she happily accepted the pajamas and put them on. Soon, she hoped for more, much more, between them, but tonight was not the night.

As they crawled into bed together, Sofia slid across the sheets and spooned up behind her. Her warm arms engulfed Lydia. All the chaos of the outside world melted away and Lydia's happy meter tipped into a zone it hadn't reached in a very, very long time.

CHAPTER TWENTY-SEVEN

On Wednesday, Lydia reluctantly bid farewell to Sofia and managed to drag herself to work, but she spent most of the day hibernating in her office. Occasionally, Tisha came to check on her and even went to the food truck across the street to get her empanadas for lunch. Tisha was the only person at work Lydia had confided in about her foray to Bowie, Maryland, to track down Britney. Lydia had detailed the ensuing scavenger hunt at Macon's, a.k.a Joe's, stinky storage unit. She'd also told Tisha about the rendezvous with Paul and Miller in the park in Georgetown and the exclusive article Paul would write if Macon's DNA was indeed tied to any of the murder scenes.

When Tisha knocked on her door again at around three o'clock, Lydia practically jumped out of her chair. She'd been staring out the window at nothing.

"Why don't you call it a day?" Tisha put her hand on her hip. "You won't be much use to any of us here until you get word back from that Detective Miller about the DNA."

Lydia rested both elbows on her desk and sighed. Her green and yellow screen saver was a dead giveaway that her computer had not seen any action in the last thirty minutes. "You're right. Sorry I've been a useless sack of potatoes all week. I can't thank you and the team enough for picking up the slack. I don't know what I'd do without you guys."

Tisha waved her off. "If you don't shoo this instant…"

Lydia pushed back her chair and stood. "Okay, okay, I'm out of here."

Once out on the street, Lydia surveyed her surroundings. No serial killer-looking guys lurked in the shadows. Still, there was this eerie sensation that she was being watched. She cut into the alley beside her office building and zigzagged through the streets of DC, constantly checking over her shoulder until, at last, she was safely back inside Jen's apartment.

Given how early it was, Jen and Eric probably wouldn't be home for a few hours. She snagged a folded pair of sweatpants from the top of the dryer, changed out of her work clothes, and curled up on the couch with the TV remote. Four *Seinfeld* reruns later, she heard a key in the door. She tossed aside her blanket, sprang to her feet, and ducked behind the refrigerator in the kitchen until Jen appeared in the hallway.

"You poor thing," Jen said and came over to give Lydia a hug. "I don't blame you for being scared shitless. Hopefully you'll hear from the police soon and this whole thing will be over." She glanced at the clock on the stove. "Eric should land at DCA in about an hour, so he'll be here soon. Don't forget, he has a black belt in karate."

Eric had been away on a business trip for the past two nights and Lydia was grateful he'd be there tonight. "I'll definitely sleep better knowing he's around."

Except Lydia didn't. She fell asleep not long after dinner but woke up at two a.m. Although she was beyond exhausted, she couldn't fall back asleep. For hours, she tossed and turned on the pullout couch in Jen's home office, causing the sheets to twist around her. When she'd fallen into bed, she'd neglected to lower the window shades and the glare of the streetlight shone in her eyes, but, at this point, she didn't have the strength to get up and lower the shades.

The furnace clicked on. Her muscles tensed and she lay perfectly still, listening to the hum of the warm air cycling through the vents. When the heat clicked off again a few minutes later, the only sound Lydia could hear was that of her own breathing, its rhythm slowly lulling her back to sleep.

She finally dozed off but jolted awake at the creak of the old wooden floorboards in the hallway. Had Eric or Jen gotten up to go to the bathroom? Lydia held her breath, listening for the sound of the toilet flushing or running water in the sink. A siren blared somewhere off in the distance and then it was silent again. The stillness of the house unnerved her. She burrowed her head under her blanket, praying for morning to come.

Feet shuffled past her closed door. The sound of a coin or marble falling to the floor was followed by two soft thumps. Lydia was overtired and on edge. Perhaps it was her mind playing tricks on her. No, there was the thump again, this time much louder.

The sound of breaking glass brought her to her feet. A moment later, someone screamed. Lydia called out, "Jen, Eric?" There was no response. She scrambled for her shoulder bag and curled her hand around the cool metal can of pepper spray she always carried. With that in one hand, she grabbed a pottery vase off the bookshelf with the other and yanked open the door to the room. When she stepped into the hallway, she collided with Jen.

"They're gone," Jen said.

"Who's gone? Lydia asked.

"Whoever broke in. Eric hit them over the head with the fire poker. There's a bunch of blood on the living room floor, but the intruder escaped through the window before Eric could tackle them."

"The broken glass," Lydia mumbled.

Jen nodded. "I was on my way back to make sure you were okay."

Lydia wrapped her arms tight around her body. "I'm okay. I mean, I'm not hurt or anything."

"Thank God."

"Did Eric get a good look at them?"

"No. It was dark, and whoever broke in had on a mask." Jen held up her phone. "I need to call 911." When she finished talking to the dispatcher, she said, "The police are on their way."

The sun had long since risen by the time the cops finished processing Jen's apartment. Lydia figured all the evidence they'd gathered—fingerprints, DNA, and whatever else—would point to Joe.

Eric filled a bucket with hot soapy water and scrubbed the blood from the floor and the windowsill in the living room. The police didn't detect any sign of forced entry, leading them to believe that whoever had broken in may have had a key. Either that, or the door to Jen's apartment had been left unlocked. Jen assured them that that had not been the case. She'd double-checked it herself before she'd gone to bed. Now they were waiting around for the locksmith.

"Do you want me to go down to the corner and get some bagels and lox?" Lydia asked.

"No way," Jen said. "What are you, crazy? You're not going anywhere by yourself until they figure out who broke into my place. Let's do Uber Eats."

Lydia didn't have much of an appetite, but she managed to get down half a bagel and some juice before curling up in an armchair with a steaming mug of coffee. Jen went off to take a shower and Eric dipped into Jen's home office to take a work call.

When Lydia's cell phone rang, she unfurled herself from the armchair and fetched it off the kitchen counter. She didn't recognize the number, but given everything that had happened lately, she figured she should answer.

"Hello."

"Lydia, it's Archibald McQueen from the Phillips Collection. I'm sorry to bother you, but after you and I met last week, I continued to examine the letter you shared with me. I believe I've uncovered something quite important."

"Okay," Lydia said slowly, eager to hear what exactly he'd uncovered.

"Do you, by chance, have a copy of the letter handy?" Archibald asked.

"No, but hold on a second. Let me grab my laptop." Lydia got up, grabbed her computer from the kitchen island, and returned to her chair. Once she found a copy of the letter, she said, "Okay, I have it up."

"Scroll down toward the bottom, to the section you and I reviewed together here at the museum, the part that starts with, *A figure dances.*"

Lydia did as he requested. "All right, I'm there."

"Underline the words *mob never* and *white tent*," he said. "Do the same for the time *5:05* and the word *cherry.*"

She didn't have a clue where he was going, but, again, she did as she was told.

A figure dances on the fringes of normalcy, wielding a brush as an extension of their soul. Their canvas is life's platter, transcending the bounds of convention.

There's a leak, drip, drip, drip. Do you hear it?

The <u>mob never</u> knows the answer. Don't follow them to the <u>white tent</u>. Red, always red.

The train is safer than driving especially on Lee Hwy. Take the <u>5:05</u> to the third stop. If you have time, stop for ice cream, but don't forget the <u>cherry</u> on top. Trust me, it will be so much fun.

"Like I told you before," Archibald said. "I love puzzles. My wife and I do the Spelling Bee in the *New York Times* every morning over breakfast."

Lydia thought this was very endearing, but she really hoped he got to the point soon.

"Do you know what an anagram is?" he asked.

"Of course," Lydia replied. "It's when you rearrange the letter in a word to spell a new word or phrase." *Joe and his damn anagrams. Lager, lager, lager…regal, regal, regal.*

"Yes," he said approvingly.

This guy must think I'm an idiot, Lydia thought as she waited for him to go on.

He cleared his throat. "According to the police reports I've read, they estimate that the taxidermist in Alexandria was killed on or about November twentieth. Look at the words I had you underline, mob never and white tent. Rearrange the letters and you get November twentieth.

"Holy shit."

Archibald let out a muffled laugh. "My thoughts exactly. Can you tell me, Lydia, the letter you shared with me, on what date did you receive it?"

"Hang on." Lydia scrolled through her email inbox. "It came in on November twelfth."

"Okay," he said. "So, well before the murder."

"Yes," Lydia replied.

Archibald cleared his throat again. "There's one more thing."

"Oh, God, what?" If Lydia had been anxious to hear what Archibald had so say before, she was now doubly so.

"Lydia, the taxidermist lived at 505 Cherry Street."

Lydia dropped her phone on the floor. "Holy fucking shit!" She'd been right all along. Joe, a.k.a Macon, was the Red Scarf Murderer.

Jen ran into the living room wrapped in a towel with Eric right on her tail. "Oh, my God, Lydia, are you all right?"

Archibald's voice rang out from the phone on the floor. "Hello? Lydia?"

Lydia opened her mouth to speak but no words came out. She began to hyperventilate.

Jen snatched the phone from the floor. "I'm sorry, Lydia will have to call you back."

Eric rested a hand on Jen's arm. "Should I get her a paper bag?"

"I don't know, yeah, maybe." Jen squeezed herself into the armchair next to Lydia and gently rubbed her back.

Lydia wriggled out of the chair and lurched across the room toward the bathroom. "I think I'm going to be sick."

Jen came into the bathroom behind her and held back her curls while Lydia retched into the toilet until her throat was raw. She closed the toilet lid and rested her cheek on its cool surface.

Eric brought her glass of water, and after she gargled that and brushed her teeth, she returned to the armchair and picked up her laptop. "That was Archibald McQueen on the phone," she explained. "He's the museum curator I shared one of Joe's letters with." She opened her computer to Joe's letter and detailed the significance of the sections Archibald had asked her to underline.

The *mob never* knows the answer. Don't follow them to the *white tent*. Red, always red.

The train is safer than driving especially on Lee Hwy. Take the *5:05* to the third stop. If you have time, stop for ice cream, but don't forget the *cherry* on top. Trust me, it will be so much fun.

"This letter from Joe landed in my inbox more than a week before the taxidermist was killed," Lydia said matter-of-factly. At this point, her entire body was numb. The whole situation was beyond surreal.

"Are you saying what I think you're saying?" Jen asked.

"Yes," Lydia said. "Joe, the guy who's sent me all those nasty letters, *is* the Red Scarf Murderer, or, at the very least, he and the murderer are tight pals."

"Right," Eric said. "Tight enough that Joe would know the murderer's next move."

Lydia's cell phone vibrated on the table beside her. She eyed Jen and Eric. "I'm scared to see who it is." She ventured a glance at the caller ID. "It's Paul Gibbons, the investigative reporter at the *Post* I told you about."

Lydia answered the call and put Paul on speaker. "I just heard from my source at the police department," Paul said.

"What's the verdict?"

"They took DNA samples from the items you gave Miller in the park." There was a long pause before he continued, "The results are back. They match DNA collected from several of the murder scenes."

Jen gripped Lydia's hand and their faces reflected a shared sense of alarm. Lydia tried to absorb the enormity of it all, the chilling realization that all doubt was now removed. Joe was the serial killer who had been terrorizing the nation's capital. After the call from Archibald McQueen, a tiny part of her had hoped that perhaps the curator had read too much into Joe's letter, that he'd twisted the words to create things that weren't actually there. But now, there was no escaping the horrible truth. DNA didn't lie.

A mix of utter disbelief and sheer terror washed over her, and she wiped her clammy palms on her pant leg.

"Lydia, are you still there?" Paul's voice echoed through the phone.

"Yeah, yeah, sorry. I'm just in shock."

"I understand," he said. "Where are you now?"

Lydia gave him Jen's address.

"A police cruiser will be there to get you in thirty minutes."

"And take me where?"

"To police headquarters," Paul said calmly. "They want to question you."

"Question me? Why?"

"You're central to this case. They'll likely ask to see all correspondence between you and Macon Hardy."

"Who's Macon Hardy?" Jen whispered.

Lydia glanced at her. "That's Joe's real name."

Jen nodded slowly. "Oh."

"One more thing," Paul said. "This will be all over the news any minute…The police just raided the last known address for Macon Hardy. He wasn't home. A full-scale manhunt has been launched. Once you're finished at police headquarters, you'll be taken to a hotel. I want you safe until they have him in custody."

"What about my friends Jen and Eric?" Lydia asked Paul. "Although I don't know for sure yet, I have reason to believe Macon broke into their apartment last night. Who's to say he won't come back?"

"We can go to my mom's house in Bethesda," Eric said. "She's got three dogs and a high-tech security system."

After she got off the phone with Paul, Lydia said, "I guess I should go pack." She stood and started across the living room but didn't get far. Her legs buckled beneath her, and she landed in a heap on the floor, narrowly missing the corner of the coffee table with her head.

Jen and Eric helped her to the couch. After a few sips of water, the dizziness began to ease. Lydia's eyes darted around the room before settling on her friends. "I'm scared."

CHAPTER TWENTY-EIGHT

Britney flung open the fridge in her parents' kitchen, on the prowl for something savory to munch on. The back room of their house doubled as her studio for Sun & Moon, and she spent half her life back there. Her folks were currently off on a cruise to the Bahamas. Given the circumstances, Britney appreciated the peace and quiet.

After the fucking cops pinned Macon to the murder scenes, they'd hauled her sorry ass in, interrogating her for what seemed like forever. The last place she wanted to be right now was at her apartment. If the cops came knocking again, Britney was determined to make herself a bit trickier to track down.

With cheese curds and chips in hand, Britney smoothed *The Washington Post* out on her parents' kitchen table. A smile crept across her face as she scanned the front-page article.

Former girlfriend aided investigation…DNA gathered from items found in storage locker …matched DNA collected…led police to…

By now, Macon had most certainly heard the news. *He must have gone ballistic.* Britney chuckled at the thought. How had he reacted when he'd discovered what she'd done? What had he thought when he'd realized she'd played him like a fiddle and left him out to dry? It wasn't her fault he was an idiot. It also wasn't her fault that Macon had gone and fallen in love with her. Once that happened, it was laughably easy to wrap him around her little finger.

She'd started small, asking him to wash her car or shoplift an insignificant item. He never hesitated even as her requests grew more daring—poison the neighbor's dog who never fucking stopped barking. Push the little girl down the street off her bike after she threatened to rat Macon out for poisoning said dog.

At first, she'd worried that the step to murder might be too big, but Macon never pushed back, always eager to please her no matter what she asked. It had all been so convenient. Britney got to knock off a long list of people who had fucked her over during her life, but she never had to get her hands dirty. She issued the order and Macon carried it out like a dutiful fucking soldier.

To the cops, the murders appeared random—they had yet to discern a connection between the victims. She cackled. "The connection between them was me, you fucking maggots."

She turned on the TV. Every channel had images of helicopters and police in tactical gear above a banner that read "Special Report" or "Breaking News." A massive manhunt was underway. They were all looking for Macon. *Such a delightful thought.* Two possible scenarios played out in Britney's mind.

Scenario one: the cops caught Macon.

If this happened, he'd probably point fingers at Britney, saying she'd put him up to the murders—one had to assume his love for her only ran so deep. But he could point fingers all he wanted; none of it would matter. There was no evidence to tie Britney to the murders. They'd only find Macon's DNA.

Scenario two: Macon grew outraged when he read the article in the *Post* about the DNA and decided to come after Britney.

Of the two scenarios, this was the most desirable. If he came after her, she'd be ready. A scuffle would ensue, and she could kill Macon, claiming self-defense. With Macon dead, there would be no one around to point fingers at her. Everyone would think Macon was the Red Scarf Murderer, end of story.

It was brilliant really. She'd grown tired of Macon, and now that he'd carried out the murders for her, she had little use for him. At the same time, it wasn't rocket science that the cops and the press—the fucking press—would never rest until the Red Scarf Murderer was caught.

This meant that Britney must dream up a way to frame Macon *without* drawing any scrutiny to herself. Although she'd tried, she hadn't been able to devise a foolproof plan. Until now. She cackled again. By some miracle, that bitch advice columnist had appeared out of nowhere and everything had fallen into place.

Now people would think Britney was a clueless ex-girlfriend who had no idea her ex-boyfriend was a murderer and had done all she could to help the police tie him to the crimes.

The twisted part was, Macon wasn't her ex. They were still a couple. Britney had seen the letter from Gainfully Employed Girlfriend on the *Post's* website. It had appeared the same day as the letter from Anxious, Anxious, Anxious, who wrote in to say she was scared and anxious about the serial murderer roaming the DC region.

Dear Birdie's response to Anxious, Anxious, Anxious had made Britney irate. She wanted to punish Dear Birdie for her mean words, get back at her in some way. That's when Britney came up with the novel idea—she'd compose letters to Dear Birdie pretending to be Joe, Gainfully Employed Girlfriend's scorned and now ex-boyfriend.

Writing the letters and pretending to be Joe had been even more fun than Britney had imagined, so much so that she'd gotten carried away. What had started out as an enjoyable way to torment Dear Birdie, turned into a game for Britney. Because she orchestrated the murders carried out by the Red Scarf

Murderer—the dumb name the press had given Macon—she decided to make Dear Birdie believe this Joe character was the murderer.

Never in Britney's wildest dreams did she think this little charade of writing made-up letters to Dear Birdie would yield such fruit. Never did she imagine that it would give her the perfect out for eliminating Macon, making everyone believe he alone was the one behind the murders.

Britney had certainly been caught off guard when the advice columnist...What was her name? Lydia. When Lydia had confronted her at the post office...Once she got over the initial surprise, she briefly panicked. How had Lydia tracked her down? Had Britney slipped up somewhere? Did Lydia know the truth? Did she know Britney was the mastermind behind the Red Scarf Murders?

But as Lydia began to explain why she was there, Britney figured it out. Lydia had somehow tracked her down via another fake email Britney had sent to Dear Birdie. This time rather than purporting to be Joe, she'd written in pretending to be Gainfully Employed Girlfriend. Maybe it had been a little reckless to write the letter pretending to be the girlfriend, but who cared? It had paid off!

Britney turned off the TV and gently set the remote on the counter. It was time to get ready. If Macon came after her, she better begin her preparations.

Not long after she jumped into action, her phone rang. At first, she ignored it, but after it rang two more times, she reluctantly pulled it from her back pocket. It was Lydia, the advice columnist woman. What the hell did she want? Britney had given her the items with Macon's fucking DNA! Couldn't the woman leave her alone? She reluctantly answered the phone, trying to mask the annoyance in her voice. "Hi, Lydia."

Lydia's voice held a sense of urgency. "Have you seen the article in *The Washington Post*?"

Britney hesitated, wanting to appear anxious—not overjoyed. "Um, yes. I saw it the article about the items from the storage place and how they led the police to Macon."

"I think we have to assume Macon has seen the article too," Lydia said softly. "Which means…"

"I might be in danger." Britney refrained from saying anything more. It was "game on." Lydia thought she was Gainfully Employed Girlfriend with a crazy ex-boyfriend named Joe. Britney needed to play the role and she couldn't slip up.

"Yes," Lydia said. "I'm afraid you could be in danger. Do you still have Miller's business card?"

"Yes," Britney confirmed.

"Where are you now?"

Britney sure as hell wasn't going to tell Lydia where she was. "Staying with a friend."

"Okay, well if you get scared, the police have put me in a hotel. I'm sure they'd offer you the same protection if you asked."

"Okay, I will," Britney said, knowing damn well that she wouldn't.

"Good," Lydia said. "Please call me if you need anything, anything at all."

"I will." Britney smiled into the phone. "Thanks for calling, Lydia."

After they ended the call, Britney got to her feet. She needed to get back to work. Macon could show up at any moment.

She stepped into the studio space off her parents' kitchen. Two years earlier, she'd used the money that her business, Sun & Moon, had made on Etsy to build herself a proper studio. The large, well lit, cabin-like space now provided ample room for her work. It also had vast amount of storage space for the tools she used to create ornate sculptures from scrap metal. Right now, she planned to use these tools for another purpose: to defend herself against Macon. She laid a series of sharp metal instruments out on her workbench like a doctor preparing for surgery. She also set out her favorite blowtorch.

Macon was a large, strong man, and if he was enraged, as she suspected he would be, it might give him superhuman strength. Although Britney worked out religiously, most people would probably describe her as petite. She, therefore, needed to come up with ways to slow him down to give her a chance to attack.

First, she strung fishing line back and forth across the doorway to her studio, leaving herself a small hole near the bottom to crawl through. Then, she went back into the kitchen and pulled her mother's Cuisinart food processor from the cupboard. If he came after her, she'd turn the tables on him, exploiting his weakness—the parmesan mashed potato and meatloaf casserole she'd made him countless times.

Using the food processor, she ground up whatever noxious ingredients she could find around her parents' house—rat poison, laxatives, and a few squirts of Scrubbing Bubbles bathroom cleaner. For good measure, she added a few pills from an expired penicillin prescription and tossed in a bunch of cashews. Macon happened to be allergic to penicillin and cashews. When the concoction reached a soupy grit state, she added it to the mashed potatoes in her mixer.

His nut allergy was moderate, usually resulting in nausea and itchy hives, so she doubted a few mouthfuls of her potion would prove fatal—a good thing, her attack on him couldn't appear premeditated. Still, she hoped the mixture would debilitate him enough to give her an advantage.

When the timer went off, she pulled the dish from the oven, set it on the counter to cool, and carefully slipped through the fishing line and into her studio. Although it was only a little past five, Washington, DC was nearing its shortest day of the year and darkness had already descended outside.

She flipped on more lights and sat down at her computer to tackle the ever-growing backlog of Etsy orders. Her mind was focused on Excel sheets and invoices until she jolted upright at the sound of someone rapping against the window above her desk. She smacked her knee hard into the filing cabinet as she leapt to her feet.

Macon stared back at her through the window, his eyes wild and his hair disheveled. The flashlight he held below his face gave him a ghostly look, like a character in the movie *Halloween*.

His face disappeared from the window as quickly as it had appeared. Had it been a mirage?

He pounded on her front door. "Britney, open the fucking door!"

Moments later the sound of shattering glass and splintering wood filled the air. Grabbing the blowtorch and a tool that resembled a pickaxe, she crouched under her workbench to wait. From her perch, she had a clear line of sight into the kitchen.

Britney's hand flew to her back pocket. Where was her phone? Her eyes roamed the room. Her gold phone cover sparkled under the light of her desk lamp. She crawled out from the cover of her workbench. As her hand went to snatch the phone, Macon barged into her kitchen, rage etched across his face.

His movements were robotic as he crossed the kitchen, his heavy boots dragging across the tile floor.

She held her breath, praying the meatloaf casserole lured him in. When his eyes locked on the glass dish near the oven she whispered, "Hook, line, and sinker."

He dug around in the silverware drawer for a fork and greedily jabbed it into the crust of potatoes, devouring mouthful after mouthful.

Britney remained as still as she could, afraid if he heard her move, it would distract him. She needed him to consume more of the meatloaf first. He weighed nearly two hundred pounds, and it would take lot of the nut-infused brew to affect him.

He belched and hurled his fork across the room. The wild look returned to his eyes, as if he'd just remembered why he was there. Britney raised her blowtorch and took a few tentative steps back toward her workbench. With the ferocity of a wild animal, Macon tried to lunge through the door to her studio. He spat profanities when he became entangled in the fishing line she'd strung across the entryway.

While he struggled to free himself, she whispered, "Game time." She stabbed 911 into her phone. When the dispatcher came on the line, she screamed, "The Red Scarf Murderer is at my house and he's trying to kill me!"

Hearing her make the 911 call only further infuriated Macon. He growled and broke free of the fishing line. When he reached her, he swatted the phone from her hand, sending it flying to the floor.

Britney could hear the muffled voice of the dispatcher. "This is not a crank call. This is real," she hollered.

Macon stomped on the phone with his boot, shattering the screen. "I did it all for you," he howled. "I'm not taking the fall alone."

Their eyes locked in a deadly standoff. Macon punched her in the arm, causing her to drop the blowtorch. The adrenaline coursing through her veins propelled her into action.

Britney was smaller and more agile than he was, and she needed to use this to her advantage. With the pickaxe tucked under her arm, she rolled over the workbench and snatched a baseball bat from a hook on the wall. The irony was not lost on her. The bat was Macon's, one his many possessions strewn across her parents' house.

He rounded the bench, his arms oscillating wildly. The floor lamp crashed to the floor. Britney set down the pickaxe and raised the bat, swinging it with all her might. A loud crack echoed through the room when it connected with his head.

He growled but seemed unfazed by the pain. When Britney raised the bat again, he caught it in his meaty hand midair, yanked it away from her, and tossed it aside. It clattered on the cement floor and rolled under a bookshelf.

Macon charged at her. She snatched the pickaxe off the workbench, twirled around, and landed a solid kick to his knee, causing him to stumble back and collide with the wall. A large wood-framed mirror fell to the ground and shattered into a million shards.

Britney had to make a split-second decision. Should she try to lodge the axe in Macon's throat or simply deliver a kick to the head and leave him for the police to finish off? Her preference was to take him out herself. It would be cleaner that way. It would also make it easier for her to escape. While stringing the fishing line across the door to her studio had seemed like a good idea at the time, it now served as a trap. Macon had left behind a tangled mess when he'd pushed into the room, and she'd have to pick her way out.

Time was running out. Macon was regaining his balance and looked ready to pounce again. But suddenly, his movements slowed. He clutched his stomach and threw up on his boots, his eyes bulging out of his swollen face as if he didn't comprehend what was happening.

Britney raised the axe and inched closer to him.

He retched again and welts peppered his cheeks, neck, and forehead. He swayed back and forth and leaned heavily against her workbench.

Sirens wailed in the distance.

"They're coming for you," Britney whispered and bit back a laugh.

Taunting Macon was the wrong move. He straightened his posture and pushed open his coat, revealing the sheath strapped around him like a gun holster.

Britney picked up one of her work stools and hurled it at him.

He blocked it with his beefy forearm. "You bitch." Macon's face twisted into a malicious grin as he withdrew the knife. Another round of vomit spewed from his mouth. He tried to move toward her but tripped on the stool and fell to the ground. Britney detected a flicker of fear in his eyes as he went to stand. Had he realized she'd outsmarted him by tainting a dish she knew he'd eat?

With Macon momentarily disoriented, Britney once again went to raise the axe, but Macon grabbed a fistful of her shirt before she could swing it. He wrapped one arm around her neck and pressed the tip of the knife against her back. She dropped the axe to the floor.

"Let her go!" a male voice said.

Macon loosened the grip around her neck to peer over his shoulder. Britney ducked her head and managed to free herself, but she wasn't fast enough. He waved the knife through the air, slicing her arm and nicking her neck in the process. Warm blood oozed from her wounds.

A uniformed officer burst into the room right as Macon leaned over to get sick again.

Britney fell to her knees and crawled across the floor. It took some effort, but she was able to make it to the dog door at the back of her studio and began to wriggle through. Once she pushed her way outside, her chest heaved in the cold December air. Blue police lights flashed over the bushes in the backyard, and she turned to run toward them. But just as she did, two gunshots echoed from inside her parents' house.

It wasn't until later, when Britney lay in a hospital bed, that she learned the police had shot Macon dead.

CHAPTER TWENTY-NINE

Lydia sat in her office and spread a "hot off the press" copy of *The Washington Post* on her desk. It had been almost three days since the police had announced that the Red Scarf Murderer had been killed. The *Post*, of course, had covered Macon Hardy's death in great length and Paul Gibbons, the investigative reporter, wrote a follow-up column detailing exactly how the cops had come to have Macon's DNA in their possession. His article appeared on the front page of today's paper.

...DNA evidence played a pivotal role in establishing Mr. Hardy as a prime suspect in the series of killings. Authorities managed to match DNA recovered at the crime scenes to genetic material provided by his ex-girlfriend, Britney Alice, of Bowie, Maryland, a law enforcement official said. A law enforcement official, speaking on the condition of anonymity, confirmed this critical breakthrough in the investigation.

Lydia Swann, the Dear Birdie *columnist at* The Washington Post, *also emerged as a key figure in connecting Mr. Hardy to the murders. For several months, Mr. Hardy sent cryptic letters to* Dear Birdie, *employing word games and riddles to conceal clues about the murders. The motive behind Mr. Hardy's correspondence with Ms. Swann remains undisclosed.*

Both Ms. Swann and Ms. Alice are being lauded as heroes for their exceptional courage and resilience. Thanks to their contributions, coupled with the unwavering dedication of law enforcement officials, the Red Scarf Murderer's reign of terror has finally come to an end...

Before Lydia could finish reading the article, Tisha knocked on her door and stepped inside. "I just got the strangest email," she said. "I can't make sense of it."

"Who was it from?" Lydia asked.

"Gainfully Employed Girlfriend."

"You mean Britney?"

"Well, that's the thing," Tisha said. "I'm not sure it's from Britney."

The hair on Lydia's arms stood up. "What do you mean?"

Tisha set a printout of the email on Lydia's desk. "Remember when you and I sent Gainfully Employed Girlfriend that first email to make sure she wasn't in danger from her ex, Joe?"

"Yeah, and we got that weird response, something about improper forwarding causing mail loop."

"Right," Tisha said. "Because of that error, we never knew for sure whether she received our email. IT told us the email probably bounced because of the error and it might not have reached her at all."

Lydia tried to think back to what had happened. "But then, about a week later, she sent us a second email, right?"

"Right," Tisha said. "We used that second email from GEG to track Britney down. It had the logo for her business, Sun & Moon." Tisha took a seat in one of the chairs opposite Lydia's desk and tapped the printout of the email that had just come in from Gainfully Employed Girlfriend. "This is where things get confusing."

"How so?"

Tisha tapped the printout again. "I exchanged a few messages with Gainfully Employed Girlfriend today. You need to read the email chain."

Lydia picked up the paper and read through it. The first email in the exchange was the one Tisha, acting on behalf of

Dear Birdie, had sent to GEG in late October to check to see if GEG was okay—the email to which they'd received the weird loop message. The second email was a reply from GEG. It was dated today, December 16th.

Dear Birdie,

Thank you so much for checking on me. It's very kind of you. I did take your advice and ended the relationship with Joe. He didn't take it well at first but eventually saw it as a wake-up call. I haven't spoken to him since the breakup, but I've heard through the grapevine that he's doing fine—he's landed a new job and has already shacked up with someone new.

Regards,

Gainfully Employed Girlfriend

Lydia threw a hand in the air. "So, the email with the loop error finally went through."

"It appears so," Tisha said.

"But the response we got from GEG today doesn't jive with the story Britney told me."

"I know," Tisha said. "Read on, there's more."

The next email in the exchange was one Tisha had written to GEG just a few hours earlier. In it, Tisha said that she was happy to hear things were going well for GEG, especially because that hadn't appeared to be the case in the email GEG sent in early November.

Lydia moved down to read the final email from GEG, received only ten minutes earlier.

Dear Birdie,

What email? Prior to today, the only other email I've sent you was the one I originally wrote back in early October.

Regards,

Gainfully Employed Girlfriend

Lydia set the paper back down at her desk and shook her head. "Huh."

"It's almost like Britney and Gainfully Employed Girlfriend are two different people."

"It does seem like that," Lydia agreed. She picked up her phone. "I'm gonna text Britney."

While they waited for Britney to respond. Lydia brought up the second email they'd received from GEG—the one Dear Birdie had gotten in early November that the original Gainfully Employed Girlfriend claimed she had not sent. The November email was the one that included the logo from Sun & Moon, the logo Lydia had used to track down Britney. If Britney wasn't really Gainfully Employed Girlfriend, then who was she?

* * *

Britney rested both elbows on her workbench and stared at the small TV on the wall in her studio. Two days earlier, the DC police had held a press conference to update the public on developments in the Red Scarf Murderer case. Britney had replayed the press conference over and over since then.

The police chief spoke slowly as he detailed the circumstances of Macon Hardy's death. He highlighted the DNA evidence the police had used to link Macon to the Red Scarf murder scenes.

Local and national news crews jockeyed for space in the packed room and the moment the chief stopped speaking, the reporters began to shout out questions.

"Do you believe Macon Hardy acted alone?"

"Can you provide more details about how the police were able to link Mr. Hardy's DNA to the crime scenes?"

"Will you give more details about the circumstances surrounding Mr. Hardy's death?"

The police chief took the questions in order, directing his attention first to a reporter from CNN. "It's still early in the investigation, but at this point, yes, we believe Mr. Hardy acted alone."

He then turned his attention to the reporter from FOX News. "Regarding the DNA evidence…"

Britney didn't care much about the rest of the press conference. Her fixation was on the chief's answer to the first question. "We believe Mr. Hardy acted alone."

She smiled like she had each of the other times she'd watched the press conference. She'd done it. She'd pinned the murders on Macon, and no one suspected she'd played a role in them.

Moments later a text came in from Lydia. *Sorry to bother you, but do you have a moment to chat?*

"Why can't that woman leave me the fuck alone?" Britney bellowed into her empty studio. It probably would not behoove her to ignore the advice columnist at this delicate juncture. Britney needed to be hyperaware to avoid doing anything suspicious. She turned off the TV and typed a response. *Sure. Does now work?*

When the call came in from Lydia, Britney answered it promptly, straining to keep her tone friendly and her breathing under control. As she listened to Lydia, her hands grew clammy, and heat rose up the back of her neck. The advice columnist relentlessly peppered her with questions, causing Britney to grow increasingly agitated.

"I'm just confused," Lydia droned. "It's almost like you and Gainfully Employed Girlfriend are two different people. Did you write a letter to Dear Birdie pretending to be her?"

When Britney didn't respond, Lydia continued her inquisition. "Because if you're not Gainfully Employed Girlfriend, then none of it makes sense—"

"Listen," Britney interjected. "I'm really busy with work and I don't have time to answer your ridiculous questions."

Lydia's voice rose a few pitches. "I need to know—"

"I said I'm busy," Britney growled. So much for keeping her tone friendly. "I helped you get the DNA evidence you needed. Now, can you please leave me alone?"

Lydia started to say something else, but Britney ended the call before she could finish. "God, fucking damn it," she screamed and hurled her phone across the room. Just when Britney thought she had this murder thing buttoned up, that bitch, Lydia, had to go stirring the pot. What if Lydia went to the cops with her needling questions?

Britney paced the room, yanking on her hair as she wore a path circling her workbench. Her next move became crystal clear. The situation left her with only one choice. Lydia had to be eliminated and there was no time to waste. Unfortunately,

Macon was no longer around to do Britney's dirty work. That meant she'd have to take out the advice columnist herself.

* * *

When the line went dead, Lydia slapped her phone on her desk. There were more questions than answers when it came to the letters from Gainfully Employed Girlfriend, inconsistencies and discrepancies that Lydia was determined to piece together.

To start, she printed out every letter from Joe, including the scanned copy of the one he'd handwritten. Afterward, she lined them up in chronological order on the table in her office. Using the whiteboard in her office, she catalogued each letter Dear Birdie had received, both from Joe and from GEG.

After pouring over each letter, she stood and wrote "Monday Nov 4th" on her whiteboard. Then she called Paul Gibbons.

When he answered the phone, she asked, "Can they collect DNA from paper, say a handwritten letter?"

"It's certainly possible," Paul responded. "Remember that string of violent bank robberies a few years ago? The cops managed to lift DNA off one of the notes the robbers passed a bank teller."

"Awesome," Lydia said. "Because I'm now convinced that Macon Hardy did not act alone, and I think I know how to prove it."

Paul let out a whistle. "I can't wait to hear what you've got."

"Can you come up to my office? It might be easier to show you what I have."

"Be there in ten," he said and ended the call.

When he arrived on the seventh floor, Lydia gestured to the letters arranged on the table in her office. "The group on the left are from Now Single Joe, the jilted boyfriend, or at least the letters we thought were from him."

"Got it," Paul said. "And the letters on the right?"

"They're from Gainfully Employed Girlfriend." Lydia picked up one of the GEG letters. "I scoured the letters again today and this one jumped out at me."

"Why is that?" Paul asked.

"Well, it was sent to Dear Birdie in early November, about two weeks before the taxidermist was murdered in Alexandria. I hadn't noticed it before, but the letter includes a reference to a groundhog." She pointed to a paragraph in the letter.

In moments of weakness, I catch myself wondering if I made the right decision. Should I have stayed and tried harder to make things work? Did I give up too easily? These doubts gnaw at me like a groundhog.

"If I recall," Paul said, "the taxidermist specialized in woodchucks. And, in many places, woodchucks are called groundhogs."

"Exactly," Lydia said. "One might brush off GEG's mention of a groundhog as mere chance, but I've reached a point where I believe every word in both GEG and Joe's letters are intentional." Lydia carefully set down the GEG groundhog letter and exchanged it for one from Joe. "Which leads me to the second thing I wanted to ask you. One of the letters we got from Joe was handwritten. This is a copy of course. Security has the original."

"Let me guess," Paul interjected. "You want to have the handwritten letter tested for DNA?"

"Yep. My hunch is that Now Single Joe isn't the person who penned it."

"Then who do you suspect did?" Paul asked.

Lydia met his gaze squarely. "Britney Alice."

CHAPTER THIRTY

Lydia drew in a deep breath, her hand hovering near the doorbell. It was one of those fancy models with a built-in camera, giving whoever lurked inside a clear view of their visitor. Lydia would have preferred the element of surprise. She held her breath and pressed the bell.

The front door swung open with an ominous creak.

Britney stood at the threshold of her parents' house; an unsettling smile etched on her face. Her eyes burned with an intensity that sent a shiver down Lydia's spine. All signs of the kind and pleasant woman Lydia had met in Bowie, Maryland had vanished.

"Hello, Lydia," Britney sneered, her tone dripping with disdain as she launched into a barrage of profanities, punctuated by a cackle reminiscent of the Wicked Witch of the West. "How wonderful to find you on my doorstep. Saves me the trouble of hunting you down." She laughed again. "Pardon my manners, would you like to come in?"

Lydia's gut reaction screamed a firm no. She most certainly did not want to come in. But she'd come there on a mission, and she wasn't backing out now. With hesitant resolve, she stepped inside, shivers prickling her skin when the door clicked shut behind her.

"Take off your coat," Britney barked.

Following orders, Lydia shrugged off her coat, feeling exposed in more ways than one.

Britney snatched the coat, carelessly tossing it into a heap in the corner of the living room before subjecting Lydia to a thorough pat down. Apparently satisfied, she stepped back and asked, "Why the fuck are you here?"

"I have a few questions for you." Lydia said, her voice barely above a whisper.

"What makes you think I'll answer them?"

"Why are you being so hostile? I've shown you nothing but kindness."

Britney scoffed, her laughter grating against Lydia's nerves. "That's a complete load of BS."

"I don't understand," Lydia stammered.

Britney put her hands on her hips and leaned forward. "On Monday, October seventh, *Dear Birdie* published a response to two letters."

Lydia tried to think back. October seventh. That was only a week or two into her tenure at the *Post*. For the life of her, she couldn't recall publishing anything that might have set Britney off. "What letters?" she asked. Right now, the only tactic she could think of was to keep Britney talking.

Britney took one step closer to Lydia. "The first letter was from Gainfully Employed Girlfriend. She wanted to know what to do about her loser boyfriend, Joe. The second letter was from Anxious, Anxious, Anxious. She wrote to Dear Birdie about her never-ending cycle of fear and anxiety in response to the constant media coverage of the Red Scarf Murderer."

"Okay," Lydia said. She tried to take a step back but Britney grabbed her arm.

"Your response to Anxious, Anxious, Anxious seriously pissed me off," Britney said.

Lydia's voice shook. "Why is that?"

"You wrote that the Red Scarf Murderer was a freakin' psycho. You called the murderer a truly deranged and evil person and said that the person responsible for the murders had demonstrated a level of cruelty that was difficult to fathom."

"That sounds familiar," Lydia said. *Was Britney about to admit she played a role in the murders?*

As if reading her mind, Britney said, "By now you've probably realized Macon was my puppet…"

Lydia hadn't quite reached that conclusion, but she kept her mouth shut and let Britney continue.

"That idiot was madly in love with me, unhealthily so. He'd do anything I asked him to do."

"Including murder?" Lydia asked.

Britney's nostrils flared. "Yes, even murder. I told him who to kill and when. He did it, no questions asked, all because he couldn't bear the thought of losing me. I reveled in that, used it to my advantage."

"How did you pick the people you told him to kill?"

"They were all people who had pissed me off at some point in my life," Britney retorted, her voice a mixture of bitterness and satisfaction. She began ticking off the murder victims on her fingers. "There was Mr. Ring, that prick of a chemistry teacher who caused me to repeat tenth grade."

Lydia's mind raced. *Chemistry teacher.* "The man who was murdered in his bed, his throat slit while he and his wife slept. She woke up to discover the horrific scene."

"That's the one." Britney's expression morphed into a sinister smile. "After that, there was the wench, Claudia Spiess, who'd bullied me all through junior high." Britney's face flushed and her eyes bulged out of her head. "But one murder brought me more satisfaction than all the others. Albert Moss, the retired psychiatrist."

"The taxidermist?"

"Yeah, fucking weirdo."

"What did he do to you?"

"In high school, I was forced to see Dr. Moss. He swore our sessions were confidential. Turned out, he was a lying fucking shithead. He snitched on me, got me fucking arrested."

"All right," Lydia said as calmly as she could. "But I still don't see how this ties back to *Dear Birdie* and the letters."

"When I read your garbage response to Anxious, Anxious, Anxious, I wanted to make Dear Birdie pay for the horrible words she'd written about the Red Scarf Murderer. I took them personally."

"Because for all intents and purposes you were the Red Scarf Murderer," Lydia spat. "Macon carried out the murders, but it was you who pulled all the strings."

Britney's eyed narrowed. "Righto. You're a quick one, Lydia." She took another step closer. "To get back at Dear Birdie, I came up with a brilliant idea. I decided to pose as Joe, Gainfully Employed Girlfriend's loser boyfriend. I thought it would be fun to mess with the righteous advice columnist." Britney laughed. "Writing the 'Joe' letters turned out to be way more fun than I expected. Taunting Dear Birdie, playing mind games...It was fabulous. I started following you around, hoping to crank up the freak-out factor. Oh, and in case you're curious, it was me who slit your car tires."

Lydia wasn't completely surprised by the revelation about the stalking. What truly floored her was that she'd been right. Now she needed to confirm her other theory: Britney also authored the second letter from Gainfully Employed Girlfriend, the one Lydia had used to track Britney down using the Sun & Moon logo. "You also wrote a letter purporting to be Gainfully Employed Girlfriend, didn't you?"

"Yes," Britney admitted. "In retrospect though, that was a mistake, a moment of weakness on my part. I was having such a good time playing Joe, but I took it too far. Although, writing a letter claiming to be from Gainfully Employed Girlfriend did end up proving useful."

"How so?" Lydia asked.

Britney looked at her like she was an idiot. "It enabled you to track me down in Bowie. When you showed up asking for something with Macon's DNA, my prayers were answered. It gave me a nice clean way to frame Macon for the murders."

"How convenient."

"Yes, it was. All I had to do was ride away into the sunset." Britney raised her fist. "But then you continued to meddle, Lydia. When you called me earlier and peppered me with all those annoying questions about Gainfully Employed Girlfriend's letter, I knew what I had to do. I had to kill you. Shut you the fuck up once and for all."

Britney edged toward Lydia until they stood only a few feet apart. The house fell into an eerie silence. Now that the sun had dipped below the horizon, a lone lamp cast long shadows, its soft glow illuminating the room.

Though fear gnawed at her insides, Lydia fought to maintain her composure, willing herself not to betray an ounce of vulnerability.

And then, like a thunderclap shattering the silence of the night, the front door exploded inward with a resounding bang, and the harsh glare of police lights flooded the room. The sound of shattering glass reverberated from the rear of the house. The heavy thud of boots echoed through the house. Chaos erupted as a wave of uniformed officers surged the room, seemingly coming from every direction.

The once arrogant expression on Britney's face crumbled, supplanted by one of raw terror as the click of handcuffs sealed her fate.

Lydia unfastened the top two buttons of her shirt, revealing the wire taped to her skin.

Britney spat on Lydia. "You fucking bitch."

Two officers flanked Britney, but before she was led away, Lydia stared into her beady dark-brown eyes. "Can I ask you a question?"

Britney just stared back at her.

"Did you break into my apartment?"

"Macon," Britney hissed.

"Macon broke into my apartment?"

"Yes."

"Because you told him to come after me?" Lydia asked.

"No."

"Then why?"

"I told him about the letters I'd been writing to Dear Birdie. He got paranoid." Britney's eyes narrowed. "He wanted to kill you. Sadly, I encouraged him not to." She leered at Lydia. "In retrospect, I wish he had."

CHAPTER THIRTY-ONE

After the police took Britney away and finally informed Lydia she was free to go, she returned to the hotel where she'd been staying temporarily. After retrieving a small bottle of wine from her minifridge, she crawled into bed. When she woke up, the sun was already high in the sky. She had to check her phone to figure out what day it was.

She texted Tisha. *I just woke up. Can't remember the last time I slept until 10 a.m. on a Thursday. Moving a little slowly. I'll be in the office soon.*

Lydia swung her feet to the floor, feeling groggy and stiff. She'd perk up with some coffee and bite to eat before taking the long way to work. The walk would give her a chance to stretch her legs and clear her mind.

Although the idea of going to work felt mildly overwhelming, Lydia had a more daunting task to conquer that evening. She intended to return to her apartment for the first time since the break-in. With Macon dead and Britney in jail, it was time for her to go home and get on with her life. A cleaning company had been enlisted to tidy up her apartment. Still, Lydia couldn't shake off her anxiety about returning there.

After Lydia polished off her breakfast, a call came in from Sofia.

"Are you okay?" Sofia asked, her voice filled with concern.

"Yeah. Just feels like I got steamrolled by a truck, but I'm okay. Physically at least."

"I've been worried sick," Sofia said. "Your name is all over the news. I wanted to call you last night, but after what happened, I didn't want to bother you."

"Sofia, you could never be a bother. Just hearing your voice lifts my spirits." Lydia rehashed the confrontation with Britney the previous evening before apologizing because she had to leave for work. "Mind if I call you tonight?"

"I'd like that. Hang in there, Lydia. You're one tough cookie."

After they ended the call, Lydia stared at her phone for a few moments. There was something truly special about Sofia. With the Red Scarf Murderer case now put to rest, Lydia hoped she could carve out more time to explore their relationship.

When Lydia arrived at the office, it took her twenty minutes to get from the elevator to her office. People stopped her to ask if she was okay, congratulate her for her role in bringing down the mastermind behind the Red Scarf Murderer, and bombard her with questions about the encounter with Britney.

She managed to reply to one email before Tisha knocked on her door. "The police are holding another press conference."

TVs hung from posts throughout the sea of cubicles outside Lydia's office. She and Tisha joined the crowd gathered around them to watch the presser.

The conference room was packed like it had been when the cops revealed the discovery of Macon's DNA at the crime scenes. The stern-faced police chief and his entourage approached a podium that sprouted more than a dozen microphones.

Only days before, when the cops had initially painted Macon Hardy as the elusive Red Scarf Murderer, the press had feasted on the story, turning Macon Hardy into a household name synonymous with terror.

But now the truth was about to unfold.

The police chief cleared his throat and the room fell into a hushed silence as he began to speak.

"Today, we are here to share another significant update on the Red Scarf Murderer case."

Cameras clicked, capturing the moment as the police chief continued, "The murder investigation has taken an unexpected turn. While Macon Hardy was initially considered the sole suspect, recent developments and forensic evidence have revealed a startling truth."

He paused for effect, allowing the tension to mount.

"It has been determined that Macon Hardy was not the mastermind behind these heinous crimes. Instead, we believe it was his girlfriend, Britney Alice, of Bowie, Maryland.

"Although DNA evidence played a pivotal role in establishing Mr. Hardy as a suspect in the murders, it appears that he was unwittingly ensnared in the sinister web woven by Ms. Alice. He committed the murders at her direction. Because we do not have any evidence to tie Ms. Alice to the crime scenes, her role in the murders was not initially known."

Lydia listened as the police chief rehashed the cryptic letters Dear Birdie had received from Now Single Joe. This time though, the chief clarified that the letters had come from Britney Alice, not Macon Hardy, as they originally thought.

The reporters furiously scribbled notes as the chief went on to explain Lydia's role in uncovering Britney as the mastermind behind the murders.

Before the police chief finished speaking, Lydia's coworkers again crowded around her, expressing their awe at what she had done. It was nearly two p.m. by the time she was able to escape back to the quiet of her office. She sat behind her desk, leaned back in her chair, and closed her eyes, trying hard to conjure up what she'd learned about meditating at the retreat in Arizona. *Had that only been two months earlier?* With all that had happened since then, it felt like a lifetime ago.

Lydia opened her eyes and sat upright at a knock at her door.

"I'm sorry to bother you," her administrative assistant, Martha, said.

Lydia forced a smile. "It's okay, Martha. Please come in."

Martha stepped inside and reached over to affix a sticky note to Lydia's desk. On it was a date and time.

"What's this?" Lydia asked.

Martha gave her a broad grin. "The mayor's office just called. She'd like to host a dinner in your honor."

"Oh, wow," Lydia said. "I'm not really sure I deserve—"

Martha held up her hand. "Hold on, that's not all." She pulled another sticky note from behind her back. "CNN, MSNBC, and a representative from *CBS This Morning* called. They all want to interview you."

"Oh, gosh, that's a lot."

"It is," Martha said. "But it's no surprise. You're a modern-day Agatha Christie." She paused before adding, "Shall I inform the mayor that you accept her invitation?"

Lydia nodded. "I can't exactly say no to the mayor. Please tell her I'd be honored. As for the TV interviews, let me mull them over and I'll get back to you."

After Martha left her office, Lydia's thoughts immediately went to Sofia. She hoped Sofia would agree to be her date for dinner with the mayor. Lydia wanted to attend the event as a couple.

As Lydia walked toward her apartment that evening, her cell phone rang. It was someone Lydia hadn't heard from in a while: Carrie. She was the absolute last person Lydia wanted to talk to at the moment, but if she didn't answer, Carrie would only call again later. Better to get it over with now.

"Hey, Lydia." Carrie's voice was exceptionally chipper. "Your name is all over the news. Quite the little hero, aren't you?"

"I don't consider myself a hero."

"Oh, come on, babe, don't be so modest. From what I've read, you're the one who put all the pieces of the puzzle together. I always knew you were an intelligent one."

"Well, thanks for calling," Lydia said, eager to get off the phone.

"How about we meet up for a drink? You know, to celebrate your cerebral-ness and courage and all that."

"I don't think so, Carrie, but thanks for the invite."

Carrie audibly sighed into the phone. "Fine, be that way, Lydia. Call me if you change your mind."

"I won't change my mind. Bye, Carrie."

Lydia tucked her phone back in her pocket and walked the rest of the way home with her head high, not because she thought she deserved to be celebrated as a hero, but because she knew, without hesitation, she was better off without Carrie. The last few months had tested her, placed her under extraordinary stress, but she'd survived. Maybe, just maybe, she was stronger than she thought.

* * *

Lydia and Sofia entered the elegant house where the mayor was hosting dinner in Lydia's honor. The gathering teemed with a lot more people than Lydia had expected. The lively hum of conversation filled the air and the chandeliers above glittered from the flash of cameras. Apparently, the press was there too.

They handed their coats to an attendant and were ushered into what appeared to be the living room. The opulence of the place was hard to ignore—high ceilings bejeweled with more chandeliers and walls adorned with blue flowered wallpaper.

From the moment Lydia and Sofia stepped into the room, they were engulfed by a wave of people. Firm handshakes and warm hugs accompanied a stream of accolades. Lydia reached for Sofia's hand and held on tight. Thank God she'd opted to wear sensible shoes. Without a doubt, the plush carpet beneath their feet would have toppled her in heels.

The mayor appeared by their side and expressed her gratitude for Lydia's exceptional courage. "Finally, we can all sleep at night," the mayor said. When she realized that neither Lydia nor Sofia had a drink in their hand, she summoned a server who promptly produced two glasses of wine.

During dinner, there was much clinking of glasses as people toasted Lydia. This time it was Sofia who reached for Lydia's hand. Things quieted down once it was time to eat. For the first time all evening, Sofia and Lydia found a few precious minutes to talk.

A glint of excitement lit up Sofia's eyes. "I have some exciting news."

Lydia set down her fork, turning in her chair to face Sofia. "What is it?"

"You know how I told you my dream was to one day work in pricing at Logan?"

"Of course, I remember. You love numbers, so it would be a perfect fit."

"Well, the head of the pricing department called me this afternoon." Sofia bounced on her chair. "He offered me a job as a senior analyst."

Now it was Lydia's turn to bounce in her chair. "That's awesome. I'm so excited for you!"

"Thanks," Sofia said. "I'm pretty excited for myself. Plus, I'll earn a lot more than I do now and work regular hours. No more graveyard shifts at the customer service center."

"What a relief."

"It sure is." Sofia turned in her chair. "There's one more thing…Now that I'll earn more, I told Marta I'd take her and her daughter to New York City. And, I was wondering, would you like to come along too?"

Lydia leaned over to brush a kiss on Sofia's cheek. "Nothing would make me happier." She had an overwhelming desire to wrap her arms around Sofia and give her a proper kiss. But that would have to wait until later.

The mayor now stood at the head of the long table and rang a fork against her water glass. When she had everyone's attention, she gave another heartfelt thanks to Lydia for ending the Red Scarf Murderer's reign of terror, this time with the press poised to capture the moment.

Under the dinner table, Sofia and Lydia's hands intertwined once more as everyone again raised a glass in Lydia's honor and cameras flashed around them.

As the night drew to a close, Lydia found herself unable to suppress the burgeoning feelings that had taken root within her. Her eyes met Sofia's and held her gaze. Sofia's eyes reflected the emotion that Lydia felt.

As they stood together waiting for their coats, Sofia whispered, "Will you come home with me?"

Lydia brought her lips to Sofia's ear. "I would be delighted to."

Sofia's face visibly relaxed.

"Did you really think I would say no?" Lydia asked.

"I don't know. I wasn't sure if…I didn't want to be…"

Lydia reached up and tucked Sofia's hair behind her ear. "You're cute when you're flustered."

Sofia smiled. "Thanks, I guess."

Lydia pulled on her coat and helped Sofia into hers before they stepped out into the crisp cool air. It was a crystal-clear night, and even with the lights of the city around them, the stars popped in the dark sky.

A car waited for them at the curb, and they huddled together in the back seat as it whisked them back to Sofia's apartment.

Lydia cupped her hands around Sofia's face and kissed her gently on the lips. When she pulled back, she whispered, "I still owe you that proper date."

"That you do," Sofia said with a smile before bringing their lips back together.

More Titles from Bella Books

Hunter's Revenge – Gerri Hill
978-1-64247-447-3 | 276 pgs | paperback: $18.95 | eBook: $9.99
Tori Hunter is back! Don't miss this final chapter in the acclaimed Tori Hunter series.

Integrity – E. J. Noyes
978-1-64247-465-7 | 28 pgs | paperback: $19.95 | eBook: $9.99
It was supposed to be an ordinary workday...

The Order – TJ O'Shea
978-1-64247-378-0 | 396 pgs | paperback: $19.95 | eBook: $9.99
For two women the battle between new love and old loyalty may prove more dangerous than the war they're trying to survive.

Under the Stars with You – Jaime Clevenger
978-1-64247-439-8 | 302 pgs | paperback: $19.95 | eBook: $9.99
Sometimes believing in love is the first step. And sometimes it's all about trusting the stars.

The Missing Piece – Kat Jackson
978-1-64247-445-9 | 250 pgs | paperback: $18.95 | eBook: $9.99
Renee's world collides with possibility and the past, setting off a tidal wave of changes she could have never predicted.

An Acquired Taste – Cheri Ritz
978-1-64247-462-6 | 206 pgs | paperback: $17.95 | eBook: $9.99
Can Elle and Ashley stand the heat in the *Celebrity Cook Off* kitchen?

Printed in the USA
CPSIA information can be obtained
at www.ICGtesting.com
JSHW021351210524
63541JS00001B/4